Spies Never Quit

BANANA GIRLS
BOOK 1

Spies Never Quit

M. TAYLOR CHRISTENSEN

MOON
ZOOM
PRESS

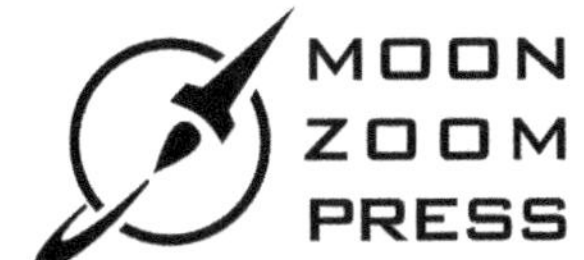

eBook ISBN: 978-1-951454-04-3

Paperback ISBN: 978-1-951454-03-6

Hardback ISBN: 978-1-951454-05-0

Moon Zoom Press - Orem, Utah

Cover Design by Myles Christensen

Copy Edit by Courtney Larkin

For Anna and her friends.

Chapter One

THE HUMID ATLANTA AIR settled around Mari like a sticky sweatshirt as she walked briskly down the sidewalk past the science building, heading toward the baseball field. Even after three weeks as a college freshman, she still wasn't quite used to the walk across campus toward Midtown. It probably would have made more sense to choose on-campus housing, but the part of the application that asked for roommate preference had freaked her out. Some of her friends from high school had come to Georgia Tech, but they all had closer friends they had wanted to room with.

At least, that's what Mari had assumed. It would have been far too embarrassing to have actually asked them. Better to just get a contract at some off-campus apartment complex and let them assign her a friend.

Days like these when she was trudging home after a long day on campus made her seriously second guess that decision.

Mari hustled to cross the street before the light changed. Tall, white-columned entries and Greek letters stared down at her as she continued along the sidewalk. As if the long walk to her condo wasn't enough, living off campus also forced her to walk through the Greek Sector on the way to and from school. She didn't mind the walk, per se. It was just seeing all of those other students clustered together with their friends, talking and laughing, belonging. Her loneliness was difficult to ignore in those moments. Not that she minded that either; she and her mother had been alone for as long as she could remember.

And now the time had come for her to be alone . . . by herself. That was rough.

Georgia Tech was her mother's alma mater and current employer, so there'd never been any question about Mari's first choice of universities. She had only asked her mother once if she could continue living at home while she went to college. Her mother's response had been firm. Mari needed to be independent, learn to live on her own, and fend for herself. Being left to raise Mari alone had taught her mother the importance of independence. But sometimes Mari wished she hadn't been forced to suffer twice for her father's decision to leave.

Mari pulled out her phone and tapped her mother's picture, hoping to see a new message.

Still nothing.

She didn't remember exactly when her mother's flight to the Netherlands had left the day before, but Mari was pretty sure the research conference in Amsterdam had started this evening. Or was it already tomorrow in Europe? Either way, she figured her mother should have texted to say she had gotten there okay.

Her mother was a self-reliant woman and a brilliant scientist, but time awareness had never been her forte. Jet lag from traveling halfway around the world certainly wouldn't help.

And did her mother even have one of those European SIM cards?

Mari tapped out a quick message.

— *How was your flight? Hope you got there safe. Miss you.*

Another breath of hot air swept by as Mari walked out onto the overpass bridge. No matter what the calendar said, it was definitely not fall yet. It wouldn't even start cooling off for another month, to say nothing of the leaves changing colors—green boughs still lined the streets as far as the eye could see. Fortunately, in addition to the trees, the midsized office buildings and condos along her walk home offered some shade from the evening sun.

As she turned right on the next road, Mari heard quick footsteps approaching. Her muscles tensed, and her heart raced. She gripped her shoulder bag tighter.

When she turned eighteen last spring, her mother had paid for her to attend an evening self-defense course. To say that it was a polite offer would have been misleading. Her mother hadn't even given Mari the option of refusing. Of course, she was grateful for her mother's insistence. Mari wondered how scary her walks home would have been if she hadn't felt confident in her ability to fend off potential assailants.

Was this the moment her instructors had prepared her for?

"Hey, Mary," a voice called out.

Mari glanced quickly over her shoulder.

A guy she recognized from biology class huffed to catch up with her. "Wow, you're a fast walker," he said.

She forced her arms to relax, but she didn't slow down. "Actually, my name isn't Mary; it's Mari. It's not *mare* like a female horse; it's more like *mar*, you know, when something gets scratched. Also—"

"Aren't your legs tired?" the guy spoke over her.

Mari's mouth hung open, her well-practiced explanation of Spanish pronunciation only half-finished. Given her very obvious Latina appearance—dark brown hair, olive skin, and brown eyes—people usually listened politely and then at least attempted to say her name correctly. But apparently not this guy. She blinked at him. "Uh, no."

"They should be—you've been running through my mind all day." He smirked at her.

A cheesy pickup line? This guy was pathetic. "Anyway . . ." Mari rolled her eyes and increased her pace.

"We're having a party at the Zag-Shack tomorrow night," he said, still hustling to keep up. "You interested?"

"Zag-Shack?"

"Zeta Alpha Gamma. My frat." The guy was seriously sucking wind now. "Can we . . . stop and talk . . . for a sec?" He grabbed Mari's elbow.

In one quick motion, she jerked her arm from his grasp and spun around. He looked amused as she glared at him. "Do not touch me," she said, backing down the sidewalk.

A slow smirk spread across his face. "Wow, you're feisty, too. I don't mind that."

Mari turned and jogged away from him.

The Zag-Shack guy surged forward. "C'mon back to my place and I'll show you—"

Mari would never find out what he would have shown her, because he chose that moment to grasp Mari's wrist. Her two weeks of self-defense classes kicked in.

In less than a half a second, she jerked his arm forward and swung her elbow out to break his grip. He winced in surprise and discomfort as his momentum carried him forward. She could have stopped at that point. She probably should have. But without really even thinking about it, she finished the move with a quick little lift of her elbow right to his throat.

The guy stumbled off balance and crumpled to his knees on the ground next to her. He was hunched over, wheezing and coughing, his hands on the asphalt.

Hoping he'd had enough, Mari hurried away, putting some distance between them. Several passersby watched her with apprehension. She hadn't really hurt him, had she? And if she had, it wasn't like it would cause any permanent damage. Not that he hadn't sort of deserved it.

A tall girl with deep brown skin and an athletic build was leaning against a tree across the street. She looked just like any of the hundreds of college students Mari saw each day except that she seemed to take particular interest in Mari as she passed. Mari watched out of the corner of her eye as the girl pushed off the tree and crossed the narrow road toward her. Even though she didn't seem in any particular hurry to catch up, Mari wondered whether she could outrun the girl. Mari was fast, but there was a limit to what her medium-length legs could do in a footrace against a woman built like an Olympic track star.

Suddenly, the Zag-Shack punk appeared in front of her, blocking her way. He rubbed his throat and scowled at her. When he spoke, his voice was raspy. "What's the matter with you?"

Mari's body tensed. What more she could do to get this jerk to leave her alone?

His eyes had a maniacal look in them. "I take back what I said earlier," he said. "You are one crazy little—"

Without warning, a hand slid gently through Mari's arm. "Hi! I wondered if I would see you today." The fact that the voice was soft and friendly was the only thing that kept Mari from lashing out. Mari glanced up to see the tall black girl who had crossed the street to follow her. The smile on her face and the lilt in her voice made it seem like they were old friends. "You wouldn't believe the kind of day I've had."

Mari gave her a bewildered look, then followed her gaze back to the boy in front of them. His fists were clenched, but his expression was just as confused as Mari's. He looked back and forth between Mari and the newcomer. Finally, he shook his head and sulked away, muttering.

Her fake new friend pulled Mari forward, talking all about what she'd been doing that day. She was easily six feet tall and muscular, but more in a fitness way than a body-building way. She wore a green shirt and jean shorts. Though it felt forced, she continued yammering for several minutes before Mari had a chance to get a word in.

"Look, I really appreciate your help with that guy," Mari said to her new friend. "Not that I couldn't have handled it," she added.

The girl gave Mari an appraising look—not a silly, sarcastic one, but a serious evaluation of her size and strength. "Hmm," she finally said before looking forward again.

They walked in silence for another half a block, surrounded by the sounds of evening traffic and shoppers, while Mari stewed over what the girl could have meant by that "hmm." At a small side street, the girl turned and tried to pull Mari with her.

Mari resisted. "I'm going this way," she said, pointing along her normal route to her apartment.

The girl smiled sweetly at her. "I don't think you want to go that way home today, Mari. You should come this way. It's much safer."

Something wasn't right about this.

How did this girl know her name?

She even pronounced it right.

The route this girl had chosen would force Mari to walk the long way through several unfamiliar streets. Mari tried to pull her arm out of the girl's grasp, but she held tight.

"You need to let go of me," Mari said through gritted teeth as she prepared to free herself, by force if necessary.

Again came the scrutinizing gaze from the girl. Mari glared back at her. She could feel her breathing increase, her muscles tightening involuntarily.

A moment later, the girl released her. Mari backed slowly away. The girl didn't move. She didn't look mad or upset, just resigned.

After a dozen backward steps, Mari turned forward again and proceeded on her normal walk home—if anything about this particular evening could be considered normal anymore. She waited half a minute before glancing over her shoulder.

No tall girl following.

Mari allowed herself to relax a little.

As usual, pedestrian traffic thinned the farther she got from campus. The buildings became shorter, too. After her run-in with the Zag-Shack guy and the tall girl, her senses were on heightened alert. Was it too much to ask that she make it back to her condo without any more problems?

She scanned the street around her, watching the few people close enough to observe. Half a block ahead, a guy caught her attention. He was headed the same direction as she was, but he seemed lost. He kept looking over his shoulder and changing speed. He was well-dressed, but nothing fancy; he looked pretty much like any other office worker with a job in that part of town.

What was going on today?

Maybe she was being paranoid. He was probably just a normal guy on his way home from work.

But why would he be lost on his way home?

Maybe he was on his way to a new job at a Midtown software company . . . doing database programming . . . on the swing shift.

Mari would have laughed at the absurdity of it all if she weren't in the middle of living it.

No need to catch up to this guy too soon. If he was just an innocent pedestrian, he'd never notice. Mari slowed way down and pulled out her phone again. She pretended to send a text, glancing up every few seconds as if absently trying not to run into anything.

The lost guy seemed to suddenly become even more confused with his surroundings. He came to a stop and squinted up at the buildings around him.

Just in case, Mari casually tilted her phone's screen to check behind her. She caught a glimpse of a similarly dressed guy walking intently toward her. It could have been her imagination, but he seemed to be looking straight at her.

Wow, the freaks were out today. What had she done to draw so much attention?

And how was she going to make it to her apartment in one piece?

She stopped and pretended to tie her shoelace. The guy behind her suddenly became as lost as the guy in front of her. He went from a determined straight line to a wandering mess in half a second flat. If this was his way to trail someone, he was completely clueless.

That's what she'd call them: Lost and Clueless.

And she was definitely their mark.

In her self-defense class, the instructor had said the best way to escape a confrontation was to avoid it in the first place.

Mari assessed her surroundings.

Were there any concerned citizens nearby who could reliably help her take on two sturdy-looking guys intent on trapping her?

There was an elderly lady across the street walking her dog. Mari couldn't quite see her as she passed behind the parked cars, but unless she was packing heat, the woman probably wouldn't be much help. If only she had one of those vicious attack dogs . . .

The dog walked out from behind the car.

Nope. It was a wiener dog.

With a quick glance ahead, she saw a side alley that would take her a different way home. It wasn't ideal, but she was closer to the alley than both thugs, and she might be able to lose them in a full sprint.

She stood up and darted forward. Giving up all pretenses, Lost and Clueless pelted after her. Mari leaned into the curve as she turned the corner down the side alley. She couldn't remember what her self-defense instructor had said about dark alleys, but this was probably a bad idea. The freedom of the open street at the other end beckoned her forward. She was halfway down the alley, and if she could beat them to the end, she might just be able to lose the jerks.

At the sound of squealing tires, Mari skidded to a stop. A silver SUV pulled up at the end of the lane, blocking her escape. Two thugs jumped out; they hadn't even pretended to dress nicely. She glanced back and saw her two pursuers slow down, blocking the narrow alley.

Ah, crap.

One against four and trapped.

They had definitely not covered this in the self-defense class.

If she screamed, would anyone on the street hear her?

The first guy out of the car looked like the one calling the shots. "Hey, sweet little thing. You need a lift somewhere?" His face pinched in a sneer, the diamond of his nose stud glinting in the waning light.

"No." She glared at him, heart pounding.

His lips pressed together in a thin, mirthless smile. "Actually, from what I hear, you do need a lift. In fact, a friend sent us to make sure you made it safe to his place."

"My friends always tell me if they're planning to send a bunch of goons to trap me in a dark alley," Mari shot back. She realized a split-second too late that she'd need to do a better job of keeping her mouth shut in situations like this.

The thug at his side chuckled. He was shorter and stockier with a spider tattooed on his neck. At least, Mari was fairly certain it was a tattoo. Either way, it gave her the creeps.

Nose-Stud scowled at Spider-Neck, jerking his head in Mari's direction. Spider-Neck frowned and moved toward Mari. She checked behind her; Lost and Clueless were moving in, too.

Mari wondered if she should go with them quietly or put up a fight. What was the worst that could happen if she went with them?

It only took a split-second's thought to know what the worst could easily be.

She decided to fight.

Mari slowly backed up, pretending she was scared—which wasn't difficult at the moment. When she could feel the goons behind her breathing down her neck, she kicked quickly backward. Her foot connected hard with Lost's crotch. He buckled to the ground and rolled over with a moan.

The other two stopped in surprise, so Mari seized the moment. She stepped forward and kicked wildly at Spider-Neck's leg. Despite his momentary shock, he was able to deflect her attack.

"How hard could this be?" Nose-Stud said in obvious frustration. "Just grab her."

Like lightning, they rushed from both directions and took hold of Mari's arms. She struggled and kicked, but they easily held her off the ground.

The Nose-Stud stepped toward her. "See, was that so hard?"

"Let me go, you jerk!" she yelled as she attempted to hook the leg of one of her captors.

With the back of his hand, Nose-Stud struck Mari's cheek. "That was for Johnny," he said, nodding to the guy still on the ground moaning in pain.

Mari's face burned as fear clutched her insides. How was she going to get out of this?

A blur of green and brown flashed from behind the thugs' SUV. The tall girl who had helped Mari on the street sailed through the air and landed a large high-heeled sandal into Nose-Stud's back. He stumbled toward Mari. With her arms pinned, all she could do was knee him in the gut on his way to the ground.

"Hey!" Spider-Neck yelled, letting go of Mari's arm to go after the tall girl.

Maybe she wasn't a trained expert in street fighting, but Mari knew when to make herself useful. With her free arm, Mari swung her open palm up into Clueless' face. He dodged and caught a glancing blow against the side of his head. The guy immediately released her and put some distance between them.

The tall girl grappled with Spider-Neck, blocking punches and landing a few in return. As she grabbed his arm and fluidly swung the thug around into a sleeper hold, the girl caught Mari's eye and nodded behind her. Mari turned and saw Nose-Stud on his hands and knees, slowly attempting to get back to his feet. She wasn't exactly sure what to do, but the tall girl obviously wanted her to do something. With a few quick steps, Mari planted her foot and kicked Nose-Stud in the head as hard as she could. He lurched sideways and slumped back to the asphalt. At almost the same moment, the tall girl lowered an unconscious Spider-Neck to the gravel at her feet.

Both ladies turned to look at Clueless, the last man standing. His expression was priceless. With wide eyes, he spun on the spot and took off at a run.

"We can't let him get away!" the tall girl called out.

Mari stared, dumbfounded, back at her. What did she expect Mari to do? Chase down her own attacker?

The tall girl grabbed one of her sandals and ripped the heel off. The rest of the shoe dangled by a long wire. She swung it over her head and threw it at the fleeing thug. The shoe-turned-bola wrapped around his legs and brought him to a chin-scrapping halt.

The girl smiled. "Good thing Susan let me borrow these."

Chest heaving from exertion, Mari surveyed the chaos around them. "Why were they . . .? How did you . . .?" Her head spun to the point that she didn't even know what question to ask.

The girl pulled a couple of long plastic zip-cuffs from a small backpack. She stared at the zip-ties then at the four men on the ground. "I only have two left. I knew I should have packed more."

Mari glanced at each of the men before turning back to the tall girl. "Two of them are unconscious," she said with a shrug.

The girl smiled and nodded. "Good point." After untangling the surprisingly fashionable bola from Clueless' legs, she bound his ankles with the zip-cuff and put her sandal back on. She tossed the second zip-tie to Mari, indicating she should take care of the other guy, then pulled out her phone.

Bewilderment began to set in as Mari glanced around the alley. She wondered if anyone else had witnessed the bizarre scene of two college girls taking down four muscly goons.

While she zip-cuffed Lost, who was still writhing in agony, Mari listened in on the tall girl's phone call.

"I need a cleanup team at this location," the girl said as she surveyed their handiwork. "No. No witnesses, so probably just a catch and release. Yeah. Thanks." She ended the call.

Hoping she would finally get some answers, Mari stood and faced the tall girl. "How did you—"

"Turn off your friend locator," the girl instructed.

"What?"

"The locator app on your phone. Disable it."

"Okay . . ." Mari pulled her phone out and fumbled through the settings menus.

"And you can't go back to your apartment for a few days."

"Wait. Where am I supposed to—"

"Crash at a friend's."

"But I don't really—"

The tall girl continued as if Mari hadn't said anything. ". . . basically anywhere but your place or your mother's home."

Mari frowned. "Wait. What do you know about my mother? What's going on? Who are you?"

"I can't tell you. You'll just have to trust me." The girl was already moving away toward the alley entrance. "Don't go back to your place and don't walk into any more alleys."

The girl jogged to the end of the street and disappeared around the corner.

Mari slowly backed away from the chaotic alley scene. She wasn't sure what the cleanup team was going to do, but she didn't want to be there when they arrived.

They might think it had been her fault.

Chapter Two

"Are you sure you don't want to come with us? It's supposed to be the biggest party of the semester. Plenty of hot guys to go around."

Mari looked up from her phone and smiled at her friend, Beth. "No, I'm fine. You go ahead."

Beth could probably be called a friend only in the very loosest sense. They'd gone to the same high school and had once worked on a group project together. Mari was grateful for Beth's hospitality, and she was doing her best not to impose on Beth's social life.

"Okay. We'll try not to wake you when we get back," Beth said. Her roommates smiled and waved as they filed out the door on their way to the big party.

The pile of books Mari had poured out of her bag still sat on the coffee table. She had shifted them, opened them, and even pretended to read them. She hadn't wanted Beth or her roommates to feel like they had to make conversation with her.

Even in high school, Mari had always hated feeling the pity of someone who saw her alone and tried to invite her into an unfamiliar group. Acting like she was engrossed with homework had been a security blanket these last three weeks since school had started up. As long as she looked busy, people tended to ignore her.

Mari adjusted the cushions on the lumpy couch. Beth's apartment was old and kind of small, but at the moment, Mari couldn't be picky. She grabbed armloads of books and slid them back into her backpack. She didn't want Beth to think she was messy.

Laying her head down on the arm of the couch, Mari pulled a worn quilt over her legs. She closed her eyes and tried to relax, but she was so shell-shocked from her encounter with the street thugs—and the warning from the tall girl—that she knew she'd never be able to fall asleep.

How had the tall girl known Mari's name? And why had she mentioned Mari's mother?

Mari pulled her phone out again and checked her messages. Still nothing from her mother. She checked her mother's social media. Maybe she had posted something about being in Europe.

Nothing.

She searched for a list of yesterday's flights out of Atlanta, partially to see if she could find the one her mother had taken and partially because she figured any news of an airplane crash would have shown up in the results. She didn't want to search for a crash, specifically, that would be bad luck.

Mari put in her earbuds and started her soothing bedtime playlist. She rolled to her other side and tried to get comfortable. Rubbing her eyes, she checked the friend locator app for the hundredth time. Her mother's icon hovered three blocks away from the airport.

Suddenly, her earbuds rang and the screen lit up with her mother's picture. Relief flooded her entire body.

Mari fumbled with the slide to answer the video call. "Mamá!" she cried.

When the video finally came in, she wasn't looking at her mother. A man's face stared back at her. He had wild blondish-brown hair, gray-green eyes, and a scruffy beard. He looked to be in his early thirties, but he might have been older. It was hard to tell with the shadows falling across his face.

Her stomach dropped as her panic flooded back. "Who are you? Where's my mother?"

"Hi. Hello. Can you hear me okay?" the man said. He was moving the phone forward and back as if trying to frame his face just right.

"Where. Is. My. Mother?" Mari was nearly shouting now.

"Are you Mari?" the man asked.

"Yes. Who are you?"

"Braxton. But you can call me Brax. That's a much tougher-sounding name, isn't it?"

Mari's eyes bulged in frustration.

Why was this simpleton talking about how his name sounded?

"You're using my mother's cellphone." Mari spoke the words slowly, as if trying to explain something to a small child. "Where did you get it?"

"Your mother gave it to me."

Mari's hopes lifted. "Really? Where is she?" She squinted at the small phone screen as if she could peer through the glass into the faraway room. She saw walls lined with dark bookcases, like an old-fashioned personal library from the movies.

"Well, I guess I shouldn't say she 'gave' it to me. She was rather selfish about it. She took some convincing."

Mari felt her insides go cold.

"I want to see my mother," Mari said firmly.

"You won't like what's happened to her," the man said with childlike playfulness. "I shouldn't show you because it'll upset you . . . but I really do want to."

The camera panned toward the other side of the room where a pitiful figure sat slumped in a lone chair. Thick ropes wound across her chest and arms, holding her down. As the camera approached, Mari gasped.

It was her mother.

"Dr. Sandoval," Brax's voice was singsongy, "you have a call." He shook her on the shoulder.

Mari's mother stirred and looked up. Her hair was a tangled mess and there were dark circles under her eyes. She flinched when she saw Brax. He held the camera close so that her face filled the screen.

"Mamá!" Mari sobbed.

Her mother's eyes swam in and out of focus as she slowly recovered awareness.

"Mari?" she asked slowly. Her eyes suddenly saw her daughter. "Mari. Don't listen to them! Don't do anything for them!"

A hand shot from off-camera and struck her in the head. She cried out then fell silent, her head hanging limply, body still bound to the chair.

"No!" Mari screamed.

Brax's face loomed on the screen again. "Oh, no. See, I knew you wouldn't like what had happened to her."

"Leave her alone, you monster! What do you want from her?"

"Your mother hasn't been trying hard enough. I thought maybe my friends could bring you over for a visit. That could've helped motivate her. But you're a slippery little thing, aren't you?" His crooked smile was playful.

Friends? Did he mean the goons that tried to kidnap her?

Mari shivered involuntarily. "I can get money, if that's what you want."

Brax gave a short, cold laugh. "I already have more money than I know what to do with." He gestured briefly to the lavish room around him.

"I'll get whatever you need then. Just please don't hurt her anymore," Mari pleaded.

"I am glad to hear you can be helpful. Your mother was not as optimistic." The airy tone had returned. "You have access to your mother's office on campus?"

Mari nodded warily.

"All you have to do is get the swarm algorithms from your mother's computer."

"Swarm algorithms?" Mari repeated. He sounded like he was asking her to pick something up at the store instead of steal something from a government funded research program.

"Yeah. The ones that control her nano-bots. Go to her office, download the file from her computer, and send it to this number. That should be simple enough, right?"

Mari nodded, her brain kicking into overdrive trying to formulate a plan to get the algorithms. She could get into her mother's office no problem, but could she figure out her mother's password? And would the other scientists object if they saw her? Not that those details mattered—Mari would tell Brax whatever he wanted to hear.

Or perhaps she should approach her mother's colleagues. Would they be willing to help? Maybe they would demand proof that her mother was being held hostage. And what if she eventually had to go to the authorities? They would need something to go on.

Mari glanced back at Brax's cruel face on the phone screen. What she really needed was a picture of her mother's captor.

"You have five days," he said with a creepy smile. "And in the meantime, I'll be *encouraging* your mother's memory."

Mari inched her free hand up to the power button. She swallowed hard. "I'll get them," she said as she pressed the button combo to capture a screenshot.

Brax's smile vanished. "Oh, and Mari?" His expression had turned murderous. "No police. No FBI. Not even university administration. Don't tell anyone. And don't try to be a hero. If you don't do exactly as I ask, this will be the last you ever see of your mother."

Mari nodded contritely.

If he knew she'd taken a screen capture, she'd already put her mother in danger.

A second later, Brax turned his phone and let it linger on her mother's body before he ended the call.

After several hours of tossing and turning, interspersed with silent crying and a bizarre half-sleep where Brax's evil face continually loomed from the darkness, Mari finally decided that staring bleary-eyed into a screen was preferable to her nightmares.

She pulled her laptop from her backpack and balanced it against her knees. She typed *what to do in case of kidnapping* in the search bar. Most of the results were tips for surviving a kidnapping or hostage situation. But unless Brax had given her mother access to an Internet browser, this information wouldn't really be helpful. It was mostly all common sense anyway, so hopefully her mother would know what to do.

She tried changing the search to include *family member*, but then the results skewed toward child abductions in custody battles. Not very helpful either.

She gave up and started searching for who to contact in case of an abduction. The results all said to contact the authorities. That was the smart thing, and probably what her mother would want her to do.

But did she dare ignore Brax's warning?

Picking up her phone from the coffee table, Mari turned it over and popped open the card compartment. Her bright yellow student ID card with its fierce little yellowjacket icon stared back at her. She could easily use it to get into her mother's research lab. But then what? She shook her head.

Mari focused on the other articles on the search page. This type of abduction was referred to as a Tiger Kidnapping—a situation where the kidnappers want a family member or friend to do something illegal on their behalf. She also found out that the FBI had jurisdiction over kidnapping investigations.

Should she try and contact the FBI somehow?

She glanced down at her phone again. Her ID card peeked out from the back of the case, screaming for her attention. All Mari had to do was duck into her mother's office, get the algorithms from her computer, and make a getaway. If she did it right, no one would ever even know she had been there.

No. She forced herself to look away from it. You were never supposed to give the bad guys what they wanted, right?

Mari stared at the computer screen again, not really seeing the words. She should just go to the police and ask them to be sensitive to her mother's safety as they investigated. That would be the safe thing to do. The right thing to do.

She sat up on the couch, throwing the quilt off her body. After quickly stuffing her laptop back into her bag, she slung the pack over her shoulder. Then she slipped her phone back into her pocket, trying not to notice the extra weight of her mother's freedom it now carried.

As Mari quietly opened the front door, she paused. Should she leave a thank you note for Beth? But what if Mari didn't get everything straightened out before she needed a place to crash again? Would it be awkward to come back? Maybe she could find another friend to stay with. Shaking her head, Mari made a mental note to text Beth a quick explanation for why she had left in the middle of the night. Maybe something about needing to be up early for a family emergency.

With a quick glance up and down the dark, empty road, Mari hurried up the sidewalk toward the stadium. She had to go talk to the police before she lost her nerve. Maybe there would be a nice detective on duty who would understand that this was a delicate situation.

Skirting freshman hill, she cut through the parking deck and up across the center of campus.

Halfway there. She only needed to keep her nerve a little longer.

But what if Brax was serious? And what if she ended up talking to a rookie police officer who didn't know how to keep hostages safe?

As she caught the first glimpse of her mother's building through the trees, Mari's chest tightened. Her mother's safety depended on her next decision. Nothing like being thrown headfirst into the adulting world. And failing at it.

Mari sat down on a nearby stone half-wall and buried her face in her hands.

What should she do?

Brax had sent those goons after her, and they had known exactly where she was going on her walk home.

Had someone been following her? What if Brax had someone watching her right now?

If she went straight to the police, Brax would know. What would he do then?

Her mother's only chance was if the police could get to her before Brax found out.

And the only thing Mari had to offer them was his name and a badly lit screenshot.

Mari pulled out her phone and opened her recent photos. Despite the warm night air, a chill ran down her spine at the sight of Brax's evil sneer. Mari tried to focus on the clues in the picture: a dark room, an ornate chandelier behind his head, large, shadowy bookshelves in the background.

How would the police ever find her mother in time?

Absently fiddling with the snap closure on the back of the case, Mari turned her phone over and stared down at her student ID card. She glanced up at the nanotechnology building across the street that housed her mother's research program.

It would be so easy. She could slip in and duck out before ever being noticed. She could give the criminal what he wanted and get her mother back safe.

Never give the criminal what he wants.

With a frustrated sigh, Mari lay back on the half-wall. She needed a minute to think things through, but her head swam with images of Brax, the Zag-Shack boy, her mother's bruised face, the thugs in the alley, and the tall girl who came to her rescue, twice.

Mari's eyes popped open.

If only she could talk to that tall girl. She seemed to have plenty of answers. But there was no way to find her again.

No. Mari was on her own.

And the weight of the decision that could save or doom her mother was crushing the air from her lungs.

Mari lay on the short stone wall listening to the predawn sounds around her—the wind through the trees, scattered footsteps on nearby walkways, and the occasional car driving by—and just tried to breathe. She might have been there five minutes or an hour, she wasn't sure. But when the sky turned from black to deep blue, she knew she had to do something.

She had to save her mother.

Sitting up, Mari rubbed her eyes and looked at the street around her.

The Saturday morning foot traffic was basically zero, which was ideal. She couldn't afford to get caught.

As far as Mari could see, there was no other way out. She couldn't go to the police without risking her mother's life. That left her with only one option. Sneak into her mother's office, get the algorithms, and get out. Then her mother would be safe. Or maybe she should hold on to the information until she knew for certain that her mother was safe.

Not having worked a hostage situation before, Mari's knowledge was basically limited to what she'd seen in movies. Not much to go on as far as the real world was concerned.

She was out of her league. And she knew it.

Once her mother was safe, she could go to the authorities and maybe they could clean up the mess she'd made. Hopefully, they would understand that she'd had no other choice.

Mari stood and took a few steps toward the road. A slow-moving vehicle drove by, its headlights momentarily illuminating her face. Mari squinted and ducked her head. Hopefully, she didn't look too guilty.

As she quickly crossed the street and approached the nanotech building, her palms started sweating. Fortunately for her mother's safety—and Mari's nascent life of crime—the building didn't have stress scanners or anything else that could reveal her plan of deception. Mari would have to remember to suggest an anxiety detector to help keep the building secure.

After this was all over.

The college would have a record of her entering the building. If they discovered the theft of the code, she would be the obvious suspect. But she didn't care about that right now. Her mother's life hung in the balance.

The student ID card got Mari into the front doors. She tiptoed across the atrium and entered a waiting elevator. After what felt like an eternity, the doors finally opened on the top floor. The silent hallway stretched out in front of her. The only sound was the hum of the fluorescent lights and the whir of machinery and computers. After walking past the long cleanroom windows, Mari stopped at the double glass entrance doors to the office suite of her mother's team. Another quick card scan unlocked the doors, and she slipped into the small foyer.

Her mother's office was just past the reception area. Mari moved across the open space to her mother's door. Over the years, she'd come with her mother to this office countless times. None of those visits had ever mattered as much as this one. None of them had ever been so illegal, either.

At the door to her mother's office, Mari scanned her card, and the lock clicked. As she pushed the door open, Mari heard a different sound from down the hallway.

Was someone in the research offices this early on a Saturday morning?

She paused and looked over her shoulder. Nothing moved in the dark hallway. She walked down to look in the windows of a few offices. No lights. No people. Nothing.

It felt like her heart was beating out the bass line from a crowded dance club. These offices had never felt spooky before, but they certainly did now. She took a deep breath. She just needed to get the algorithms and leave.

When she arrived back at her mother's office, the door was wide open, and the light was on. A young woman sat behind her mother's desk. She was slim, fair-skinned, with long silver-blond hair and crystal-blue eyes. Leaning back in her mother's chair, the girl looked at Mari with a bored expression.

With a frown, Mari took another step toward her. "You shouldn't be here," Mari said curtly.

"Neither should you," the girl replied, her gaze fixed on Mari.

Mari scowled at her. "I have more right to be here than you do."

The girl rolled her eyes and reluctantly stood. She was a little taller than Mari. "Go home, Mari." It sounded like she was used to bossing people around.

Mari felt her temperature rise. "What? You can't tell me what to do. You need to leave before I call security."

The girl smirked. "Oh? And tell them what? That you were out for a Saturday morning stroll and decided to stop by your mother's high-security research lab?"

Mari's eyes narrowed as she considered the presumptuous girl. "How do you know my name? And how do you know I'm Dr. Sandoval's daughter?"

The girl strutted out from behind the desk, exuding authority. She stopped in front of Mari and stared down at her. "Leave now."

Mari's heart banged in her chest. If she let this girl boss her out of her mother's office, when would she have a chance to come back and get what she needed? And what if this girl meant to destroy the algorithms that would save Mari's mother?

As the girl put her hand out to take her shoulder, Mari reacted with a quick wrist grab and flipped the girl around. The blonde grunted as she continued the spin and swept Mari's legs from beneath her.

Mari quickly rolled away and stood to face her aggressor. The bored expression on the girl's face was replaced by a sneer as she stepped forward and blocked the office door.

"You're tougher than I expected," the girl said in a condescending tone.

Mari glared back at her. "I surprise a lot of people." She lunged forward, lashing out with a punch to the thin girl's face. The girl flinched but easily deflected Mari's fist before delivering a return punch to Mari's ribs.

Pain shot through Mari's side. She tumbled backwards, rolled, and jumped up again.

How was she going to get into her mother's office with this nosey brat in the way?

Mari circled back and forth, just out of the girl's reach, watching for some sign of weakness. The blonde girl was ready for everything. Mari needed to try something new.

Mari lunged forward again, but this time she knowingly gave the girl an opening for another punch. When the girl's hand shot forward, Mari was ready. Gritting her teeth against the pain, she grasped the girl's small wrist and, with a firm jerk, dragged her away from the office door. But just as Mari tried to release her, the girl twisted her arm and grabbed Mari's wrist, pulling her along, too.

Mari wrenched her arm free and lunged for her mother's office, hoping to get through the door and lock the girl out. The girl attempted to trip her, but Mari leaped over the girl's outstretched leg.

Unfortunately, the girl was too quick. With her second effort, she snagged Mari by the shoe and brought her facedown on the thin carpet.

In a flash, the blonde girl was on top of her with a knee on Mari's butt and Mari's arms pinned flat behind her back.

Mari twisted and fought, but she couldn't upend the girl.

Suddenly the outer door to the research offices opened and in walked the tall, black girl who had saved Mari from Brax's goons

"Hannah! What's taking so long? Security's going to check this floor any minute. We have to get out of here."

Mari's jaw would have dropped if her chin wasn't already rubbing the brownish-gray carpet.

"She wasn't coming quietly," the girl named Hannah replied through gritted teeth.

The tall girl moved forward and knelt next to Mari.

Mari shifted her head toward the girl. "I need your help, please. I have to save my mother."

The girl considered her for a moment. "You were going to trade your mother's research for her freedom, weren't you?"

Mari didn't understand what these girls were doing here, or why they knew her name, or what was happening to her mother, but the weight of what she was doing finally settled on her. She squeezed her eyes closed, sending a small tear trickling down her cheek, and nodded as best she could.

The girl continued in a soft, caring voice. "We want to help you and your mother, Mari, but this isn't the way," she said, motioning to the research offices. "Will you come with us?"

"I just want to save her," Mari squeaked.

The tall girl nodded for Hannah to get off. Taking her sweet time, Hannah eventually lifted her knee from Mari's back.

Mari stood carefully, eyeing her recent adversary. "You could've just asked," she said to Hannah.

"Would you have come with me?" she asked dryly.

Mari scowled. "Maybe if you had explained things as nicely as . . ." She turned to the tall girl and realized she didn't know her name.

"Anna," she said.

Mari stared at her, then looked back at Hannah in disbelief. These girls' names were Hannah and Anna?

Hannah rolled her eyes. "Yes, Anna and Hannah. Ha, ha. It's so funny. Let's get out of here." Her long blonde hair fluttered as she stalked past them and out the door.

Anna smiled at Mari. "C'mon. We'll explain later."

CHAPTER THREE

THE LOBBY OF THE Midtown condo high-rise was opulent at a level Mari had never seen before except in movies. Polished marble floors met silver-accented white walls that rose to the ceiling three stories up. Modernly austere silver chandeliers dotted the space high above their heads. The room smelled fresh—and extravagant. Even in the early morning hours, the expansive room glowed brightly.

Hannah strode past the waiting attendant without even the smallest acknowledgment. Mari assumed this was standard fare as the attendant did not react in the least, though he did give a small friendly nod when Anna waved as she went by. The ride to the top floor of the tower was silent. Obviously, the state-of-the-art elevator made no noise, but neither did the occupants. Hannah scowled at the doors as if willing it to go faster. Anna simply smiled at Mari without speaking.

Hannah bolted from the elevator as soon as the doors opened. A single, long hall stretched away from the elevator. Morning sunlight streamed through a window at the far end. There was a single door on the left side of the hall, and a matching door on the right. Hannah stepped up to the left door, touched her thumbprint, and pushed it open in one well-practiced motion.

Before entering, Hannah looked over her shoulder, leveling a stare at Anna. "*You* have to call Stacia and tell her what you volunteered us for."

"Don't worry, I will," Anna replied calmly.

"And you know the policy on *guests*." Hannah's emphasis of the last word was accompanied by a pointed look at Mari.

"Hannah, do I need to remind you to mind your manners around *guests*?" Anna replied.

Hannah huffed and stormed through the open door.

Mari glanced at Anna. "If helping me is going to cause trouble, I'm sure I can—"

"Ignore Hannah. She's in one of her moods." Anna replied. She stepped over the threshold ahead of Mari and swept her arm with a flourish as they walked through the foyer into a large living room. "Welcome to Club Banana."

The room was enormous. Dark hardwood floors stretched out to meet giant, floor-to-ceiling windows. The living room had a cluster of white leather couches, love seats, and armchairs, each dotted with yellow accent pillows shaped like bananas. Medium-sized mirrors hung on the walls interspersed with small, yellow wall art, all banana-themed. The decor on one wall of the living room didn't look quite right. It had the same type of art and mirrors, but art was flat, and the mirrors were just pictures—no reflection. Mari realized that it was a full-wall video screen currently showing an image to match the rest of the room.

A girl about Mari's age with deep-red, long, wavy hair sat lounging with a laptop in front of her. She wore frayed white shorts and a lace-edged blue blouse, making her look somehow casual and fancy at the same time. She waved at Anna. "Hey, you're back," she called. Then she seemed to notice Mari for the first time. "Who's this?"

"This," Hannah said, motioning in Mari's general direction, "is the reason I had to be out of bed so early on a Saturday morning." She flopped onto an extra-wide, yellow chaise lounge tucked into the corner and draped an arm over her face.

The redhead pulled a silly face at Hannah, which Hannah obviously couldn't see.

Anna shook her head. "Oh, hush, Hannah. You're just grumpy because you haven't eaten breakfast yet. What if I make some of my mom's famous waffles?"

Without moving her arm, Hannah grunted something that sounded like acknowledgment.

Anna stepped up next to Mari and spoke to the girl on the couch, "This is Mari."

Mari gave a small wave.

The redhead waved back. "Hi. I'm Susan." She smiled and gestured broadly to the penthouse. "So . . . what brings you to our humble abode?"

"Anna volunteered the Banana Girls to help rescue Mari's mother," Hannah piped in from her corner.

"I guess that makes sense," Susan continued.

"Wait. That makes sense to you?" Mari asked.

Susan nodded vigorously. "Well sure, that sounds like the type of thing we would do."

Mari suddenly felt drained. She sunk onto the edge of the nearest couch.

Anna touched her on the shoulder. "You poor thing. You must be exhausted after fighting with Hannah—I always am. Oh, I'm supposed to be making waffles! Just sit right there, and I'll get breakfast going."

Anna bustled across the living room to a spacious, immaculate kitchen. It was large enough that Mari's entire condo space could have fit inside. In fact, the island counter alone was the size of Mari's bedroom. Anna set to work making breakfast, clanking cabinet doors and mixing bowls as she went.

"What I really need is to know what's going on," Mari mumbled, mostly to herself.

"Well, we've been monitoring the situation with your mother's disappearance," Susan explained.

"You have?" Mari asked. "Why?"

Susan made a very dramatic surprised face. "Because of her research, of course." She narrowed her eyes at Mari. "You do know about her research, don't you?"

If she hadn't been so worn out, Mari would have felt insulted. These strangers could never know as much about her mother's research as she did. "You mean that she developed the technology to manufacture a nano-bot the size of a grain of rice that can monitor city infrastructure, national roadways, and global weather patterns? That research?" Mari had only heard about it her entire life.

Susan shook her shoulders and wagged her head as if to acknowledge Mari's fancy response. "Well, did you know that recently her research group was able to make them autonomously mobile? And that she developed a swarm algorithm that allows them to move synchronously to accomplish a task?"

Mari's confidence slipped. Her mother had talked about a possible new breakthrough that she would be sharing at the conference, but she hadn't said what it was. "I'd heard something about that."

"And did you know that with a little reprogramming of the algorithm, your mother's nano-bots could be used as a weapon? They could attack infrastructure rather than monitor it. There's even the possibility that the nano-bots could be used to infiltrate the human body." Susan added a theatrical shudder.

Mari's eyes went wide. "How could you possibly know all this?"

Susan smiled gently. "We have certain . . . resources."

"And now it's the same as always," Hannah called from under her yellow, fruit-shaped pillow, "Banana Girls to the rescue, again."

Mari felt like she had been politely patient long enough. "And what's with the whole banana thing? What's actually going on?" She said it with more huff than she'd intended.

Susan set her laptop next to her on the couch and faced Mari. She settled her hands dramatically in her lap as if preparing to tell an epic saga. "Well, once upon a time—"

Simultaneous groans came from the kitchen and the corner chair.

Susan rolled her eyes. "You two have no appreciation for a well-told tale."

"Just tell the story," Hannah complained. "And make it short this time."

Susan stuck out her bottom lip in a mock pout. "Fine." She turned back to Mari. "We call ourselves the Banana Girls. It started with Anna and Hannah. They were on a mis— . . . I mean, they had a project they were working on together, and the other ag— . . . uh team member . . . made fun of the fact that they were Anna and Hannah. You know, Anna, Hannah, banana? It just sort of flows."

"You call yourselves Banana Girls . . . because it rhymes?" Mari wasn't sure how that made sense.

"Well, there's more to it, but that would be the longer version." Susan pulled a face in Hannah's direction. "Let's just say we're a group who likes helping people."

"Helping people . . ." Mari said, hoping Susan would clarify. But the redhead picked up her laptop and went back to work. Apparently, that was the end of the short version of the story.

Mari looked around at the three ladies. They were the picture of college relaxation. Hannah in her name-brand shorts, designer sandals, and purple, sleeveless summer blouse. Anna's outfit was more down to earth: well-fitting jeans and a sleek tank top. More of a girl-next-door look. And this luxury apartment with its posh furnishings and expensive decor. These women lived in an enormous double penthouse in Midtown Atlanta. There was no way they could afford this type of opulence on college budgets. Where did that money come from?

Was there something going on beneath the surface?

She studied them with new eyes. They definitely had information sources. They had known about her mother's abduction. And Anna had followed Mari yesterday to make sure she got home safe. Not to mention that Anna and Hannah had shown up just in time to stop Mari from stealing her mother's research.

Plus, they certainly had fighting skills. Mari absently touched the sore spot on her ribs from her fight with Hannah. And she recalled what Anna had done to those punks in the alley.

"You aren't spies, are you?" Mari blurted out.

Anna and Susan laughed, but it sounded forced. Hannah lifted her pillow momentarily, but then went back to pretending to be tired.

"We help people," Susan repeated.

"Yeah, but not if those people are nosy and ungrateful," Hannah added.

Anna walked into the living room with the first two plates of waffles. "Hannah, why don't you do something with that mouth of yours besides insulting our guest." She set a plate on the end table next to Hannah and another on the coffee table in front of Mari and went back to the kitchen for more.

Mari hadn't realized how hungry she was until she saw the plate of waffles. Anna returned with plates for Susan and herself. It was Mari's first solid meal in nearly twenty-four hours, and her first really good breakfast since she left home for college. She polished off the first waffle in a minute flat.

"Let's talk about how we're going to rescue Dr. Sandoval," Anna said between bites.

"Who has her?" Susan asked.

All eyes turned to Mari. She choked on a bite of strawberry. "I have no idea. You guys are the ones who help people; I thought you would know."

Hannah huffed from her corner, but her attitude seemed to have improved slightly now that she was eating. "We don't get told everything.

The information we got was that Dr. Sandoval might have been abducted for her research, so Anna was sent to keep an eye on you. That, plus there's been some black-market chatter about nano-bots."

"Well, that's more than I knew," Mari pointed out.

"Who contacted you about stealing from your mother's lab?" Anna asked.

Mari shuddered. "A guy named Brax. He used my mother's phone to video chat with me. He said I had to send him the algorithms for the nano-bots or he'd hurt my mother."

Susan set her empty plate aside and pulled her laptop closer. "What did he look like?"

"Um. He was white, sort of a pinkish complexion. Blondish hair. A short beard. Light eyes. Hang on." Mari fished her phone out of her pocket and pulled up the screen capture of the call. "Here. I thought this would come in handy if I needed to convince anyone my mother had been kidnapped." She handed the phone to Susan.

"Ooh, he looks sort of like Kenneth Branagh. Except the eyes. Those are some mean eyes." Susan shivered, for real this time. She tapped the phone screen, sending the image to her laptop. Then she started clicking away at her keyboard. "Let's see if facial recognition pulls up any hits."

"Great, while that's searching, let's try and figure out location," Anna said.

The ladies looked at each other for ideas.

"What about the locator app on my phone?" Mari suggested.

"I thought I told you to turn that off," Anna scolded.

"I did. I mean the location it shows for my mom's phone." Mari grabbed her phone back from Susan and pulled up the friend locator. It showed her mother's last known location. The one she had stared at all day yesterday, wondering where her mother could be. Her mother's icon hovered in the exact same spot about half a mile from the airport on Highway 6. She handed the phone to Anna.

Anna examined it for a few seconds. "Doesn't your mom live in Decatur?" she finally asked.

Mari nodded.

"So she'd be coming at the airport from the opposite direction, wouldn't she?" Anna asked.

"Yeah, we usually come down on the 285," Mari replied. "I just thought that her location was a glitch from losing connection or something."

"It could be off by a few dozen feet, maybe." Susan held her arms wide then squinted as if trying to judge the width of the room. "How far away from the airport is she?"

Anna handed the phone to Susan who inspected the map before handing it back. She picked up her laptop and started typing. Before long, Susan was almost bouncing off her seat.

Mari glanced over at Anna in concern. Anna simply shook her head as if to tell Mari not to worry about it.

"We have to make a few assumptions for the model to work," Susan explained, her leg nearly jostling the computer out of her lap. "We're assuming this position is after she was abducted—that she didn't just take a weird detour on her way to the airport." Susan looked up, and Mari, not knowing what else to do, nodded in agreement.

Anna leaned over and whispered to Mari. "She gets this way when she's excited."

Susan continued. "We're also assuming that the abductors didn't intentionally drive in the wrong direction before disabling the locator app."

"That's giving them way too much credit," Hannah scoffed.

Susan's fingers flew across the keyboard. "We'll need a little more information about the location." She held out her hand. "Picture?"

Mari brought up the picture of Brax again and handed it back to Susan.

"Could he have been in a library, Mari? Not the public kind of library, but like a private library."

"Yeah. It was dark, but it was definitely a library."

Susan squinted at the screen. "Is it a fancy, old library, like in those mansions on British romance movies? Or is this just a small home library?"

"Oh, definitely a mansion. The room was huge." Mari bit her lip, trying to remember her conversation with the disgusting man. "And he bragged that he had more money than he knew what to do with."

"Okay, that does narrow it down a little bit," Susan said. Then she looked up with a wry smile. "Assuming she's not in England somewhere."

"For now, let's assume that the abductors are not sophisticated enough to get Mari's mother on an international flight without arousing suspicion," Anna said.

Susan tapped on her keyboard and swiped across her screen. "Most of the mansions are north of Midtown. There are only a few dozen above five million dollars that are west of the city."

Hanna set her plate down and sat up straight. "You need eyes on them?"

The girls all looked up at her in surprise.

"What?" she replied casually, slipping back into her detached attitude. "That's sort of my thing."

"Yeah, if we're going to make a positive ID, we need some footage to work with," Susan said as she waved Hannah away.

Hannah walked purposefully into an adjacent room. Anna also stood, having just finished her breakfast, and motioned for Mari to join her. They followed Hannah into a large room filled with technology and gadgets. Hannah pulled two quadcopters from a rack on a wall and set them on a workbench.

The quadcopters were about a foot square, plus the eight-inch rotors. Hannah hit the power buttons on both. "Send me the locations, Suz," she called out as she activated a nearby computer.

"You got it," Susan yelled from the living room.

Hannah zoomed in on the locations on the map and tagged each with a miniature icon of a quadcopter, like she was assigning the real quadcopters their targets.

"This is my favorite part," Anna whispered with an air of excitement.

As interesting as quadcopters were, Mari didn't see anything that would elicit this kind of anticipation. Wouldn't they need to take the little copters outside before anything interesting happened?

After a few more commands on the computer, one of the quadcopters' rotors started up. The whine of the electric motors filled the workroom. The first drone lifted from the workbench, and Hannah and Anna looked toward the ceiling. Mari followed their gaze and watched the large skylight slowly peel back and open a portal to the outside air. The drone rose above their heads and disappeared through the opening. A few seconds later, the second drone followed.

Hannah went to the rack of quadcopters and selected two more. After giving the new drones their targets, she sent them away like the others. The process repeated itself twice more.

Anna nodded toward the living room. "C'mon. It's more fun to watch their progress out here."

They sat next to Susan on the longest couch, facing the wall-turned-video screen. The display was divided into nine pictures, one aerial view from each drone plus a map view of Atlanta's western suburbs.

"We'll need to get you moved in," Anna remarked to Mari in an offhand way.

"Moved in where?" Mari asked.

"Here, obviously."

"Oh, uh," Mari spluttered. "That's very kind, but I don't want to impose on your—"

Anna gave Mari a look that reminded her of when her mother thought she was being intentionally obtuse. "You obviously can't stay at your apartment anymore. And I can't imagine that you want to keep staying at your high school friend's house." Anna gave a knowing smile when Mari looked surprised. "Besides, that will save us the trouble of having to race to your rescue."

"That was only once," Mari protested.

"What about this morning?" Anna asked.

Mari frowned. "That was a rescue?"

"Mm-hmm. From yourself."

Mari opened her mouth to argue, but there wasn't much she could say.

"We'll go after the show," Anna added, eyes still riveted on the wall display.

Hannah came back into the living room and sat down with the others. She picked up a tablet and opened an app to monitor the drones. "Number Three will get to its target first. Just a few more minutes," she said.

They watched as the view from one of the drones descended on a spacious mansion tucked in the green of surrounding trees. Tiny paths wound through manicured gardens. Three tennis courts sat next to a large swimming pool. Mari could barely fathom living in a home like that.

The drone descended until it was even with the treetops directly in front of the mansion's main gate. The picture panned down to the branches directly below the drone, and suddenly, a small object fell from the drone and snagged itself in the canopy of the tree.

Hannah tapped her tablet's screen, and the square showing Drone Three's view changed to another image of the same mansion, but with a few leaves on the edges of the view.

"Each drone has several tiny camera pods that it can leave behind," Anna explained.

"Let me see if I can get a better view." Hannah swiped a few instructions, and the image wobbled then stabilized. "That's probably as good as we'll get."

The image panned from the mansion to the road to the surrounding fields. The camera pod of the first mansion was perfectly situated to see the front gates and even a good part of the front grounds.

"Don't you want the pods closer to the house? You know, like inside the grounds?" Mari asked.

"Sure we would," Hannah said. "But technically, that's illegal." She entered a few commands then switched to controlling Drone Seven.

Mari's brow furrowed. "Wait, don't we need to watch the video to see if anything happens?" she asked.

"It's programmed to watch for activity and upload a synopsis report," Susan explained. "And the system has the screenshot of Brax, so the facial recognition software will be looking for him."

"But what if the camera is looking the wrong way when he goes by?" Mari pointed out.

Hannah scowled. "These are full 360-degree video pods. They can see all directions. What you see on the screen is just our panning through the full sphere of view."

Mari had seen some pretty amazing technology before. She loved to follow the latest developments in high tech. But what these ladies had was borderline science fiction. They were definitely more than just some altruistic sorority. No regular do-gooder society had access to this type of technology and information.

She looked at the girls on the couches next to her—Anna intently watching the video feeds, Susan tweaking the facial recognition parameters on her laptop, her legs bouncing and her eyebrows going up and down dramatically the whole time, and Hannah leaning slightly as she flew another drone down toward a nearby mansion. If somehow these women really were secret agents, how had she lucked out and found them? She couldn't believe these complete strangers would do so much to help her rescue her mother.

Tears welled up in Mari's eyes. Embarrassed, she stood and walked to the tall windows overlooking Midtown. The morning sun reflected off the nearby buildings, scattering bright flashes of yellow and white amid the blues and greens of the surrounded buildings and trees.

Half a minute later, Anna stepped up next to her. She was quiet for a long time. When she finally spoke, she said, "Well, it looks like it's going to be a beautiful day."

Mari didn't trust her voice, so she simply nodded.

"How are you holding up?" she asked.

After a long shuddering breath, Mari tried her voice, "Not great," she said.

Anna placed an arm around Mari's back. It was awkward at first, but Mari leaned her head against the tall girl's shoulder, and Anna rested her head softly on top of Mari's. "We'll do everything we can to get your mom out safe," Anna said.

"I only wish there was something I could do to help," Mari replied.

With a quick squeeze to her shoulder, Anna said, "I know what we can do. Let's go get some of your stuff. It'll make you feel more comfortable here. Plus, we can enjoy the morning breeze in the convertible."

The elevator doors opened on a tiny parking garage—much smaller than expected for a high-rise condo building—and Mari was blinded by a dozen bright yellow cars. It looked like the happiest taxi station she could ever imagine except that none of the vehicles were the same. A yellow utility van sat next to a yellow Mercedes sedan with a yellow SUV on the other side, and a yellow convertible next to that. The other row had a yellow minivan, a yellow midsized car, a yellow compact car, and a yellow micro car.

Mari had met people who had an affinity for a certain animal or fruit or flower, but this was taking it to a whole new level. "What is this, the banana garage?" she asked.

"Actually, we call it the Banana Cave. You know, the secret lair where we keep all our special vehicles," Anna replied with a laugh.

Mari wondered how sane—or even normal—these women were. She searched for a tactful comment. "I have always liked bright, happy yellow."

Anna led Mari to a sporty yellow BMW convertible. "Yeah, we thought new-banana-yellow looked better than old-banana-yellow. But don't get too attached to it; we're not going yellow today." Anna's matter-of-fact tone caught Mari off guard. She'd never heard someone talk about the color of their vehicle in such temporary terms.

Once in the car, Anna touched a small yellow square on the dashboard. Swiping sideways through a rainbow of colors, she stopped when the display showed metallic silver and tapped twice. The exterior of the car slowly morphed to match the color on the dash display.

"What color would you say this is?" Anna asked.

Still shocked at seeing a car change color at all, Mari stammered, "Uh, maybe a silver-gray."

Anna beamed. "Exactly what I was going for. See, the other girls don't appreciate this. The most common car color is black, but that's only if you count silver and gray separately. Together, they definitely outnumber black cars." She didn't give any additional explanation.

After a few seconds, Mari ventured a question. "So, you want your car to be the most common color?"

With a shrug, Anna replied, "Today we do. Sometimes it's important to blend in."

On the way to Mari's apartment, Anna explained the plan. Basically, all Mari had to do was pretend like she was going to her apartment, then wait for the bad-guys to show up before rushing back outside. Anna would take it from there, hopefully leading them far away. It sounded easy enough, and the way Anna explained it made it sound relatively simple to pull off.

A few minutes—and about a dozen city blocks—later, they turned onto Mari's street. Her apartment was nothing like Club Banana—or any of the high-rise condos in Midtown—but it was one of the nicer places off campus. She lived in a six-story red brick building that looked like a row of very tall townhomes attached to each other. Of course, in reality, it was six floors of small two-bedroom condos, but Mari liked the quaint look of her street.

Driving slowly toward the apartment, Anna pointed to a dark sedan with tinted windows parked on the street. "That's why you couldn't go back to your condo last night."

Mari craned her head to look as they drove by. It was hard to make out who was in the car, but it wasn't empty.

"Good idea. Make sure they get a really good look at you so the plan will work," Anna said in all sincerity.

Mari's cheeks heated. She hadn't even thought about that. Good thing the plan called for being seen instead of ducking down or she would have ruined the whole thing before it even got started.

Anna pulled up, jack-knife-style, onto the curb on the wrong side of the road, right in front of the door. "Remember to move fast, like you're nervous," Anna said as she nodded for Mari to jump out.

"That won't be hard," Mari said.

She slammed the door to the silver convertible and ran for the front entrance. Once inside, she ran up the stairs to the fourth floor. She hurried to her apartment door, fumbling with her keys. Once she had the door opened, she stopped and waited. Half a minute later, she felt the buzz in her pocket of a single ring on her phone.

That was the signal.

Holding the doorknob in a death grip, Mari strained to hear the anticipated footsteps. The sound of rapid footfalls echoing up the stairwell grew louder. Mari slammed her apartment door shut as hard as she could. The sound reverberated through the hall. After a momentary pause, the approaching sound on the stairs increased its pace. Mari bolted down the hall away from her condo toward the building's second set of stairs.

Half a dozen steps away from the door to the other stairs, Mari heard the door to the main stairs clang open.

"Hey!" an unknown voice called out.

Mari spared a quick glance over her shoulder as she wrenched open the door of her escape route. Two tall men in athletic gear ran down the hall toward her. The pounding of their loud steps matched Mari's heart. She slammed the stairwell door behind her as hard as she could and bounded up the steps to the landing half a flight above her floor.

Once on the landing, out of sight of the door from her floor, Mari pressed herself flat against the wall. Instead of trying to slow her breathing, she took several very quick, deep, heaving breaths. As the stairwell handle rattled, she took one last gasp and held her breath. The door flew open, and the two large men stepped into the stairwell.

Then silence.

Mari was sure they would hear her racing heart as it tried to beat its way out of her chest. The door clanged shut and Mari jumped. A single footstep tapped on the stairs leading up toward her.

Suddenly, racing footsteps clattered on the stairs far below them, followed by the bang of the exit door. Her pursuers took the bait and raced down to catch what they thought was their quarry. As the sounds of men being led on a wild goose chase reached the bottom of the stairs, wheels squealing on pavement reverberated from the small lane outside. Mari could imagine Anna leaving two ten-foot tire marks on the sidewalk. Hopefully, the building supervisor wouldn't know it had been because of Mari.

The stairwell exit door clanged shut, and Mari finally allowed herself to breathe easy. She didn't have the luxury of waiting to make sure they were really gone; her time was limited. She raced back to her apartment. Once inside, she ran to the bathroom, grabbed her overnight bag, and stuffed in a few necessities. In her room, she grabbed clothes by the handful and crammed them into a duffel bag she pulled from the closet. Returning to the front door, she stopped for a second and looked around. Hopefully, she hadn't forgotten anything. This was the first time she'd ever had to pack for a trip in under two minutes.

She locked the door and—reminding herself she wasn't trying to get anyone's attention anymore—she pulled it softly shut. Mari forced herself to take normal, measured steps on her way back down the main stairs. Halfway down, she passed a neighbor whose name she didn't know but that she recognized from her floor. The girl smiled, and Mari did her best to smile back. Could the girl tell Mari was fleeing for her life? Mari always thought that sort of thing would be obvious on the outside, but apparently it wasn't, because the girl simply continued up the stairs as before.

Back on the street, Mari glanced around, wondering how long it would take Anna to lose the stakeout jerks. A moment later, the silver sports car pulled rapidly—but reasonably—around the corner and stopped in front of her.

This woman had some serious driving skills.

Mari threw her bags into the back seat. "That was amazing. How did you lose them so fast?"

"Uh oh," Anna said, looking into her rearview mirror. "I guess I didn't."

Mari glanced up the street in time to see the black sedan careen, much less gracefully, around the curve. So much for their easy getaway. Mari fumbled for the door handle.

"Hurry!" Anna cried.

Without a second thought, Mari gave up on the handle and somersaulted over the door into the car. She had barely hit the leather seat before the tires squealed again. By the time Mari had righted herself and was safely belted in, the close-set townhouses two blocks down were flashing past in a blur. Mari flinched as they swerved around a parked car. She debated simply closing her eyes until they were out of the worst of it.

Anna threw the car into one screeching turn after another as they zigzagged through the increasingly more residential neighborhoods. Mari craned her head around to watch the street behind them and was satisfied to see the black sedan fall farther and farther back with each turn.

"We can't keep this up without getting caught by the police," Anna yelled over the wind as she pulled onto another small lane.

"I'm surprised they haven't noticed you already," Mari called back.

Anna turned onto a larger, two-lane road and weaved in front of a lumbering delivery truck. Their pursuers pulled onto the street half a block behind them. As Anna pressed forward through the Saturday traffic, it became harder and harder to maneuver. Every advantage that she gained by passing slow-moving cars seemed to be negated by the recklessness of the goons on their tail.

"They're getting closer," Mari declared after glancing once more over her shoulder.

"Yep," Anna said, her mouth a grim line. "But unless we want to start jumping curbs or running people off the—hang on!"

The traffic light half a block ahead had turned yellow, but the car in front of them was going to stop. Anna swerved around the slowing car and gunned it through the intersection just as the light turned solidly red.

Anna shook her head. "I hate it when that happens."

"Yeah, and right in front of a church." Mari smirked and pointed to the steeple-topped red brick building flashing past.

"Hey, at least it's not a Sunday. That really would be a sin." Anna's face relaxed a bit now that they had some breathing room.

When she heard the sound of tires squealing behind them, Mari turned around just in time to see the black car swerve to avoid a crash as it ran the red light at the church.

Anna glanced in her rearview mirror. "Now that's a sin even if it's not a Sunday." She gunned the engine and drifted around another turn.

The black sedan made the same turn about the time that Anna was again forced to slow because of traffic.

She checked her mirror. "We're going to have to bend the rules a little bit." She pulled around a car waiting at the light and drove over the shoulder and onto the sidewalk. With a friendly wave at the short line of cars honking at her, she swung into the sharp, hairpin on-ramp to the freeway.

As they sped through the turn, Mari saw that the black sedan didn't even hesitate to match their maneuver. They were within spitting distance now.

Once on the straight part of the on-ramp, Anna pushed the little speedster up to freeway speed in three seconds, leaving the lumbering sedan in the dust. Mari felt like they were about to launch into orbit.

The on-ramp had a long stretch running parallel to the interstate before merging. Anna didn't wait for the lanes to combine, however. As soon as they passed the cement barrier, she lurched across the gravel strewn no-man's-land into the flow of traffic.

Mari's mother would have muttered some choice words about a driver like Anna. They sped along the freeway, weaving in and out of traffic until Anna suddenly pointed to the cars ahead. "There! That's perfect."

Mari wasn't sure what Anna wanted her to see. It looked like a normal line of cars. Anna accelerated forward and Mari saw it—a small silver convertible. It wasn't the exact model of their car, but it looked pretty similar from a distance.

Anna checked the rearview. "We're going to have to time this just right."

Mari looked back and saw the sedan gaining speed. Anna pulled up within a few cars of the other silver convertible and slowed slightly.

"They're going to catch us!" Mari said, watching their pursuers closing in on them.

"That's what they think," Anna said with a broad grin.

She gunned the car forward and veered across traffic to pull on the other side of a large eighteen-wheeler. The sedan changed lanes to follow. They lurched forward, ahead of the long truck, and as soon as the sedan had reached the back of the semi-trailer, Anna swerved in front of the cab and slowed down on the other side. It was a do-si-do with their chasers and the eighteen-wheeler was in the middle.

With several quick swipes on the dash display, Anna changed the car's exterior back to yellow and the car's top started lifting out of its storage compartment.

"We can't close the roof at freeway speeds!" Mari yelled over the wind and traffic noise.

"Sure we can! It's reinforced," Anna shouted back.

A few seconds later, the roof of the small car sealed and the cabin fell silent.

"Wow," Mari murmured.

They were slowly losing speed, allowing the semi-truck to pass them. Mari watched under the trailer as the sedan flashed ahead of the cab on the other side and swerved back into their lane, in front of them now.

"Better duck down a little," Anna said as she tapped a few more commands into the system and the windows slowly darkened.

Peeking barely over the dash, Mari saw the black sedan pull up next to the other silver convertible, crowding into its lane. The small car swerved slightly, obviously wondering why a strange car was driving so close. The goons in the black sedan never even noticed the little sports car with the newly-yellow exterior as it slowed down behind the semi-trailer.

"Oh look, there's our exit," Anna said.

With extremely conservative and courteous driving, Anna signaled and merged slowly across several lanes. She took the Midtown exit, and five minutes later, they were driving into the condo tower's parking garage, taking a side ramp through an automatic security gate into the private garage reserved for the penthouse.

Mari stepped gingerly from the car. "That was, hands-down, the most exciting thing I've ever done in a car."

Anna raised an eyebrow at her. "I should hope so. You've only been in college for a month."

Mari glanced at the other yellow cars in the hidden garage. She stepped up to an SUV and peeked in through the glass. It had a similar layout of special displays on the dash.

"That's Big Banana. We take that when we have guests." Anna pointed toward the other cars and rattled off, "Fat, Posh, Family, Business, Teen, and Bitsy."

Bitsy Banana was the adorable micro car. It would have looked better in candy-apple red, Mari decided.

Her head spun with the level of wealth these cars represented, not to mention the penthouse which took up the entire top floor of the most expensive high rise in Midtown Atlanta. It was hard to fathom. If what Susan had said was true—that they help people—at least the money was being put to good use. Her attention was drawn back to the convertible sports coupe as the top slowly folded back inside its compartment. "And this one?"

"My favorite," Anna said with a wide grin. "Hot Banana."

Chapter Four

B y the light of the sun streaming in through the guest room windows the next morning, Mari realized how stupid the decision to rob her mother's lab had been. She was almost grateful that Hannah had overpowered and stopped her.

Almost.

She didn't know if these Banana Girls could actually save her mother, but they stood a much better chance than she did on her own.

Mari quickly dressed and went out into the living room. The smell of something fresh-baked and delicious met her.

When Susan saw Mari, she leaned forward from her spot on the couch and gestured wildly for Mari to hurry. She pointed at a small piece of something in her hand. "Anna made blueberry muffins," she said through a mouth full of food.

"Don't talk with your mouth full, Suz," Anna called from the kitchen in a motherly tone.

Susan grinned and blocked her mouth with her hand. "Go grab some before they're gone."

"How many muffins can three girls eat?" Mari asked as she strolled into the kitchen.

"You'd be surprised," Anna answered. She held out a plate of fresh muffins and a glass of juice. "Plus, with you there are five of us. You just haven't met Katie yet."

Mari had been so exhausted the night before, she'd barely made it till nightfall before she passed out in her bed. "When do I get to meet her?" Mari asked as she made her way, breakfast in hand, to sit next to Susan.

Hannah spoke from her yellow chaise lounge in the corner. Mari hadn't even noticed her there. "As soon as her *study session* is done." Hannah made air quotes with her fingers, a very sarcastic expression on her face.

A few minutes later, the balcony door at the far end of the living room slid open, and another twenty-something girl walked in. She was shorter than the others and had long, jet-black hair and dark eyes. Mari guessed that she was of Asian descent. She wore a yellow polka-dot bikini and was pulling a guy by the hand. He was tall and muscular, wearing only wet shorts, with a shirt draped over his shoulder. His light brown hair was still dripping.

Mari blushed and thought she should look away, even though she didn't want to.

"Hey everyone!" the short girl said in a very high-pitched, flirty voice. "This is Greg. He came over to help me with my calculus."

"Hi, Greg," the other roommates answered in identical deadpan voices, like welcoming someone to an anonymous help group.

"Hey," he replied. That was all he said. Then he just stood there smiling at the girls as if he was happy to let them admire him for as long as they wanted.

The girl in the bikini rolled her eyes. "Anyway, he was just leaving. Thanks, Greg."

The muscular guy smiled and walked across the living room, dripping all the way. As soon as he was gone, the small girl in the bikini spun around and faced them. "Would it kill you guys to get to know the boys I like?" she asked in a much less high-pitched, much more intelligent-sounding voice.

"There are just so many of them, Katie," Susan said with an exaggerated widening of her eyes. "And you go through them so fast."

"Yeah, how'd the *studying* go?" Hannah asked without looking up from her phone.

Katie walked around the couch and sat down next to Susan. "Well, we started studying in here. Then we decided we would do better studying in the hot tub—"

"Better studying of what?" Hannah mumbled.

Katie continued as if Hannah hadn't spoken. "—and since I was already wearing my new bikini, and he didn't mind getting his shorts wet, well . . ." Katie held up her arms in a shrug that clearly meant there wasn't anything else she could have done.

Susan shrugged to match Katie's gesture. Hannah muttered something unintelligible.

Then Katie seemed to notice Mari for the first time. "Hi," she said with a smile.

"This is Mari," Susan explained. "We're going to help rescue her mother," she added in a mock whisper.

Katie nodded. "Good idea."

Apparently, this was a common enough thing that Katie didn't think twice about it.

"Um, I can help you with your calculus, if you need," Mari offered to Katie. She wanted to do something to repay these girls.

"Oh, aren't you so sweet," Katie smiled back. "I'm actually pretty good at calculus. But I don't let the boys know that," she added the last part with a mischievous giggle. Susan joined the giggling.

From behind the couch, Anna waved a wire whisk in Katie's direction. "Katie, you know what my mom always says, 'if you can't respect yourself, the boys sure won't.'"

With a guilty cringe, Katie replied, "I know, I know. But the hottest guys always tend to be the dumbest. I have to act dumber than them if I'm going to get them to help me."

"You could always offer to help *them*," Mari suggested.

Katie laughed. "Yeah, like that'd ever work."

Susan's watch dinged with a notification. She swiped across the screen and read the message. Her face stretched into an expression of pure delight, and she started bouncing. "Hey girls, guess what? We just got a positive ID!"

Hannah perked up and set her phone down. "Really? Which drone?"

"What difference does it make which drone?" Susan replied with a dismissive wave of her hand.

"It makes a difference to me," Hannah huffed.

Susan rolled her eyes and glanced down at her computer. "Fine. It looks like it was number four."

"What does a positive ID mean?" Mari asked.

"One of the drones caught a match to your picture of Brax." Susan pantomimed taking a picture.

Mari immediately stood up. "Great! Let's call the police."

"Wow. Nice enthusiasm." Katie patted Mari on the arm and pulled her back down onto the couch.

Mari looked around at the girls, desperation rising in her chest. "Don't you understand? He said I've only got five days! And it's been nearly two already! We have to call someone to get my mother out before it's too late."

Katie smiled patiently. "Mari, if we call the police, they'll just charge in there and make a mess of everything."

Mari frowned. "Then who should we call? The FBI or the CIA or something?"

A wide grin spread across Katie's face. "If you call the FBI, how do you know they won't just call us?" she asked playfully.

"Yeah, the CIA usually texts," Hannah muttered drily.

Katie must have seen the confused look on Mari's face because she leaned over and said, "Let me explain the way this usually goes: we get our first lead, Anna asks some questions, we do some research, Anna gives us some assignments, and the plan starts coming together."

"How long have you been doing this sort of thing?" Mari asked.

Katie scrunched her forehead and looked up as if searching for something. "Let's see, it was near the beginning of my sophomore year, so I guess I've been on the team for about a year now. They asked me to help out on a . . . project . . . because they didn't have anyone who could do the electrical and computer stuff. Well, Susan can do some very basic coding; she's majoring in applied mathematics, and she's always loved computers. But they needed someone who could design the circuits and program the PCBs and stuff. That's my specialty."

Mari nodded. "What about Anna and Hannah? What are their specialties?"

Katie smiled. "Well, you've already seen some of Hannah's. She's in mechanical engineering with a minor in aerospace because she loves drones so much. Anna's major is chemistry, which might be why she's so good in the kitchen." Katie lowered her voice slightly. "You wouldn't know it by looking at her, but she's quite the pyromaniac. In fact, Hannah and Anna's first mi— . . . er . . . project together was Anna's pyrotechnics combined with some crazy drone flying by Hannah and it ended up—"

"Katie . . ." Anna chided. "Don't annoy Mari with our boring stories."

Katie grinned. "Sorry." She turned back to Mari but spoke loud enough for everyone to hear. "Anyway, Anna's good at planning stuff and mothering us all to death, and Hannah is good at being rich and pessimistic . . . and sulking."

Hannah shot Katie a withering glare that made the other ladies laugh.

"So, getting back to Mari's mom." Susan activated the main screen on the wall and sent it the results of the drone pods' video surveillance. "This was shot outside the Keating Mansion at 8:27 AM this morning."

The video showed a car rolling down the drive from the large house then waiting for the main gates to open. As it pulled out onto the main road, the video paused, and the frame zoomed in on the driver.

Mari gasped.

It was Brax.

"I guess that means the facial recognition software is working correctly," Hannah said dryly.

"What do we know about Keating Mansion?" Anna asked Susan.

Susan tapped her keyboard, somehow able to hit the right keys even while it was bouncing up and down. "Belongs to Charles Henry Keating, founder of Keating BioMedical," Susan read from the screen. "At closing bell on Friday, the market-cap of the company was 15.2 billion dollars," she looked up, "rounding off a few million. Mr. Keating's personal assets are estimated around 102 million."

Anna looked at the screen and squinted. She pointed to a section of the picture behind the mansion. "Can you enlarge that area?"

Hannah grabbed the display control tablet and zoomed the image. On the screen, there was a large building behind the mansion that looked different from the main home.

"What's that building back there?" Anna asked.

Susan searched furiously. "County website says it's a workshop."

"Big workshop," Hannah observed.

"Let's see . . ." Susan continued. "Here's an article that says Mr. Keating manages the entire business from his home, including a select team of research and development personnel."

Anna's eyebrows went up. "Hmm. This is getting interesting." Anna pointed to the large building behind the mansion. "If this is Keating BioMed's headquarters, and Brax was seen driving away from the grounds, they might be connected because of the possible application of Dr. Sandoval's research to the human body."

"Or the company could just be a front for black-market arms dealing," Hannah added.

Anna gave a non-committal sound of agreement. She stepped up to look closer at the screen, scrutinizing the perimeter of the grounds. "Looks like the mansion has a fair amount of security in place. I think this one might require a soft touch." Turning away from the screen, she sat on an empty loveseat and looked at the other three ladies. They all leaned forward slightly as if they were in a huddle. "Here's the basic plan. We get someone in there. We figure out where they're holding Mari's mother, and we get her out."

Mari looked around at the others. They all nodded in agreement.

That was it? Mari couldn't believe the plan could be that simple.

Anna pointed to Katie. "Let's see if we can get someone inside."

"You got it, boss," Katie replied as she stood and walked into another room. Mari assumed she was going to change clothes, but maybe it was an assignment that could be done in a polka-dot bikini.

Anna continued, "Susan, check that county information again and see if there's an active utility easement anywhere along the property line. It'd be great if we could drop a few more pods." She nodded in Hannah's direction.

"I'm on it," Susan said as her fingers flew over her bouncing keyboard.

"We could always do my fence crawling trick to get some eyes out there," Hannah offered.

"You've walked along a fence before? Like a cat?" Mari could hardly believe that any of this was real.

Hannah grinned. "Not me. My mecha-pillars."

"The actual fence line itself is sort of a gray area when it comes to surveillance," Anna said. "We can usually make the argument that the camera wasn't technically on anyone's property because it was exactly on the line. Of course, somebody owns the line, but legally, it might take a while to figure out who."

First, all of the hints about missions—or "projects" as they kept calling them—then the comment about the FBI, and now evidence that they had apparently been involved—more than once—in the legality of close-up surveillance.

Mari couldn't think of any other plausible explanation.

"I'm not saying you have to tell me—you barely know me—but I'm still pretty sure you're spies."

No one reacted right away. Mari saw several furtive glances exchanged.

Finally, Susan spoke. "Actually, we're more like ninjas," she said with a sly smile as she continued typing. "Freelance ninjas who help people."

Mari turned to Anna, who gave her a noncommittal shrug.

Katie walked back into the room a few minutes later. "Got something," she announced. "We can get someone in as a personal assistant to the lab's technology manager. But it's a full-time job. There aren't any part-time spots available. That's the best I could do."

"So, whoever goes in, we're talking full-time undercover for . . . what?" Anna paused to look at the others. "Maybe a week or two?"

The others nodded.

Anna continued. "Let's decide who should go. Then I can call Stacia."

"Who's Stacia? Is there another Banana Girl?" Mari asked.

Katie laughed. "No, Stacia's our bo—"

Three sets of eyes quickly turned toward Katie.

". . . uh, I mean, she's our . . . sponsor?" Katie finished.

Susan tried to suppress a giggle.

"Well, Anna and Mari have already been seen by the hired muscle, so they're both out of the running," Hannah said, clearly trying to change the subject.

Mari whipped around to look at Hannah. "Wait. Why am I out? I want to be the one to go in and find my mother."

"First off," Hannah replied," You're not trained for this type of assignment—"

"I had a temp job as a secretary once. How hard could it be?"

"Second," Hannah continued as if she hadn't been interrupted, "you've been visually ID'd. In addition to the fight with the street thugs, you actually had a video call with the suspect."

"She'd go in disguise, obviously," Katie pointed out.

Hannah shot Katie a scowl. "Third, she's too emotionally close to the situation. It could compromise the mission."

Anna took up the cause. "One might argue that her love for her mother would make her the best candidate for the job."

Hannah gaped at Anna. She looked around at the rest of the team as if she couldn't believe they were arguing in favor of Mari going in. Hannah folded her arms and glared at Mari. "She's not one of us," she declared finally.

Mari did her best to hold Hannah's stare.

"That's true, she's not a Banana Girl," Anna conceded. "But I think we can make an exception in this case."

"Yeah, I can't miss my classes for two weeks," Katie volunteered. "That embedded systems class is kicking my butt, plus I just claimed the seat next to the hottie in my signal processing class. There was this gorgeous blonde—no offense Hannah—who thought she was going to get that seat. But I made sure she—"

"Katie . . ." Anna gently cut in.

Katie giggled. "Sorry."

"And I have an in-class midterm next week I can't miss," Susan pointed out.

Anna shrugged and turned to Hannah. "They're out. So it's either you or me. Or we can have Mari do it."

Hannah huffed. "Fine. But I still think this is a bad idea."

"When does the position open up?" Anna asked.

"Tomorrow morning," Katie answered.

All attention turned to Mari. Her eyes went wide.

Tomorrow morning. She'd have less than twenty-four hours to learn the ins and outs of undercover work or her mother would suffer the wrath of a lunatic.

No pressure.

She took a deep breath and nodded. "I'm ready. Just tell me what I need to do."

With an affirming smile to Mari, Anna turned to Katie. "You and Susan get working on a disguise for her."

"Makeover time!" Katie cheered and ran out of the room.

Anna called after her. "Not a makeover, Katie. A disguise."

Susan followed after Katie, strutting like she was on a catwalk.

Anna sighed and turned back to Mari. "While they're working on that, why don't we do some basic self-defense training." She stood and beckoned Mari to follow.

"Do you need any help?" Hannah offered.

"I think you already tested her skills yesterday," Anna said with a grin.

Mari was glad that it wouldn't be Hannah testing her on fighting skills. That girl always seemed so grouchy around Mari.

Mari followed Anna out of the penthouse and across the hall to another enormous suite that had been completely opened into one large workout area. With one wall entirely covered with mirrors and racks of fighting equipment scattered throughout the space, it looked like a cross between a dance studio and a dojo. Mari also caught a glimpse of a dozen exercise machines in a side room.

Mari brushed her hand along several martial arts weapons before resting her hand on the ballet barre mounted against the mirrors. "Do the ballerinas dance with nunchucks?"

Anna laughed. "We don't do fighting instruction at the same time as dance instruction. That would be silly."

Though Mari had meant it as a joke, it was obvious that Anna's reply was serious. Clearly, these ladies were no ordinary college coeds. Mari would make sure not to underestimate them.

Anna led Mari over to a corner with foam mats on the floor. She turned to face Mari and crouched slightly. "Okay, I've seen you fight against street thugs, but let's see what you can really handle," Anna said.

Mari had barely turned to face her new friend when Anna came at her. On pure reflexes alone, Mari was able to deflect Anna's grab and push her away.

"Not bad," Anna said. "You've had a self-defense class or two?"

Mari nodded. "Two weeks, actually. My mother wanted to make sure I was safe when I started going places on my own."

"Can you handle a trained attacker?" Anna asked.

Just as Mari opened her mouth to say no, Anna charged. Mari swung and ducked, working on pure adrenaline. She was able to deflect some of Anna's barrage of kicks and punches, but not most. Fortunately, Mari could tell that Anna was pulling her punches.

"You gave up too much ground." Anna nodded to the floor where Mari was now standing six feet off the end of the mat.

"Gave up ground? I was trying not to get pummeled."

"We'll need to practice a few of these." Anna showed Mari several quick arm movements that would work as blocks. "But what you really need to learn is to follow a block immediately with an attack. You didn't throw a single punch at me."

"Yeah. I realize that now."

With a smile, Anna moved back to her starting position. "Are you ready?" Anna said after a pause.

Mari lowered into her stance. "Yep."

As Anna moved forward, Mari went on the offensive. She jabbed a fist for Anna's midsection, but Anna blocked. Anna countered with her own attack. This time, Mari withstood her assault without ceding ground.

"Much better," Anna said, breathing hard.

Mari nodded in response. "I wish I had known this stuff yesterday morning."

Anna grinned. "We don't teach the good stuff until we know someone's on our side."

For the next hour, Anna tested Mari's abilities in hand-to-hand combat. They didn't touch any of the weapons because Anna said Mari wouldn't really need them on this particular assignment.

"We'll skip the dancing lesson, too," Anna said as they walked back across the hall. "Some missions require dancing, but this one probably won't."

Mari's eyebrows went up. "Probably?"

Anna simply grinned back at her as they walked through the penthouse door.

Before Mari had made it five steps through the door, Katie had her by the arm.

"It's makeover time!" she said as she dragged Mari across the living room to a room that looked like a beauty salon. There was a hair-washing station, a professional makeup vanity with lights, and several racks of clothing. Susan stood at a shelf browsing through bottles of the entire rainbow of hair dye colors.

Mari protested. "You know, I don't usually worry about makeup and hair, so I don't think I need a makeover."

Katie threw up her hands. "Fine, we won't call it a makeover then. It's a disguise overhaul for a covert mission. Is that good enough?"

Susan went to work on Mari's hair, beginning with the cut.

Katie busied herself picking the outfits Mari would wear: a navy pencil skirt, a red flared skirt, three pairs of business slacks, blouses in a rainbow of colors, and a small, sleeveless black dress.

"We won't lead off with this one," Katie said, holding up the dress. "But it could definitely come in handy later."

While Susan dyed, washed, and styled Mari's hair, Katie tested different shades of pencil and blush to complement Mari's Latina skin tone, trying—unsuccessfully—to stay out of Susan's way.

The attention and pampering were completely foreign to Mari. And she felt a little guilty for enjoying it so much.

After her hair was dried and styled, Katie added makeup, casual jewelry, and trendy black-rimmed glasses—no prescription.

The girls walked back into the living room a few hours later to show off Mari's new style. From the gasps and stares of the other three girls, Mari assumed the look worked. Susan and Katie hadn't let her check a mirror as the finishing touches were put on, so when Mari finally got a glimpse, it was a shock.

Her normally straight black hair—while mostly still the original color—was now layered, shoulder-length, highlighted with strands of platinum and blonde, and flipped up at the ends. She wobbled a little on the short heels. It was a completely different girl staring back at her.

Katie looked at Hannah. "Well?"

"It could work," Hannah grudgingly admitted before going back to her phone.

"You look fabulous." Anna said as she pulled Mari away from the mirror with a gentle smile. "You can admire your new look later, but right now, we need to get your brain ready." Anna led Mari to sit next to her on the couch. She picked up a tablet and tilted it toward Mari. "Here's the information on your new job. Your name is Charlotte Preston—"

Mari pulled a face. "Charlotte? Isn't that an old woman's name?"

Anna looked over at Hannah, who lifted a skeptical brow.

"I suppose we can change it," Anna said. "What did you have in mind?"

"I've always liked the name Brooklyn."

Hannah set her phone down with an abrupt huff. "Unless it's a name you've used before, like a nickname, it won't work," she said. "Agents train for years to work undercover. If you can't respond to your alias instinctively, you will be discovered."

Katie eyed Hannah. "Agents?"

Hannah returned her attention to the phone, muttering, "That's what I've heard, anyway."

"How about Marina?" Anna suggested. "That's pretty close to Mari."

Mari thought for a moment. Could she be a Marina? It shouldn't be too hard.

Mari's smile slowly broadened as she imagined walking into a new job with a new wardrobe, a new hairstyle, *and* a new name.

"Marina it is, then," Anna said, adding a few notes to her tablet before continuing the briefing. "You're a recent graduate—"

Mari's eyebrows shot up. "A college graduate?"

"—Associates Degree in Secretarial Science—"

"Is that even a real degree?"

Anna set the tablet down, cocked her head, and gave Mari a look that reminded her very much of when she had pushed her mother too far. "We're never going to get through this if you keep interrupting me," she scolded.

From across the room, Susan scowled and playfully wagged a finger at Mari, imitating Anna's reproving tone with her hands and over-exaggerated facial expressions. Mari giggled.

Anna flashed Susan a look that made her hands fall innocently back to her laptop. Anna turned back to look at Mari.

Mari dipped her head. "Sorry."

Anna straightened and took a breath. "You'll be assisting Carol Fleishman, head manager of technology at the mansion lab. She's forty-two years old. She's a career Keating BioMedical employee, moving up within the IT department before switching to equipment technology. She's tough on her own assistants, probably because of what she sees as a lack of dedication to the work. With your degree in secretarial science, you'll have an automatic in."

"But I don't have a degree in secretarial science! The only degree I have is from high school last year." Mari's head spun with all the ways she might mess things up.

Setting down the tablet again, Anna gave Mari a very maternal look. "If you're worried about it, maybe we could work a different angle—"

"No!" Mari said quickly. "It's just a lot to process at once. I can do it."

Anna considered her for a moment. "Okay, we can come back to this. Let's switch to something else for a bit," Anna said, nodding to Hannah.

Hannah stood from her lounger in the corner and moved to the wall that separated the living room from the entry hall. She swirled a circle with two fingers near the center of the elegant white wall. A long horizontal seam suddenly appeared in the middle of the wall's matte surface and the top half lifted open like a clamshell, revealing what appeared to be a hidden jewelry counter.

"These items—" Hannah turned to see that Mari was still sitting on the couch. Her impatient look instantly conveyed that Mari should have followed her.

Mari jumped up and ran around the couch to join her.

Without even acknowledging she'd arrived, Hannah continued, "Are mission-specific. The regular jewelry is in the salon room, but these have a very different purpose."

Stepping to the side, Hannah pointed to a large glass display case. "You'll need some simple business-professional jewelry." She pointed to a matched set of watches in gold, silver, white, and rose. "These should cover just about any outfit you would want to wear to work." She lifted the glass top and picked up the rose-gold one. "They're smart watches, so they'll connect to your phone and let you make calls or text. But they also have next-generation GPS, so we'll be able to locate you within a few inches at all times. Plus, the watches have a tiny camera that you can activate, just in case you need to take a picture of something."

Hannah reached for a higher display and pulled out a bracelet from a set that perfectly matched the watches. "And in case you need to do more, each of these bracelets has a ten-inch snaking camera for peeking under doors and an ultra-sensitive microphone array. It will constantly monitor and record your surroundings throughout the day. For even better audio clarity—and the ability to listen through obstacles—it's also got a piezo mic, but you'll need to bring it into contact with the door or wall for that to work. Don't worry if you can't always do that, the regular mics can actually pick up pretty good sound even if you're just walking by a room."

With great effort, Mari kept her jaw from dropping. Inch-accurate GPS? Microphones that could listen through walls? She stared in awe at the watches and bracelets. "Any other toys? Like a pair of pump heels that are really flamethrowers?"

"She's not taking my favorite heels out on her first mission, is she?" Katie asked from the kitchen.

Anna and Hannah both turned quickly in Katie's direction.

"I mean . . . just joking about my favorite heels having anything to do with flamethrowers," Katie called out.

Anna looked past Mari with a meaningful glance at Hannah.

"Remember to grab a watch and bracelet every morning," Hannah instructed, her tone all business. "You can pick whichever color matches your outfit. Once you reconnect it to your phone, it'll download the requirements of the mission."

"Just so we're clear," Anna waited until Mari really focused on her, "your primary job is to be Ms. Fleishman's assistant. You have to do that job well, or you'll never get the chance to find your mom. So don't do anything that would jeopardize your cover job. And never talk about us. Ever. If they find out you're working with the Banana Girls, it would compromise the entire operation—your mom's safety, your safety, our team—everything."

At first, Mari wondered if she was joking. Who could possibly be concerned about a bunch of college girls belonging to an odd sorority named after a fruit? But Anna's expression clearly meant she was serious, so Mari nodded her understanding.

The weight of what must really be going on beneath the innocent exterior began to sink in. Her mother's freedom—and her own safety—depended on how well she could pull off this mission.

No pressure.

CHAPTER FIVE

THE NEXT MORNING, MARI rode with Hannah—who posed as the ride-share driver and wore a short black wig and dark, goth makeup—through the suburban Atlanta countryside to the mansion of Charles Henry Keating. They'd taken Business Banana—the sensible sedan—figuring that a ride-share driver wouldn't have a convertible BMW sports car or a luxury Mercedes. The exterior paint job was currently set to a nondescript charcoal.

Hannah had insisted on driving her. Mari wasn't sure if it was because she wanted to talk her out of it—she hadn't tried yet—or if she wanted to give her some last-minute warning. Maybe Hannah was the only one who didn't have classes that morning.

Sunlight dappled the road as it twisted and turned, and green walls of shrubbery and trees whizzed past in a blur. Mari wondered what kind of people lived in these neighborhoods.

What kind of neighbors did kidnappers have?

"You've got your mission phone?" Hannah asked.

"Yes. It's right here." Mari held up the phone.

"And you didn't bring your personal phone with you, right?" Hannah pressed.

"Uh, no. Where would I even keep it?" Mari looked down at the fashionable—though somewhat form-fitting—pencil skirt. "This thing doesn't have any kind of pockets large enough to—"

"Remember to text your friend 'Bianca' whenever you need to contact us," Hannah reminded her. "And you'll get a text from Bianca if we need to contact you."

"I know." Mari sounded more annoyed than she'd meant to, but it got Hannah to shut up.

Mari's palms began to sweat as they approached the front gate and stopped at the security guard's booth. She stared straight forward as Hannah greeted the guard, but then she wondered if that's what a calm, non-spy-type girl would do in this situation.

Hannah explained—in a very blasé attitude—why she was at the front gates and who she was dropping off. The security guard checked his tablet and allowed her through, adding that her car would need to exit the grounds within three minutes to avoid a security incursion. Hannah's eyebrow ticked up slightly, and Mari wondered if Hannah was itemizing the requirements to infiltrate the mansion's tight security.

The long driveway to the mansion wound through perfectly manicured gardens and compact magnolia tree groves. As they rounded the last bend, Keating Mansion came into full view. With its long marble staircase, porticoed entry, and gabled windows dotting the roofline, the front of the mansion could have easily been used on one of those BBC Jane Austen movies.

As they approached the mansion, Hannah finally spoke again. "Don't do anything crazy. Do your job well and observe. Susan will pick you up this evening."

Mari took a deep breath. "Thanks."

She grabbed the small folder with the documents for getting hired under her fake identity and stepped out of the car. The long, white front steps bordered by green shrubs and manicured lawn stretched up to the front door. As she reached the top of the stairs, the front doors swung open to reveal a grand entry hall with two sweeping marble staircases. Mari stepped cautiously through the doors and gaped at the luxury surrounding her. A man in a black tuxedo stood with impeccable rigidity just inside the doors.

"Your name, miss?" he asked.

"Marina?" Mari squeaked the name out like a question.

"Miss Marina . . .?" the butler prompted.

She drew a quick, fortifying breath. "Marina Preston. I'm Ms. Fleishman's new assistant." She couldn't help but gaze up at the thousands of crystals winking at her from the chandelier over their heads.

The butler nodded and closed the doors. "Follow me," he instructed as he set off down the large central hall.

They walked down a hallway of dark panels and ornate rugs past a dozen closed doors before the hallway opened into a small parlor that had been converted into an office foyer. Through an archway in the opposite wall, a newer, more modern hallway of tiled flooring and tall glass windows stretched away from the parlor room out the back of the mansion. The archway was obviously not a part of the original mansion, and it stood as a line of demarcation between the old house and the new addition. The contrast of decor between the old and the new was striking.

Peering through the opening down a long, wide hall, Mari could see workers in white coats walking together, coming and going in and out of different rooms. This must be the laboratory building that was listed as a workshop on the county register.

Some workshop.

At the confluence of the old mansion and the opening to the new addition, a beige and gray cubicle sat next to an open office door. The butler lifted an arm to indicate that she precede him around the cubicle to the door. If this was Ms. Fleishman's office, then the cubicle must belong to her assistant. Mari imagined how hard it would be to get any work done with a constant flow of people going back and forth down the corridor.

She would have to take the Banana Girls' advice and keep her head down. Literally.

The butler presented Mari at the office door and promptly returned to the main part of the house.

"Come in," Ms. Fleishman said curtly. "Welcome to the team, Miss Preston. In the future, please use the employee entrance." She waved vaguely toward the back of the mansion before continuing. "This position is about following instructions and doing what needs to be done. Do you understand?"

Mari nodded. "Yes, ma'am."

"Good. Take these replacement circuit boards to Lab 5. Deliver them personally to Dr. Sorensen." She held a small box across the desk toward Mari.

Even though Mari had no idea how to find Lab 5, she was pretty sure her boss had basically told her to figure it out. She grabbed the box and scampered from the room.

Mari had intently studied the county blueprints of Keating Mansion the night before, hoping that would translate into not looking like a bumbling idiot this morning.

She turned left at her cubicle and faced down the long corridor to the research labs. Hoping that she looked like she knew what she was doing, Mari strode off with all the determination she could muster. As she stepped into the modern addition to the old mansion, sconce lamps, ornate walls, and hard-wood floors gave way to tile, neutral charcoal-gray panels, and fluorescent lights. The rooms were numbered, so it would be easy enough to find Lab 5.

She considered the package in her hand. This would be the perfect chance to explore a little of the laboratory wing without arousing too much suspicion. After all, what could be more innocent than a new employee searching for the right place to go?

Lab 5 was obviously down the hall ahead of her, so Mari took the first set of stairs up to the second floor. The labs on the second floor looked much like the ones on the first floor, except that the windows into these labs had an amber tint, much like the cleanrooms in her mother's building on campus. The halls radiated an eerie, yellowish glow.

With a glance at her smartwatch, Mari checked to make sure the bracelet was detecting and recording sound. Maybe it would pick up her mother through one of these doors.

Not wanting to attract undue attention from the workers inside, Mari walked confidently down the hallway, doing her best to memorize the layout and purpose of each of the rooms.

As she came to a branching hallway, she peeked around the corner to see which way she should go next. Two men dressed in long white lab coats—one older, angular, and balding, the other young, tall, with terrific hair—stood in the middle of the hall.

She ducked back behind the corner.

The older man was facing the other way, but the younger man had been facing her.

Had he seen her?

Their conversation continued without a pause, so after a few moments, Mari risked another peek. The younger man had shifted slightly so that he had a perfect view of her as she peered around the corner. With the subtlest glance, he looked her way and winked.

Mari pulled back again, her heart racing.

The nerve of some guys!

There was nothing else she could do now but confidently continue and hope for the best. After a deep breath, Mari channeled her inner catwalk model and strutted out from her hiding place, continuing down the main hallway. She hoped the three seconds she would be in their view would be short enough to not attract any more attention. A sideways glance told her that the younger man was staring at her, no subtlety this time.

Tipped off by the brazen stare, the older man turned around just as Mari ducked out of view.

"Hang on a minute!" the older man called out.

Run or stop?

Mari knew she couldn't run in the situation, but the urge was strong. With a cringe, she stopped and turned.

"Who are you?" the man puffed once he caught up to her.

"I'm Marina Preston, Ms. Fleishman's new assistant," she said with her most confident voice.

"What are you doing on the fabrication floor?" he shot back. His shifty eyes searched her face.

"Oh, I'm delivering this package to Dr. Sorensen in Lab 5." She timidly held out the package, hoping it looked like a good excuse.

"Lab 5 is on the first floor," he countered. "Can't you read signs?"

The younger man stepped forward. "If this is Miss Preston's first day, she may not know where all of the labs are yet." The younger man's voice had a subtle, almost knee-melting drawl to it. His broad smile was easy on the eyes, too. "I'm sure Miss Preston didn't mean any harm by it. Why don't I show her the way?"

He had a casual way of speaking, as if he wasn't in any hurry to finish his words. With his wavy, unkempt brown hair and captivating green eyes, Mari was having trouble looking anywhere but at him. And to top it off, there was a dimple in his left cheek when he smiled.

The older man huffed. "Fine." He strode off down the side hall.

When the older man was gone, the handsome young man turned back to her and smiled. "I'm Trey Brooks," he said.

"Hi," Mari said as she tucked an escaped strand of platinum-highlighted hair behind her ears and tried not to stare at Trey's chest.

"Don't worry about Dr. Cluff," Trey said in a low voice, jabbing a thumb in the direction of the departing, annoyed older man. "He sometimes gets cranky when he finds strangers in his research facility."

"Oh, is Dr. Cluff in charge? I thought it was Mr. Keating's company."

Trey's eyebrows went up. "Well, I suppose it is."

"Hopefully, Mr. Keating has better manners than Dr. Cluff," Mari added under her breath.

Trey tossed his head back in a bark of laughter.

Mari really had to get better at keeping her commentary to herself. Besides, she hadn't thought her comment was that funny.

"I think you'll find Mr. Keating's manners are impeccable. Overly so," Trey said with a crooked, dimpled smile.

They walked together to the end of the hall and down the stairs. Trey escorted her to Lab 5 and introduced her to Dr. Sorensen, a laid-back scientist in her early fifties with brown hair highlighted in gray and an intense expression. Mari found it easy to talk to Dr. Sorensen because she reminded her so much of other researchers she'd met in her mother's lab over the years.

Following their visit to Lab 5, Trey gave her a quick tour of the rest of the research wing, including his own office on the third floor. Though he insisted it was nothing fancy, Mari couldn't help but admire the view of the well-manicured mansion gardens he had from his windows.

After the informal tour, Trey accompanied Mari back to her cubicle and stood talking with her for another twenty minutes about the nanotechnology research they were doing in the lab. Most of the terms he used were familiar from her mother's work, but she did her best to act like she didn't really know what he was talking about.

"Hey, I forgot to show you the bistro cafe. That's where most of the employees take lunch," Trey said with a big smile. "Why don't I swing by around noon and show you where it's at?"

Mari watched his expression for a moment. His grin only grew under her scrutiny. She narrowed her eyes at him. "Did you intentionally leave out the bistro part of the tour?"

He laughed. "Carol, you've got a bright one on your hands here," he called through the open office door.

"Not quite bright enough to know how to get rid of you," Ms. Fleishman shot back from her office.

Mari's eyes went wide.

Trey saw her reaction, and his laughter trailed off into a soft chuckle. "She's harmless," he said in a low voice. "But we won't press our luck on your first day." He stood there staring at Mari for several long seconds before finishing with a loud, "Bye, Carol."

"I'm billing your department for her time," Ms. Fleishman informed him without missing a beat.

With a dismissive wave in the direction of Ms. Fleishman's office, Trey smiled at Mari and walked off down the hall to the research wing.

Mari heard footsteps coming toward her from Ms. Fleishman's office.

Was she going to get fired on her first day on the job? She hadn't even had a chance to search all of the research wing yet, to say nothing of the mansion.

She turned to face Ms. Fleishman.

"I thought he would never leave," Ms. Fleishman said.

"I'm so sorry. I didn't realize that—"

"Oh, bless your heart. You're cute enough that men probably swarm to you like yellowjackets to a ripe pear. If you need me to be the bad guy, I'm happy to shoo them away for you."

Mari felt her cheeks heat. She definitely wasn't used to catching men's attention, certainly not to the level that would ever get her in trouble.

"There are a handful of sweet-talkers here at Keating that you need to watch out for," Ms. Fleishman continued. "I could tell you who they are, but I don't want to taint your interactions with them. They're mostly harmless. But like I said, let me know if you need me to come through with a broom and beat them off."

Mari couldn't help but smile at Ms. Fleishman's overprotectiveness, especially since they'd barely met. "Thank you," she said.

Ms. Fleishman waved off the gratitude and launched into a half-hour-long orientation in the various duties Mari would need to perform. It was mostly stuff Mari was familiar with already, and some she could even do in her sleep.

After the orientation, Mari did her best to spend the rest of the morning focusing on her job and not on the fact that her mother might be somewhere in the mansion or the research wing.

True to his threat, at one minute before noon, Trey sauntered down the hall to Mari's cubicle. He stopped and leaned on her cubicle's high counter. "So, I'm taking an informal survey. What are your general feelings about lunch?"

Mari stifled a giggle. "I'm generally in favor of it."

"Are there any specific things that make you interested in lunch?"

She smiled up at him, unwilling to play so easily into his hand. "Well, I do have a few favorite foods, but I'll pretty much eat any kind of lunch."

"What about the company?" he asked.

"Yes, I'd eat food from most companies as well." Mari glanced up, hoping he caught her attempt at a joke.

Trey's wide grin brought out his adorable dimple again. "I meant, is there any particular person you'd be inclined to each lunch with?"

"Maybe . . ." she said shyly.

Trey leaned a little over the counter and lowered his voice. "In the interest of full disclosure, I'll tell you that I'm particularly interested in buying lunch for intriguing new co-workers who also happen to be witty and captivating."

Mari's face heated, and she glanced down at her desk. She wondered if Trey would have been on Ms. Fleishman's list of men to watch out for. Without replying to his obvious flattery, Mari stood and walked to Ms. Fleishman's door. "Would it be okay if I take lunch now?"

"Certainly," Ms. Fleishman said, then lowering her voice to a whisper, she added. "But don't let him bully you into it."

Mari lowered her voice to match. "I actually think I want to."

Ms. Fleishman nodded and waved her away.

Trey pointed, and they walked down the hall together. Not that Mari would have needed any directions—she could have simply let her nose guide her.

After several seconds, Trey turned to her. "What did Carol say?" he asked.

"She said 'certainly,'" Mari replied with a grin.

"No, I mean, what did she say after that? Did she warn you about me?"

Mari felt a blush creep into her cheeks, but she fought to keep her steps steady and confident.

"She probably should have," Trey added with a dimpled smile.

Despite not having years of experience with men, Mari definitely knew a sweet-talker when she saw one.

Over lunch, they chatted about food and the weather and Atlanta.

Between bites of fries, Trey said, "So tell me about yourself."

Mari took a quick drink, forcing her mind into acting mode. She gave him generic answers of the persona that she'd rehearsed the night before. Knowing that she wasn't a terrific liar, she stayed vague anytime the persona departed too much from her own life.

Trey watched her with interest, nodding in all the right places. After she had finished telling him about herself, she asked him the same question.

"Well, obviously, I'm a scientific genius. How else could I have gotten such an important job?" Trey said with his chest out.

His response caught Mari completely off guard. She blinked back at him, unsure of what to say.

With a hand to the side of his mouth, Trey whispered. "That was a joke. I'm really only a so-so scientist, but I like to pretend I'm amazing."

His self-deprecating grin brought out a smile in Mari as well. Perhaps she could give him a chance; there was definitely something likeable about him.

He told her that he'd grown up in Tulsa until he was twelve, when his family moved to Austin for his mother's job. He said he'd graduated from

UCLA and had started working for Keating BioMed. Mari wondered what his mother's job had been in Austin, but she was a little too jumpy about all these personal questions going back and forth to be willing to ask.

After he finished his abbreviated life story, they drifted to other subjects, chatting comfortably until the end of lunch.

On her way back to her desk, Mari caught herself wishing that this undercover job was actually her real job. She shook her head in an attempt to dislodge that thought. Not only was rescuing her mother the top priority, but she had a college career ahead of her—one that she was already falling behind in. She should have been sitting in her physics class at the moment.

It would be worth it, though.

Back at her cubicle, Ms. Fleishman kept Mari busy for the rest of the afternoon, reading through order procurements for fabrication equipment in the lab. Despite her best efforts to stay focused on her cover job, Mari's mind kept wandering to ways to get away from her desk to do some exploring.

Then finally, Ms. Fleishman came out of her office and walked past Mari's cubicle.

"I'm going to a meeting in Mr. Keating's office. If people come by asking for things, make sure you force them to fill out the online request. The worst thing is to take their request verbally and tell them you'll take care of it. That's only babying them. We have to hold them to the established process."

"Yes, ma'am." Mari tried to think of something intelligent that would show her new boss she was doing her job. "What should I do if they ask for you?"

"Tell them to message me. I probably won't see you again this afternoon." She leaned in and added with a conspiratorial whisper, "These meetings usually last for hours." She let out a long sigh and proceeded to climb the small rear staircase leading to the second floor of the old mansion.

Mr. Keating's office must be somewhere in the original mansion.

A few minutes later, Mari looked up to see Trey grinning at her over her monitor.

She allowed a small smile, but did her best to hold her professional demeanor. "Hello, Trey."

"Marina. How was your afternoon?"

Mari fought the urge to dive into a long conversation with this kind, handsome guy. She couldn't get sucked into small talk. Ms. Fleishman was away from her office. This was Mari's chance to sneak away and do some snooping. She needed something boring to get rid of Trey. "I'm reviewing requisition orders for Ms. Fleishman."

Trey simply nodded and stared at her. Those green eyes were a bit too intense for Mari's liking. She busied herself typing gibberish on the computer, hoping Trey wouldn't look around at her screen.

He hovered over her, grinning.

What was his job that it let him waste time chatting half the day with the new employee?

Finally, she looked up at him and abruptly asked, "Do you need to put in a work order for tech maintenance or a requisition for supplies?"

Would he get the hint?

His smile only grew. "Nah, I'm just on my way to a meeting," he jerked his head toward the ceiling.

Mari's eyes widened. "Oh, with Mr. Keating."

Trey nodded solemnly.

"Ms. Fleishman is already there. Hopefully, you won't be late."

He shrugged.

Mari tilted her head toward the stairs. "Really, Trey, I don't want you to get in trouble because you stopped to talk to me." It was true—she didn't want him to get in trouble. She also wanted to get rid of him.

He lifted a shoulder nonchalantly. "Some things might be worth getting in trouble for."

Mari's cheeks flushed, so she went back to typing gibberish. How was she ever going to pull off her new confident vibe if she couldn't even handle a little office flirtation? In order to resist the urge to look up at him again, Mari switched her screen back to the requisition orders and pretended to find them extremely interesting.

Trey cleared his throat, and Mari instinctively looked up.

He winked at her.

Again.

Before she knew it, he was halfway up the rear staircase. Mari watched his retreating form, grateful that he couldn't see the extra shades of red creeping up her cheeks.

She waited a minute for her temperature to return to normal. Then she grabbed a small file folder that Ms. Fleishman had left on her desk. The only thing it contained was several pages of job description, but Mari hoped that carrying something would make it look like she was meant to be walking around the research wing. Or at the very least, that she wasn't lost.

Just as she was about to stand from her cubicle, she caught sight of someone approaching. A man in his mid-twenties, wearing an expensive gray three-piece suit, strode into the mansion from the research wing. He had perfectly set blond hair. Just dark enough to indicate that he wasn't a teenager anymore, but so well-combed that he could have passed for a model in a business school magazine. His well-defined jaw was clean shaven, and his skin was lightly bronzed, though it didn't quite look naturally tanned.

He was yammering away on his phone, and as he passed her desk, he casually glanced at her. Half a second later, his head swung back toward her in the most awkward double-take Mari had ever been a part of. His mouth hung open, mid-sentence, and he just stared at her.

Mari forced her eyes back to her computer monitor. This was so awkward. She silently berated herself for not insisting that she stick with her casual hairstyle and frumpy wardrobe. What good was the perfect disguise if it attracted this much attention?

Mari heard the handsome professional quickly end his phone conversation. With her peripheral vision, she could still see that he was standing there in front of her desk.

Unable to stand the tension any longer, she glanced up. He was still staring at her, but not in a kindly, curious way, more like the way a wolf would consider his prey.

She opened her mouth to break the silence, but at that exact moment, he held up a finger to quiet her as he checked his watch.

"Sorry," he said with a flat smile. He turned and marched up the back staircase.

Mari stared after him, unsure of what had just happened.

One thing she was definitely sure of: he would have been on Ms. Fleishman's list of men to watch out for.

With her file folder as a security blanket, Mari spent her final hour of the afternoon discretely sneaking around the research wing, knowing that she wouldn't be missed for the rest of the day.

That night, sitting around the penthouse living room, Mari told the others about her day. She'd hardly needed to, though, given that they were listening to a sped-up version of her day recorded from the bracelet. Fortunately, the recording hadn't caught Trey's winks—or Mari's blushing.

Good thing it couldn't read her thoughts, either.

"Trey likes you," Katie observed. "What does he look like?"

Mari smiled to herself but tried to keep a calm exterior. "Athletic build, wavy brown hair, tan skin, captivating green eyes, and his smile is a little . . . bit . . ." Mari stopped talking when she saw the way the girls were looking at her. "What?" She asked as innocently as she could manage.

"You're breaking Rule Number One," Hannah muttered.

"What's Rule Number One?" Mari asked.

"Never, ever, under any circumstances, get emotionally involved with a guy on a mission," she replied.

"Oh hush, Hannah," Anna said with a wave of her hand toward Hannah's corner. "You break Rule Number One all the time. Sometimes more than once per mission."

The other ladies laughed. Hannah scowled.

Susan quickly changed the subject. "I've scanned the data from the bracelet. No trace of your mother's voice in the parts of the lab you visited."

Mari's shoulders sagged. It wasn't a huge surprise, but still a disappointment. "Well, I didn't get a chance to see all of the labs or any of the mansion, plus I hear the research facility has a basement."

Katie and Susan nodded their encouragement.

"But you heard my day," Mari said in exasperation. "I was stuck at my desk reading requisitions all afternoon. How am I ever going to search the whole place?" She threw her hands in the air.

"I have an idea," Susan said as she stood from her usual spot on the couch. "Just do this." Susan proceeded to fidget slightly, then bounce on the balls of her toes. Her eyes started getting larger and larger, and she pressed her hands between her thighs. Eventually she was hopping around in such a convincing imitation of the potty dance that Mari wasn't sure Susan didn't legitimately need to use the restroom.

"That'll get you away from your desk anytime you need," Susan said, plopping back down on the couch.

"Suze, what did we say about potty humor around guests?" Anna asked.

"Sorry." Susan didn't look very contrite, though. She held an arm out toward Mari. "But it's not like it's a regular guest. It's Mari."

Mari was both pleased and a little embarrassed. She smiled at Susan, her spirits lifting a little.

"You know," Hannah joined in. "You're assuming your mom will be talking at exactly the time you walk by. You're assuming she's still in a condition to be talking at all."

Mari slumped even farther down on the sofa. So much for her rising hopes.

Anna shot Hannah a nasty glare, then put a hand on Mari's arm. "Just do your best."

Mari let out a shaky breath, doing her best to push out thoughts of where her mother might be or what condition she might be in.

A cellphone on the coffee table buzzed.

"That's yours, Mari. Better grab it," Susan said.

"No, I have my phone—" Then Mari realized it was her mission phone. She looked at Anna. "Who could be calling me besides the four of you?"

Anna shrugged. "Answer it and find out."

"Hello?"

"Marina. It's Trey. How are you?"

Mari's heart-rate jumped. She stood up and paced behind the couch. "Hi. I'm good. How did you get my number?"

"Don't be mad. I got it from Carol. I gave her an excuse about needing to talk to you."

Mari remembered that Ms. Fleishman had insisted on having her cell number.

"Who is it?" Katie whispered eagerly.

Mari held the phone back and silently mouthed, "Trey," to Katie.

Then into the phone she said, "I hope you didn't get me in trouble."

"No, no. I told her I needed to call and tell you the parts you brought to Dr. Sorensen were perfect."

"Really? That's great," Mari said.

"What's great?"

"That the parts were perfect."

Trey laughed. "Oh, I have no idea about the parts. That's just the excuse I gave Carol. I'm actually calling to see if you want to go out to dinner."

"What, tonight?"

"What does he want?" Katie asked with excited eyes.

Mari whispered, "He wants to take me to dinner."

Oblivious to Mari's other conversation, Trey continued. "Sure. Have you eaten yet?"

Mari looked around at the girls in search of what she should say.

The ladies exchanged a few glances that Mari didn't understand. "What should I say?" she hissed.

"Do you want to go out with him?" Katie asked.

Mari nodded and shrugged at the same time.

"Marina?"

Mari pressed the phone back to her cheek. "Yes. I'm still here."

"Is it that hard to figure out if you've eaten?"

Mari laughed. "No—"

"Say yes," Katie whispered.

"Yes," Mari quickly added.

Trey chuckled, the amusement apparent in his voice. "Is that, no, you won't go out with me and yes, it is hard to figure out if you've eaten? Or—"

Mari smiled at the way he could make her laugh. "No, it's not hard. And yes, I will go out to dinner with you tonight."

"Great. I'll pick you up in ten minutes. Where do you live?"

Mari had a sudden vision of Trey arriving at the penthouse and asking too many questions and ruining the whole mission. "How about I meet you there? Where are we going?" She hoped her voice didn't sound as panicky as she felt.

"It's no trouble," Trey countered.

"No," Mari insisted a little too forcefully. "Actually, it'd be great just to meet you there." She cringed as Trey paused for several seconds. A date with Trey wasn't critical to the mission, but she really wanted to go out with him. Purely for distraction purposes, she convinced herself.

"You ever been to Cafe Agora?" Trey finally asked.

"Yeah, that's a great place."

"Meet you there in fifteen minutes."

"Okay," Mari replied.

As soon as she hung up, she looked at Katie and Susan who were smiling back at her. Mari broke into a huge grin and the three girls squealed in unison.

Katie stood up and grabbed Mari by the arm. "C'mon. We have to make you presentable."

Mari looked down at the conservative outfit she'd worn all day at work, the one that had gotten Trey's attention to begin with. "Isn't this—"

"No," Katie cut her off as she led Mari to the wardrobe room.

Ten harried minutes later, Katie led Mari back to the living room wearing cutoff shorts and a lacy purple blouse. Susan had put Mari's hair back in a messy bun, saying that it was cute but still casual enough for the end of the day.

"Perfect," Anna said. "Do you want to drive Hot Banana on your date?"

Mari's eyes went wide. She wasn't sure she was ready to drive any of the cars yet. "I'll call a ride-share." She pulled out her phone and her stomach dropped.

Staring back at her on the screen was a message from her mother.

Or from her mother's phone, anyway.

— *Tick Tock, Mari. Two days left. What have you been doing?*

The room felt like it had tilted. She grabbed the back of the closest sofa and slid down onto it.

Anna moved toward her. "What happened?"

Mari showed her the message.

"Ooh, this guy is a mean one," Anna said.

Mari stared at Anna. She glanced down at her new outfit. "What am I doing? My mother is being held hostage by a maniac, and I'm going on a date?"

Anna set a hand on Mari's shoulder. "No, you're going to make social contact with a potential information source. This is part of the mission. This is how we save your mom."

Mari had never had a panic attack, but she wondered if this was what it felt like. She pointed to her phone screen. "He said I only have two more days! How am I ever going to get what I need to rescue my mother in just two days?" Tears spilled down her cheeks.

Anna waved her hand dismissively. "Don't worry about that. They always give a deadline and then they let you beg for more time. How good are you at begging?"

Mari sniffed. "When it comes to my mother, I'm a pro." She fumbled to unlock her phone. "Should I call him right now?"

"No, no. Don't beg for more time right now. We'll wait until the deadline. Otherwise, it looks like you're planning to fail." Anna pushed Mari's phone back into her lap. "Just relax; we'll help you through this."

Mari took a shuddering breath and nodded.

Five minutes later, after another quick touchup from Katie to remove the evidence of her tears, the ladies ushered Mari into the elevator.

When the ride-share driver dropped her off at the restaurant, Trey waved at her from a small table out on the sidewalk. He stood when she approached.

"Hi, I hope you don't mind, I picked a table outside," he said as they sat.

"No, it's a beautiful night."

"And I ordered the hummus to start. Do you like hummus?"

"Yeah."

Trey pushed the plate toward her. She forced herself to wait a few seconds before diving in. They talked about Atlanta and the nightlife and

Florida and school. Fortunately, Mari had reviewed her cover story while Katie had picked out her clothes, so it was fresh in her mind. She fought the urge to relax too much—Trey made it easy—for fear that she would slip and mention something about growing up in Decatur or going to Georgia Tech.

"So, how was your first day of work?" Trey asked as they examined their menus.

Mari wasn't sure if Trey could really help her get what she wanted, but she figured it couldn't hurt. "Not bad," she said with a lift of her shoulder. "But I wish I didn't have to sit at my desk all day. I would love to be up and walking around, meeting people, seeing more of how things run." It was a ridiculous stretch of the truth for her to pretend to be a people person. Normally, she would have relished a job where the only requirement was to sit at a cubicle acting busy.

"Hmm. I wonder if Carol would let you be the company gofer."

"If only," she muttered, thinking of how much freedom that would get her.

"You never know. It might happen."

Mari shrugged. "I don't want to complain. It's a good job."

As her voice trailed off, Mari found herself staring at Trey's gorgeous face. He gazed back at her with those entrancing green eyes of his. For a short moment, he almost looked as if he wanted to say something. Mari leaned forward, wondering what a girl could do to make a guy say what was on his mind.

The moment was shattered when movement over his shoulder caught her eye.

In an instant, Mari realized the danger of sitting at a table out on the sidewalk so close to campus. Groups of Georgia Tech students walked by on their way to or from dinner. And among them—much to her horror—was Zag-Shack boy.

She quickly lifted her menu high on top of the table while simultaneously sinking down in her chair. She wasn't wearing her fake glasses; she hadn't figured she'd need them. Her hair was up in a messy bun, so the length didn't look any different. Would the blonde and platinum highlights be enough to throw him off? She glanced down at her outfit. It certainly wasn't drastically different enough if he got a good look at her. She suddenly felt completely exposed without the rest of her disguise. She took a deep breath. She needed to remain calm and definitely not draw any attention to herself.

A large hand reached over the top of her menu, then grabbed and pulled it down slightly. Mari's stomach jumped into her throat.

Just momentarily.

"Didn't your mother ever teach you not to have secrets at the dinner table?" Trey asked with a sly grin.

Mari gaped at him.

Was he asking about her mother specifically, or mothers in general? It wasn't even something mothers typically taught their kids. In fact, it didn't even make sense.

And why did he have to pick that exact moment to be charming?

"Mary?" Zag-Shack guy gawked at her from the sidewalk.

She pretended not to notice him, not because she had thought through how a person would react if they were mistaken for someone else, but because she was absolutely frozen with panic.

After several awkward seconds that positively felt like hours, Trey cleared his throat. "Maybe you've mistaken her for someone else?"

Zag-Shack boy considered Trey for a second. The way he shook his head left no doubt that the guy was certain he knew who Mari was. He sidled over closer to Trey and lowered his voice. "Let me do you a favor, buddy. You should just walk away from this girl. The chick's wacko. Look at this." He held his hands out. There were several small red spots on his palms. "Well, they've healed, so you can't really see them anymore. But she elbowed me right here." He pointed to his neck, though nothing was visible. He rounded on Mari. "After what you did to me, you're lucky I don't—"

Trey's chair crashed to the floor as he stood abruptly. "I think you need to keep moving, friend."

"Hey, I was just trying to be helpful, dude. I'd hope somebody else would do the same for me if I was ever caught dead with this little b—"

The punk stopped dead as Trey grabbed the front of the shirt and cocked back his other fist. "You won't insult her like that while I'm here."

Mari stood quickly and reached out a hand to Trey's arm. "Please, Trey. It's okay. Just let him go." She glanced warily up and down the street.

Trey studied her for a moment and nodded. He released the Zag-Shack punk and shoved him in the chest. He staggered backward into a parked car.

Regaining his footing, the guy narrowed his eyes at Trey. "You're both nuts. You deserve each other." With several backward glances, he disappeared down the street.

Breathing hard, Trey sat back down. As his gaze followed the Zag-Shack guy's retreating form, the fire in his eyes slowly diminished.

Mari felt the familiar blush in her cheeks. She'd never had a man willing to stand up for her like that. Her mother had made sure she had the skills to protect herself physically, but to be with a guy who would protect her from verbal insults, too—that was a new experience.

"Thanks for not hitting him," Mari said with a shy smile.

"He was about to call you . . ." Trey's expression turned from fury to something like chagrin. He absently ran a hand through his hair. "Yeah, I guess you're right. I should have kept my temper. Sticks and stones and all, right?"

Mari shrugged. "Something like that."

"I know my mom taught me to ignore words and insults, but she also raised me to treat a woman with respect," Trey said, a bit of the fire returning. "I guess she never told me what to do when the 'sticks and stones' advice conflicted with the 'respect women' advice."

Several seconds of silence stretched between them.

"Thank you for that." Mari tilted her head in the direction of the sidewalk.

A broad grin spread on Trey's face, and he nodded.

Speaking of maternal advice, Mari's mother never told her what to do when her advice to avoid a man who had a temper conflicted with her advice to find a man who respected her. To say nothing of what to do if he was also moderately handsome and exceptionally charming.

Hopefully, she'd have the chance to talk to her mother about it.

Soon.

CHAPTER SIX

WHEN MARI ARRIVED AT work the next morning, a large package was sitting on the counter above her cubicle desk. The label was addressed to Keating BioMedical, and it had stickers saying 'RUSH,' 'HANDLE WITH CARE,' and 'LIVE SPECIMENS' plastered all over. Mari picked it up and stepped to Ms. Fleishman's door.

"This box was on my desk. Do you want me—"

"Aghh! Put it back. I can't stand those things near me." Ms. Fleishman closed her eyes and shuddered.

Mari quickly put the box back at her desk. "What is it?" she asked.

"Those are the lab mice."

"What are they doing here?"

"I have no idea; they should have gone to the lab. I wasn't about to touch them, though. With their long wiry tails and their beady little eyes . . ." Ms. Fleishman shuddered again. "That's your top priority this morning. Get them out of here and over to the lab where they belong."

Mari picked up the box and marched down the long hall connecting the mansion to the lab facility. She smiled that she had gotten exactly what she wanted again—a chance to be away from her desk exploring—and she'd been at work less than ten minutes.

She dropped off the box with one of Dr. Sorenson's assistants and hurried around the corner to walk through the back wing of the lab—the one she hadn't explored yet.

The halls were dark, as if this part of the facility wasn't used as much. She stopped every few steps and casually pressed her bracelet against the wall for several seconds. She knew direct contact with the surface meant it could use the piezo-mic to pick up the sound better. Plus, Susan had shown her how to use the detection software. Each time she stopped at a door, she checked her watch. So far, it had only ever said:

ROOM EMPTY

She didn't know where her mother would be, so she wanted to make sure she checked everywhere she could. But every door she pressed the bracelet against gave her the same result:

ROOM EMPTY

Would she need to go back to all of the halls she'd walked through yesterday because she hadn't used the detection software? What if Hannah was right and she walked right by her mother's would-be cell only to miss it because her mother wasn't talking? And how would she explain her obsession with stopping at every door if someone asked her?

After ten minutes of snooping, she decided she should head back to her cubicle to avoid arousing any suspicions with Ms. Fleishman.

She had barely rounded the corner back into the main hall when a voice called out, "Marina!"

Mari jumped in surprise. She realized it was probably a good sign that she could react so instinctively to her alias.

Trey jogged toward her from the direction of Lab 3, the bottom of his open white lab coat trailing behind him. "Fancy meeting you here." He grinned.

There was something about his smile that raised suspicions. Mari cocked her head. "Yeah, I had a message for Dr. Sorenson."

Trey looked surprised and somewhat disappointed. "Really? It wasn't a delivery?"

"How would you know about . . ." Mari's eyes grew wide. "It was you!" She swatted him on the shoulder.

Trey ducked under his arm for protection, grinning from ear to ear. "I thought you could use a little errand to start your day." Then he looked pensively off into the distance and scratched his chin theatrically. "Hmm, I wonder what else I can arrange for you."

Mari felt her heart skip a beat. She'd never had this kind of attention from a handsome man before. Granted, she usually dressed in sweats or shorts for classes. And her hairstyle hadn't changed in the last seven years. Was Trey only noticing her because of her disguise? She continued walking back toward her desk. "Please don't do anything too crazy. I don't want any trouble."

Trey matched her pace. "Don't get myself into trouble. Check."

A small giggle escaped Mari's lips. "I meant don't get *me* into trouble."

Trey continued his overly dramatic reactions. Palming his forehead, he said, "Ohhh . . . not get *you* into trouble. Okay, I think I can do that."

They parted ways at her cubicle, Trey continuing up the back staircase to the mansion. At the top, he crossed paths with the handsome businessman that had gawked at her yesterday afternoon. Trey nodded as they passed, and the businessman—wearing a well-tailored dark-blue suit today—gave him a chummy pat on the back without interrupting his phone conversation.

There was no double-take this time as the businessman passed Mari's desk. His eyes were riveted on her the entire time. She did her best to ignore his gaze. She had been tempted to call Ms. Fleishman from her office when the man had been on the staircase. Mari would have liked to know the man's identity, but more importantly, she wanted to know if he was on Ms. Fleishman's list of men to be wary of.

Ms. Fleishman did come to Mari's desk a few minutes later—too late to ID the ogling businessman—and gave Mari an errand. It was the first of several errands she had for Mari that afternoon. Mari was sent to do a maintenance check on the centrifuges in Lab 2, to record the part number on the vacuum pump, and even to the gardener's storage shed to see if all the battery packs were fully charged.

She didn't want to complain, but Mari was tired by the end of the day. She wondered what had caused the change in Ms. Fleishman's assignments.

Did Trey have some magical clairvoyance? He certainly could have arranged the lab mice misdelivery that morning. But could he have changed Ms. Fleishman's tasks as well?

On the way back from her last errand of the day, she came across the handsome businessman again. He was still on his phone call, or maybe on a new phone call; Mari couldn't be sure. She dipped her head and averted her eyes, hoping he wouldn't notice her. To her dismay, he held up a hand as she approached. It almost looked like a wave, so Mari waved back as she was about to pass him.

The man's brows furrowed and his expression grew annoyed. He motioned to her with his hand again, but this time it looked less like a wave and more like an officer halting traffic. Mari skidded to a stop. The man continued his call with his hand held up. She assumed that meant she needed to stay put. Mari glanced around the hall, wondering if anyone was watching this strange scene. How long should she stand here in front of him? And should she try not to eavesdrop on his conversation?

The man finished his call and slid the phone into the inside pocket of his well-tailored navy suit jacket. He scrutinized Mari for several seconds before saying. "My name is Charles Keating."

Mari was sure something had gone wrong with the building because it felt like the ground had just fallen out from under her. She opened her mouth to say her name—whatever it was—but Mr. Keating stopped her.

"Can I ask if you're on your break right now?"

The urges to either shrink into a corner or run away in a panic were having an all-out brawl in Mari's brain. That was probably for the best, as it meant she could only shake her head vaguely. This was it. She was sure. This was how she would get fired, right in the middle of the hall, and that would be the end of her ill-fated attempt to rescue her mother.

Mr. Keating gave her a patronizing smile. "We'll just say that you *are* on break now. It wouldn't be appropriate for me to flirt with a subordinate while she's working." He gave her a meaningful nod and held out his hand. "Call me Chaz." He took Mari's hand. Holding it firmly, he pulled her ever so slightly closer to him. "And you are?"

"Marina Preston," she choked out.

"Very pleased to meet you, Marina."

Mari nodded mutely.

"I'm sorry I didn't have time to stop and chat with you at your desk yesterday afternoon. I was in the middle of a very important phone call. Plus, given the fact that you were clearly on the clock, I wouldn't have been able to invite you to dinner at my club."

Mari stared at him. "Dinner? Club?" she managed to repeat.

Chaz chuckled lightly. "Yes, dinner at my club. You would come for the dinner, but you would stay for the dazzling conversation . . . and the amazing view." Flashing her a gleaming white smile, he reached into his jacket pocket. He pulled out a business card and handed it to her. "Show this card to the maître d' at the Corinthian Club and he'll take care of you."

The business card glinted in her hand. Laser engraved on its metallic surface were the words Corinthian Club — Platinum Exclusive — Charles Henry Keating.

Unsure of how to react to this type of invitation, Mari simply gazed up at him. She could hardly believe this was really Charles Keating. The owner of Keating BioMedical, a company valued at however many billions of dollars. And the owner of Keating Mansion, the place where her mother was being held captive—probably.

Could she bring herself to go out to dinner with Charles Keating? Did she even have a choice?

"I take dinner at the Corinthian most nights, so any evening would work. But let's say tonight at seven because I really don't want to wait until later in the week to spend more time with you."

When Mari opened her mouth, the only thing that came out was, "I . . . uh . . ."

Chaz's expression changed to one of deep concern. "Do you not like the Corinthian? Was it the fish? The chef once tried to pass off a pan-seared tilapia as a garlic butter baked cod. I could hardly believe it. I mean, can you imagine?"

Mari blinked. She fought a smirk tugging at the corners of her lips. Was Chaz being serious? "No, I think the Corinthian is fine," she finally said. Best not to mention that she'd never actually been to the Corinthian Club.

His expression relaxed slightly.

Searching for something that might give her a tiny bit of control over the situation, she finally said, "I'm just not sure if I'm free this evening. I had plans with some friends."

Did that sound vague enough that he might buy it?

Chaz's brows pulled together. "Oh." He seemed unsure what to say next. Maybe he'd never had a girl try to get out of a date with him.

"Well, it would be great if those plans were flexible, then you could come to dinner with me. I would enjoy getting to know you better."

Mari nodded. Hopefully, he'd take that as a "maybe I'll think about it" and not a "yes, I'll come."

Chaz considered her for a few more seconds then turned on his heel and strode away.

As she watched him go, Mari couldn't help but wonder how much he knew about the activities that went on in his company—or his mansion.

Susan looked up when Mari walked into Club Banana. "How was—"

"Mr. Keating asked me out to dinner," Mari announced as she fell onto a couch.

Susan's eyes went wide. "Charles Keating, the owner of Keating BioMedical, asked you on a date?! How old is he?"

"Late twenties, maybe."

Katie jumped in. "What's he like?"

Mari tried to be diplomatic. "He seems very confident and self-assured."

"Probably used to getting his way," Katie said.

"Yeah, but it just comes across as spoiled and conceited," Mari replied. "Plus, he's been gawking at me every time I see him. It's sorta creepy."

"What does he look like? Is he hot?" Katie asked.

Susan pulled a face like she'd just eaten a moldy strawberry. "Eww, Katie. Did you miss the creepy part?" She jumped up from the couch and looked at Mari. "Next time you see him, you should be like 'Get away from me, you creep!'" She swung both arms up, palms out, then stalked away.

Mari giggled. "This *is* the boss we're talking about, Susan. You know, the owner of the whole company. I don't want to make a scene."

"So, what did you say about dinner?" Katie asked.

"I gave him some lame excuse about not knowing if I had plans. He said I should change my plans and go out with him."

"Maybe you should," Hannah said.

The girls all turned to stare at her.

"Having Charles Keating's attention could work to your advantage," Hannah continued. "Sometimes you have to use whatever tools you've got at your disposal for the success of the mission."

Mari's jaw nearly dropped. "What?! No! I don't want anything to do with him! He could be part of the plan to kidnap my mother!"

Hannah looked at her and raised an eyebrow. "Exactly."

Mari took a deep breath and looked down at her bracelet. Hannah was right, she needed to set aside her aversion for Chaz. Her mother was the only thing that mattered.

"Stay focused and work the facts," Hannah suggested. "We know that the one responsible for Dr. Sandoval's abduction was seen coming out of Charles Keating's mansion. But we don't know whether she's being held at the Keating Mansion. That needs to be our focus right now." She eyed Mari. "And Charles Keating can help you with that, even if he does it unknowingly."

She didn't like it, but Hannah had a point. Mari sighed. "Okay, I'll see what I can do."

"Be on your guard, though," Hannah continued. "He can't know what you're trying to do. Remember, he still might be in on it. And if he finds out—"

"Hannah. I may be new at this, but I'm not stupid." Mari said with more edge than she meant.

Hannah blinked at her. Mari wondered if she should apologize. She hadn't meant to antagonize Hannah. But before Mari could say anything, Hannah stood and walked down the hall to her room.

It only took about twenty minutes for Susan and Katie to have Mari ready for her dinner with Chaz. After this was all over, and she had her mother safely back, Mari hoped those two girls didn't mind if she dropped by for help before any other important dates she might have.

They had put her hair up in a fancy top bun with several stray strands of blonde and platinum trailing down the sides of her face. Katie had selected a short gold skirt and a playful white blouse with sheer sleeves. She said it could pass for fancy or casual. Dangly gold hoops and strappy gold heels completed the ensemble.

Hannah insisted that she take Business Banana—the sensible sedan—to the Corinthian Club, arguing that she couldn't be taken seriously showing up at a luxury club like the Corinthian in a ride-share, or anything economy. Mari set the exterior to a bright purple pearlescent color for the evening.

As she approached the street of the Corinthian Club, Mari took a deep breath. She could do this. She had to. Sliding as gracefully as possible out of the car, Mari handed the keys to the valet, doing her best to remember the Hannah's instructions to not act weird about it. A pair of attendants held open the glass double doors as she tentatively mounted the steps to the entrance. Knowing the embarrassment she'd feel if she tripped on the literal red-velvet carpet beneath her heels, Mari stepped carefully across the entryway, advancing on the maître d' with Chaz's metal card extended in front of her like a weapon.

The maître d' examined the card and glanced up at Mari. She tried not to shrink under his fleeting scrutiny. "Welcome to the Corinthian Club, miss. Please allow Joshua to escort you to your table." The maître d' motioned to a young man standing by a set of ornately decorated elevator doors who moved quickly to his side. He slipped Chaz's metal card into the young man's hand and nodded him away.

"Thank you very much," Mari said to the maître d'. He bowed slightly in acknowledgment.

The young waiter held the elevator door open for Mari and pressed the button for the top floor once she had joined him. "Wow, I've heard about these," he said as the elevator rose.

Mari glanced down at his hands and saw him fiddling with Chaz's card.

"Are they rare?" Mari asked.

"Rare? Yes, ma'am. I've never seen one myself, but I know what it means."

Mari glanced up at his face. His youthful pink complexion and unruly sandy hair told her he couldn't have been younger than twenty. "You don't have to 'ma'am' me. I'm sure we're about the same age."

He cast her a brief, sidelong glance. "I doubt it, ma'am. A sophisticated lady like you? This waiter uniform might make me look older, but I'm only halfway through college."

Mari turned fully toward him, cocking her head to the side. "This outfit might make me look refined and sophisticated, but I'm not even nineteen yet."

The waiter's eyes nearly bulged out of their sockets. "Seriously?!"

With a satisfied smirk and nod, Mari turned to stare back at the elevator door. It wasn't technically breaking her cover since she hadn't ever told anyone how old Marina was. Besides, this was just a random waiter.

Knowing that her persona had fooled an upperclassman gave Mari an extra boost of self-assurance. When the elevator doors opened, she walked confidently out into the Corinthian Club's top-floor dining area.

Her poise slipped a bit when the young waiter led her through the large dining room to a dais set apart in the middle of the windowed wall of the room. It was almost as if someone had taken a gazebo and made it into a bay window. Half of the raised platform extended out over the side of the building.

A single round table sat in the middle of the gazebo-balcony. Two tall white candles stood on an immaculate white tablecloth. The panoramic view of downtown Atlanta was breathtaking.

It looked incredibly romantic.

Until she sat down.

She looked back at the other tables filled with guests. All eyes were on her. She assumed they were curious who was important enough to warrant the table of honor. Patrons in the farthest tables were leaning out of their seats to get a look.

Mari did her best to ignore them as the young waiter pulled her chair out and helped her get seated.

"Can I start you off with something to drink?" He sounded very official again.

"You don't happen to have any Coke products, do you?" Mari whispered.

He barked a short laugh. "I wish." He looked around at the other guests then quickly added. "I apologize for the inconvenience, but unfortunately, we do not."

Mari leaned toward him and lowered her voice. "What would you suggest for someone in my . . . situation?"

The young man nodded, hopefully understanding that more than half the drinks on the menu would technically be off-limits for her. "Might I suggest a San Pellegrino?"

She had no idea if that was a good drink or not, but she was willing to trust her young waiter. "Yes. Let's do that."

Two and a half minutes later, the waiter returned with a glass of clear, sparkling liquid. Mari thanked him as he left and waited a few moments to take a sip. She wondered if it was too late to call him back and ask for a bowl of sugar to go with her drink. She took another small sip and decided that if one was expecting water, this fancy stuff might not be half bad. Unfortunately, she'd always imagined that expensive drinks would taste good.

After another five minutes, the waiter returned. "Would you like to begin with a selection of appetizers, or would you like to wait for your host to arrive?"

Mari glanced around, hoping to see Chaz. "I suppose I should wait until he arrives." It came out more like a question. She still felt like she was an oddity on display.

The waiter nodded. "Sounds good. I'll come back and check with you in a little bit."

To take her mind off the surrounding guests, Mari looked out over downtown Atlanta. The setting sun bathed the surrounding buildings in orange and red. On the streets below—straight down, really—pedestrians scurried to their favorite clubs or restaurants. They felt so distant—so far removed from her perch in the Corinthian Club.

She hazarded another glance toward the entrance. Still no Chaz.

While she waited, her gaze wandered, taking in the decor of the room. She didn't know much about art or history, but the decorations reminded her of pictures she'd seen from the roaring twenties—bold trim in yellow and gold, embellished lighting, and blue and turquoise accents throughout. It was lovely. It would have been perfect except that she sat alone, the center of curious attention.

Absently, Mari glanced at her wrist to check the time. Chaz was only fifteen minutes late. That wasn't the end of the world. She fidgeted with the watch—not the one she wore during the day to record her circuits around Keating BioMed, a stylish gold piece that looked like it only kept the time but which Anna had told her would also emit an ear-splitting alarm if she were ever in danger—wondering how long she should stay. The watch reminded her why she was there. This was for her mother. And she'd be willing to endure much, much more if it meant she could help rescue her.

Other waiters crossed the large dining floor, taking orders and bringing elegant meals. The smells of various spices and oils wafting through the air made Mari's mouth water. She saw her waiter making his way toward her. Their eyes met, and she hated the look of pity she saw there.

When he arrived at the dais, he was all business. "Could I interest you in the basil tomato bruschetta or the lobster tarts?"

Mari looked around once more and sighed. "Yeah, I might as well."

"Which would you like?"

"What would you recommend?" she asked.

The young waiter looked surprised.

"Don't tell me no one has ever asked you for a recommendation before."

His cheeks colored, and he shrugged. "I haven't been working here very long. Plus, I don't think I look like I know what I'm doing."

"I know the feeling," Mari muttered. "So, which should I try?"

He smiled. "Well, the bruschetta is amazing. It's our toasted Italian bread brushed with extra virgin olive oil and rubbed with fresh garlic, topped with buffalo mozzarella, diced Brandywine tomatoes, and a tart basil drizzle."

"That sounds amazing. Will that be . . . I mean, if my host never arrives . . . how much—"

The waiter held up a hand to stop her. "You are the guest of a Platinum Exclusive member." From his vest pocket, he produced the card she had given the maître d' and leaned in as if sharing a dirty secret. "This card means you don't ever pay a thing."

As grateful as she was that he had understood her concern, Mari still blushed. She nodded and said, "I'll have the bruschetta, then."

The waiter gave her an approving nod. "I'll bring that right out to you."

Mari glanced around at the nearby tables—none of which were closer than twenty feet—hoping the other guests hadn't overheard the exchange. She played with the stem of her water glass as her eyes roamed the interior space of her small bay window gazebo. Once the appetizer had arrived, that gave her another item to keep her nervous hands busy.

The bruschetta was long gone—as were three more glasses of sparkling water—when the young waiter approached her table again. The look of regret on his face told her that he didn't bring any good news.

He stopped a few feet from her and straightened. "Miss, I . . . uh . . ."

"You have to kick me out, don't you?" Mari guessed.

His eyebrows shot up. "No, no. It's not that. You can stay as long as you like and order as much food as you can eat." He glanced over his shoulder. "I've been sent with a message that, unfortunately, Mr. Keating is not available to dine with you this evening." He concluded by exhaling a long sigh of either relief or commiseration.

Mari blinked up at him and swallowed. She looked down at the glass in her hands. She hadn't really wanted to have dinner with Chaz Keating, but the snub still stung. She moved to push her chair back.

"You don't have to leave, though," the waiter said quickly.

"No. I think it's time I go." Mari glanced again at her watch. It was past eight.

The waiter deflated slightly, but nodded that he understood. Glancing around, he reached into his vest pocket again and stealthily pulled out Chaz's metal membership card. "I think you deserve to keep this. I would hate for you to have waited this whole time for nothing."

Mari meant to protest, but stopped herself. She took the card with a quick dip of her head. Maybe she could have another dinner at Chaz Keating's expense some time.

The purple sedan was waiting for her in the drive-through portico when she reached the lobby. The young waiter held the door for her as she exited the Corinthian Club. "Thanks for everything," she whispered as she slipped by him. He had been the only thing that had made the evening bearable.

CHAPTER SEVEN

W HEN SHE ARRIVED THE next morning, Mari expected at least five minutes at her desk before the errands began.

Ms. Fleishman didn't even let her sit down. "Here. Take this to Mr. Keating's office for his signature."

Mari looked at the paperwork in her hand then glanced up the grand staircase toward the personal offices of Mr. Keating. This would be the perfect opportunity to do some searching upstairs in the original mansion—the only part of either building that looked even remotely close to the snippets she'd seen on the video call from Brax.

Unfortunately, she would be forced to interact with Mr. Keating. She wasn't excited about that.

With great effort to hold the papers still in her hand, Mari mounted the rear staircase.

How much did she dare wander around the second floor investigating? And what would happen if she got caught?

She paused for a moment at the landing to get her bearings. A small, laser-etched brass plaque indicated that Mr. Keating's office was to the left. She looked to the right and saw a long hall curving out of sight.

How big was this house?

She hurried and held her bracelet against the first door. Then again on the wall between the first and second doors. At the fourth door, she heard footsteps coming toward her from the end of the hall.

As quickly as she dared, Mari ran back toward the other wing of the mansion. She slowed to a walk at the top of the stairs and continued toward Mr. Keating's office. She stopped at the door that had "Charles Henry Keating – Chief Executive Officer" emblazoned in gold lettering on it. The door was ajar and she could hear a one-sided conversation coming from inside—probably Mr. Keating on his phone.

She straightened and took a fortifying breath. That small amount of snooping was hardly worth what she was likely about to go through. She knocked lightly then peeked her head in to see if Mr. Keating was alone.

Unsurprisingly, he was on his cell phone. With a quick wave of his free hand, he motioned Mari inside. Doing her best to look everywhere else around the room except directly at him, she walked to his desk and held the paper out to him.

Mr. Keating took the form and signed it without sparing it much more than a cursory glance. His gaze was on Mari the entire time. To avoid those intense eyes, she forced herself to stare at the wall paneling above his head.

He held the signed copy out to her. As she took it, he didn't release the piece of paper. She looked down to see what he wanted. Mr. Keating cocked an eyebrow as if inviting her to say something.

"Thank you for your time, Mr. Keating," Mari said.

A puzzled look flashed across his face, and he released the form. Mari spun around and made her escape. By the time she was out in the hall, Mr. Keating had already resumed his end of the phone conversation.

Mari took the signed form to Ms. Fleishman and returned to her desk. Though her immediate feeling was one of disappointment, she knew she was making progress. What little she'd seen of the mansion halls looked like a perfect match to the room her mother had been in. She needed to stay focused on the goal.

Several minutes later, Trey and another scientist walked by her desk, deep in conversation. Though she certainly wanted to catch his attention, Mari fought the urge to look up or stare or do anything else crazy. At the moment when she thought Trey had gone too far to have noticed her, he looked back over his shoulder and winked at her. Mari smiled despite herself. Trey smiled back with that crooked grin of his. When his coworker turned to see what he was looking at, Mari quickly looked down at her monitor and pretended to be working.

Half an hour later, when they returned, Mari really did her best not to watch them. Without missing a beat in his conversation, Trey slid his hand along her cubicle counter, tapping it playfully as he passed by. Mari kept her eyes focused on her screen, but she felt a small smile creep up the corner of her lips.

Not more than ten minutes later, and Trey was at her desk again. "This is three times I've passed and you've been at your desk every time. That must be a record."

"Are you keeping tabs on me or something?" Mari replied playfully.

His hand went to his chest, and his eyes grew wide in feigned indignation. "Would I do such a thing?"

Mari touched a finger to her chin and considered him. "Maybe not. But I'm ninety-nine percent sure you've managed to make me the company gopher. I just don't know how you pulled it off." His smile grew, so Mari had no inclination to stop. "Do you have some under-the-table deal with Ms. Fleishman? Are you a favorite of hers or something?"

"Carol, am I your favorite?" he called through the door behind her.

"Favorite smart aleck, maybe," Ms. Fleishman called back.

Trey laughed.

"Good morning, Trey." Chaz Keating had snuck up on them.

Trey's laughter faded, but not awkwardly so. "Hey, Chaz," he said with a nod.

Chaz gave Trey a tight smile. "Don't you have a big project you should be working on? I'm sure Miss Preston would enjoy the chance to do her work as well."

Still smiling, though not as broadly, Trey nodded curtly at Chaz. As he turned away, he raised his eyebrows at Mari. The expression looked like both an apology and a warning.

Mari wanted to glare daggers at Chaz, but that wouldn't get her any closer to saving her mother.

She did her best to focus on her work until finally Chaz leaned over her computer screen. Mari pasted her best customer-service-style smile on her face. "Can I help you, Mr. Keating?"

"Yes, you can stop calling me Mr. Keating. It sounds like you're talking to my father. I told you to call me Chaz."

"Can I help you, *Chaz*?" Mari repeated with exactly the same chilly intonation.

Chaz's eyes narrowed. "Are you mad at me?"

She certainly was, but she couldn't tell him that.

Forcing her fake smile even bigger, she said, "Do I look mad?"

"I suppose not. But you're not really acting happy to see me."

Oh, I'm definitely acting, Mari thought.

"Hmm." Mari kept her happy expression in place. "You were right; I do have work to do, but it would be inconsiderate to *keep you waiting*."

Chaz stared at her for several long moments, then his eyes widened and he touched a palm to his forehead. "Oh . . . you're probably upset because some things came up, and I didn't make it to the Corinthian Club for dinner last night." His tone made it sound like the whole thing had been a misunderstanding on her part.

Mari did everything she could to keep her facade from cracking.

How self-centered could this guy be? If that's what passed for an apology in Chaz's world, she might decide to figure out a way to save her mother without his help.

Chaz looked at Mari, obviously waiting for her to say something. When it was clear that she wouldn't, he huffed a sigh and said, "I'm sorry I didn't have dinner with you last night." The petulant tone made it sound like his mother had forced him to apologize to a playmate he'd taken a toy from.

Mari debated making him suffer a little longer. He certainly deserved it. But that might be the best apology she was going to get. Plus, she really could use his assistance. She tried to imagine how Katie might act to get a boy to do what she wanted.

Her mouth twisted into a small pout. "I suppose I can forgive you."

Chaz's face broke into a broad grin. "Let me make it up to you. How about a private lunch up on the dining balcony?"

"No," Mari said a little too quickly. She took a breath and smiled. "We don't want everyone to think you're giving me special attention."

"But I *am* giving you special attention," he said very matter-of-factly.

Mari paused and tapped a finger to her chin as if pondering what he could do for her. "How about a tour of the mansion? I've seen where you work, but I've never seen where you live."

One of Mr. Keating's eyebrows shot up, and he gave her a suggestive smirk.

"Not that kind of tour," she said coldly.

His expression fell slightly, but he shrugged it off and tilted his head toward the rest of the mansion. "Let's go."

"Now?" Mari looked back toward Ms. Fleishman's office.

"Why not? I am the boss, aren't I?" Self-importance oozed from every word. "Ms. Fleishman?" he called toward the office door. "I need Marina to come with me on an inspection of some of the facilities."

"That's fine, sir," Ms. Fleishman replied.

Mari couldn't keep the sly grin from her face. She hoped it looked coy instead of mischievous. Somehow, she'd convinced Chaz Keating to do exactly what she wanted.

"A proper tour of the home should start at the front of the house," Chaz said as he led her through the halls to the main doors that Mari had mistakenly used on her first day.

As he walked her through hall after hall and room after room, Mari did her best to ooh and aah at all the right times. She also did her best to keep her distance from him without making it look like she was keeping her distance.

In several of the rooms, Mari leaned back against a wall, making a show of taking in the entirety of the room, while she stealthily pressed the bracelet against the surface. In other rooms, she would stand very still, hoping that the ultra-sensitive microphone array would pick up something. Everything had the general appearance and style of the room in the video of her mother, but none of them was an exact match.

She created a mental map of the many halls and rooms Chaz led her through. It was obvious that there was a portion of the east wing they hadn't visited that he was specifically avoiding. Mari grew suspicious of what could be in that part of the house.

"I've saved one of my favorite rooms for last," Chaz said with a sly grin as he guided Mari up the third-floor grand staircase.

With a flourish, Chaz pushed open a set of ornate wood double doors. Mari walked into an enormous library. Light streamed in through giant windows on the south wall, flooding the space with warmth.

As Mari wandered the expansive room, an ominous feeling crept over her. The furniture and fixtures looked more than vaguely familiar. She imagined what the room would look like in the dark through the camera of a cell phone.

Mari stopped dead in the middle of the room.

Two chairs sat facing each other by the large fireplace.

Identical to each other, and identical to the one her mother had been tied to.

Looking up at the light fixtures, Mari wasn't surprised to see spot lighting, perfect for creating the effect she'd witnessed in the video call.

Mari felt like her lungs had suddenly lost the ability to function. The walls were closing in on her. Sounds around her began to diminish, drowned out by the pounding of blood in her ears.

"Marina?" Chaz touched her shoulder.

She flinched.

"What's the matter?"

Mari shook her head, trying to clear her thoughts. She would be no good to her mother if she lost her cool. She looked up into Chaz's ice-blue eyes.

Could he have helped abduct her mother? How could her mother have been here—a prisoner in this very room—and Chaz not know?

She wanted to scream and use some of the punches Anna had taught her on Chaz's very solid-looking body.

"It's a lovely library," Mari nearly whispered.

"Are you usually this emotional about books?" he asked, watching her.

Mari needed to get away from this room. And Chaz. But she could barely think straight. She grasped at some thread of the conversation. "I can see why you are so proud of it." She did her best to recover some control of the situation. "Do you spend much time here?"

Chaz shook his head. "Hardly ever, actually. I sometimes have my morning coffee in here on Sundays. But that's about it."

The constriction in Mari's chest eased ever so slightly. Maybe she wasn't standing right next to the man who'd abducted her mother. She reluctantly followed him around the room, doing her best to avoid looking at the chairs.

As they walked back out into the corridor, Mari glanced toward the rest of the east wing. She waited patiently as Chaz closed the doors but was surprised when he turned away from the east wing to go back to the rest of the house.

Mari pointed the other way. "What about this part? Are you trying to short-change me on my tour?" she added playfully.

Chaz frowned. "No. But that's my cousin's wing. We shouldn't disturb his privacy."

"Your cousin?"

"Yes, my grandfather left the mansion to me with the stipulation that I let my cousin have this part of the house."

"Have I met your cousin?"

She wanted to ask if his cousin's name was Brax, but she didn't have the nerve.

"He is a minority-owner in Keating BioMedical, so you'll probably see him at some point. But he comes and goes at strange times. In fact, I haven't seen him in a week at least."

Mari gazed down the dark hall. She felt a glimmer of hope for the first time in days. Her mother might be down that hall.

And Chaz might not know anything about it—that was a reassuring thought.

They parted ways at the top of the rear staircase, Chaz for his large office, Mari for her small cubicle.

At exactly one minute to noon, Trey appeared at her cubicle.

"Hello, Trey," Mari said, trying to suppress a satisfied smile.

He leaned over her counter and lowered his voice. "You didn't have lunch on Chaz's private balcony, did you?"

"No—" Mari eyed him. "How did you know about that?" She glanced around the converted parlor and whispered, "Were you eavesdropping on my conversation with Chaz?"

"As a matter of fact, I got about fifteen feet down that hall," he pointed toward the research wing, "and I had to stop to tie my shoe."

Mari's eyebrows went up in a look of skepticism. "How long did it take you to tie a shoe?"

"Oh, you know, I can never remember if the bunny goes around the tree and back into the hole or if it comes out of the hole and then . . ." He trailed off with a wide grin on his face. "Wanna join me for lunch?"

Mari felt heat creep up her neck. She clicked a few times on her computer and pretended to consider whether she wanted to go to lunch with Trey. He waited patiently, a silly smirk on his face. Mari wished she could bring his confidence down a notch or two without having to reject him and miss out on lunch together.

"Sure," she said with a shrug.

They walked together to the small cafe at the end of the research wing, joining a dozen coworkers at the small round tables.

As they settled in with their meals, Trey said, "So, I meant to ask, where did you go to school?"

Mari barely stopped herself from saying, "Decatur." Trey was asking Marina, not Mari. And he wasn't asking about high school. "Valdosta," she said, quickly scanning her brain for the other details of her cover story in case he asked.

"Valdosta? That's a long way from home."

"Not really," Mari said with a shrug that she hoped didn't look rehearsed. "Remember, I'm originally from Tallahassee."

"Oh yeah, right. So, what brings you to Atlanta?"

The brainstorming sessions about her cover hadn't included anything about that. Was it always going to be this hard pretending to be someone else?

"You know. Big city. More jobs." She cringed. What a lame answer.

But it must have satisfied Trey because he nodded and continued on to other subjects for the rest of their meal.

When she arrived back at her desk, Ms. Fleishmann had left her the perfect gift. Another form needing Mr. Keating's signature.

Mari grabbed the piece of paper and hid it in a drawer. This was the perfect chance to explore, but she couldn't use it right away. She had to be patient.

She watched the rest of the afternoon for an opportunity, perking up every time she heard footsteps coming from the direction of the mansion. She needed Chaz not to be in his office when she went to get his signature.

Finally, her patience was rewarded.

Chaz strode down the back staircase, phone pressed to his ear, heading for the research wing. When he passed Mari's cubicle, he pointed at her and scrunched his eye in a half-wink.

Maybe the novelty of being the new girl had worn off, but he didn't do any double-take or gawk at her when he walked by. Not that she wanted him to.

If one of the Banana Girls were here in her place, would they do more to hold his attention? She wondered if they always ran the risk of breaking Rule Number One—or of enticing the men around them to break it.

She might have to ask them that later. At the moment, she had more important things to consider.

Mari watched Chaz's departing form, letting the fantasies of the pampering and indulgence that being Charles Keating's girlfriend would include—the restaurants, the parties, the vacations—disappear with him.

With a quick shake of her head, she pulled the hidden document out of her desk. Clutching the paper to her chest, she scampered up the stairs and down the corridor toward the east wing, slowing as she passed the double doors of the grand library.

Guessing that her mother's abductors would likely keep her as far from prying eyes as possible, Mari tiptoed past dozens of doors until she reached the very end of the hallway. She paused, studying her surroundings. The curtains on the windows were drawn, letting in very little of the afternoon light. Particles of dust floated in the few rays of sunlight filtering through.

Mari stood and listened.

Nothing.

On her watch, she activated the detection app for the bracelet.

No reported activity.

She pressed her wrist against the last door and watched the app display.

ROOM EMPTY

Her watch indicated the same on the next two rooms.

She saw a small side hall, like the ones she had seen in large hotels. There were only two doors. Placing the bracelet against the first door, she saw the sound monitor immediately flash to life.

BREATHING DETECTED

Mari's heart pounded in her ears. Could this be her mother?

She left the bracelet touching the door, waiting for more information. The bracelet app flashed again.

ONE PERSON

SUBJECT CONSCIOUS

SUBJECT LIKELY AT REST

SUBJECT LIKELY FEMALE

Mari fought to control her swelling elation.

This could be it!

Mari crouched to examine the lock. She needed to know which lock-picking tool to fish out of the sole of her shoe. She stared at the doorknob for several seconds, trying to figure out what she was seeing. She wouldn't have to pick the lock after all. The locking tab—normally on the inside of a room—faced the outside. Her captors must have been too lazy to get a double-locking doorknob. They had simply flipped the doorknobs around.

She glanced back up the short hall to the main corridor and softly twisted the locking tab. The doorknob unlocked with an audible click that sounded like it echoed down the hall and throughout the entire building as if announcing—Hey! Someone's breaking in!

Very quietly, Mari opened the door, slipped inside the room, and silently closed the door behind her. The room looked like it might have once been a guest room before it was stripped of most of its furniture.

A small woman lay on the solitary mattress against the back wall. At the sound of Mari's entrance, she covered her head with her arm and curled her body away from the door, whimpering slightly.

Mari choked back a sob. "Shh," she whispered softly as she stepped slowly toward her mother. Hot tears coursed down her cheeks. Even as she soothed, she felt a burning desire to hurt the ones who had done this to her.

The woman turned and squinted at Mari in the semi-darkness.

"Mari?" she croaked.

"Yes," Mari cried quietly as they embraced.

"What are you doing here?" her mother asked with obvious confusion.

"It's a long story. I'm here to—"

"Mari." Her mother held her at arm's length. Her eyes grew wide and terrified. "You must leave right now! Get out of here before he finds you!"

"You mean Brax?" Mari squeaked out.

Her mother flinched at the name and nodded.

Mari gritted her teeth. She was no match for her mother's abductor and his henchman, but in that moment, she would have relished the chance to try.

"I'm working undercover trying to get you out of here."

Her mother stared at her. "What? I don't understand. Mari, you can't be here!"

"Trust me, Mamá. We have a plan. Just hold on for a few more—"

A noise outside startled her mother. They both listened intently.

Her mother's eyes grew frantic. "It's him! You have to get out of here!"

Mari looked around the small room. There was no furniture to hide under or curtains to duck behind.

She ran back to the door and pressed the bracelet to it. Tapping her watch, she changed the mode from Search to Escape.

MOTION DETECTED—ESCAPE INADVISABLE

Mari's heart raced. She glanced back at her mother who sat trembling on the bed.

The bracelet app displayed the waveform of the sounds coming from the hall.

Regular, sharp spikes.

Those were footsteps.

The waveform height continued to increase.

They were coming closer.

The steps stopped.

Mari held her breath.

A sudden bang made Mari jump. The display went blank, then a few seconds later flashed.

SPACE CLEAR

She let out a long breath.

"Go, Mari," her mother whispered.

"I love you, Mamá," Mari said through a sudden lump in her throat. "We'll get you out of here soon."

Her mother nodded. Mari slipped out into the hall then noiselessly closed the door behind her. It nearly broke her heart as she clicked the lock back in place.

She glanced across the dark hall and saw a light coming from under the room opposite her mother's. Mari wished she could barge in and take down the criminal who dared to hurt her mother. But it wouldn't do any good to get caught right now. Her mother's freedom depended on Mari's ability to keep her head and follow through with the plan.

Stepping lightly down the staircase past the hall leading to Chaz's office, she wondered if he realized that his mansion was currently doubling as a prison.

"We could easily get a mouse from a pet store. They sell them as snake food," Katie said.

Mari sat lounging with the rest of the team in the living room of Club Banana later that evening. The ladies typically congregated on the couches at the end of the day, but this gathering was particularly important because Mari had found her mother. They were working on the plan to rescue her.

"I'm not against the mouse idea—though I do feel bad for Ms. Fleishman." Mari wondered if it had been unfair of her to tell the girls that Ms. Fleishman was deathly afraid of mice. "I'm just wondering how I would sneak it into the mansion. They search all bags at the door."

"She could pull the Garter Blade maneuver," Susan said with a grin.

"We'd have to sedate the mouse," Hannah added drily.

"And she'd have to wear one of the longer, flared skirts," Katie said.

"What's the Garter Blade maneuver?" Mari asked.

Susan stood and walked across the room. She turned around and took a few steps back toward them. Bending down, she inched up the hem of an invisible dress and grabbed for something above her knee. She held the imaginary item in one hand and then flung it forward like a throwing knife.

Mari flinched. She didn't like the direction this was going.

Anna turned to Mari. "Stand up and take a little walk around the room."

Mari frowned but did as instructed.

Katie walked over to crouch next to Mari. "Hmm, we could tape it right above her knee," she said, pointing at Mari's leg.

Mari stopped and faced the other girls. "Tape what above my knee?" she demanded.

"The mouse," Hannah said bluntly.

A cold shiver went down Mari's spine. "What?"

"You said they search all bags going into the mansion," Hannah continued, "so the only way to get the mouse inside is to pull the Garter Blade maneuver which is basically strapping the item—in this case a heavily sedated mouse—to the inside of your thigh. Then you walk inside and hope the sedation doesn't wear off before you get a chance to set it free in the right place."

Mari shook her head. "Absolutely not. There is no way you're going to strap a live mouse to my body."

The smirk on Hannah's face told Mari exactly what the skinny blonde thought of Mari's courage in the face of imminent grossness.

"Do you have a better idea?" Anna asked.

Mari's breathing increased as she contemplated whether she would even remain conscious with a mouse taped to her leg. She closed her eyes and pictured her mother lying on a bare mattress waiting to be rescued. She took a deep breath and opened her eyes. The girls stared at her, waiting for a decision. "If that's the best we've got, I can do it."

"Good girl," Anna said. "And while Katie and Susan work out the details of their dastardly plan, you and I will go for a drive."

Not surprisingly, Anna chose Hot Banana for their drive, but at least she asked Mari what color she wanted it to be—cherry red.

The tires squealed as Anna pulled onto 14th Street.

"Where are we going?" Mari asked.

"Isn't today the deadline Brax gave you?" she called back over the wind.

Mari's stomach sank. She nodded. It was the deadline. What would Brax do when he found out she hadn't gotten the swarm algorithms from her mother's computer?

"We're going to campus. To your mother's office," Anna explained.

"Are we going to steal the algorithms?" Mari couldn't believe they would have gone to so much trouble only to end things this way.

Anna laughed as she gunned the convertible forward onto the long freeway on-ramp.

"And shouldn't we be going that way?" Mari pointed behind them in the direction of the Georgia Tech campus.

"Only if we don't want to go above thirty-five miles an hour. What's the point of taking the convertible if we don't get out on the freeway?" Anna yelled back.

Anna pushed the sports car at breakneck speed along the winding access ramp, through underpass tunnels, under an elevated parallel ramp, and onto the freeway. She immediately accelerated to ninety, both girls screaming and laughing the whole way. A few miles later, she took the first off ramp and looped around, now heading the opposite direction, and repeated the acceleration—and screaming and laughing—process.

There was no exit to the north end of campus, so they had to take the freeway down to the exit that dumped them onto the south end. As silly as Mari thought Anna was being in taking the much longer freeway route, she couldn't help but feel as if she'd shed a few layers of stress with the top-down, high-speed joyride.

Once they were back on city streets and could hear each other again, Mari continued her questions. "If we're not going to steal the algorithms, then what are we doing?"

"Don't you think you'll be getting a call from Brax pretty soon?" Anna asked as she hung a left at the light.

"Probably. But what has that got to do with being on campus?"

"We're going to help you make your case of begging for more time."

Anna turned into the parking lot across from the nanotechnology building and pulled sideways into two parking stalls with the passenger side facing directly toward the entrance.

"See?" Anna pointed to the building entrance. "He'll be able to tell you're actually on campus while still giving us enough time to get away in case he has someone waiting nearby."

"But what do I say? I mean, what's the best way to beg for more time?" Mari asked while staring down at her phone.

"If he thinks you've been trying, and you were able to get close, he's more likely to give you a little more time."

"Well, I was pretty close a few days ago. I might have succeeded if two particular *someones* hadn't interfered." Mari grinned at Anna.

Anna laughed. "You sure gave Hannah more than she bargained for. She thought all she'd have to do was boss you around and you'd go slinking home."

Mari joined in the laughter. Her heart lightened a little at the thought of making Hannah's morning just a bit more difficult.

"It's probably best to embellish on that attempt. I doubt you're very good at lying yet, so you'll be able to convince him much better if you're telling stuff that's mostly true. Make him think you just tried to break in, but be vague with the details from Saturday. Remember, if the plan goes well, your mom will be safe by this time tomorrow. We just need him to not do anything stupid in the next twenty-four hours."

Mari felt her heart begin to race. She wondered if the anticipation of a call like this was worse than when it was a surprise.

From the center console, Anna produced two bottled iced teas and handed one to Mari. They sat in silence for several minutes, looking at the campus around them and enjoying their drinks.

"I love this part of campus," Anna finally said. "Especially this time of day when the sun is setting. It's so beautiful."

Mari fiddled absently with her phone case as they watched the sun turn the buildings and trees around them a fiery orange. Finally, she let out a sigh. "What if I screw everything up, Anna?" She didn't risk looking at her new friend, worried that she might see doubt in the girl's face.

Anna sat in silence for a few moments. "My mother always says that you can't learn to walk without a few face-plants."

With great effort, Mari swallowed a mouthful of tea through her laugh. "Does she really always say that?"

Anna grinned and gave a noncommittal shrug.

Mari's smile faded as she turned serious. "But what if my face-plant leaves my mother at the mercy of a desperate criminal?"

At that moment, Mari's phone buzzed. When she saw the picture of her mother on the screen, her heart started beating double-time. Mari tilted the phone towards Anna who smiled back encouragingly.

Anna's eyes suddenly went wide. "Wait, don't answer it yet!" She held her hand out. "I almost forgot; you still look like Marina."

"Should I hide my face with something?" Mari asked, glancing around for anything she could hold in front of her.

Anna reached into the back seat, grabbed a baseball cap with a large Buzz emblazoned on the front, and handed it to Mari. "Tuck your hair up in this." Then she handed Mari her own sunglasses. "And use these to hide the makeup."

Mari twisted her hair up under the hat, put on Anna's sunglasses, and turned her back to her mother's research building. She swiped across the screen, and Brax's disgusting face appeared.

He scowled at her. "What took so long? Do you normally take that long to answer calls from your dear mother?"

If Mari's glare could have shot daggers through the phone, Brax would have keeled over at that very moment. "Where is my mother?"

Without even acknowledging her question, Brax said, "It's almost as if you don't care about your mother. I mean, you don't answer her call right away. You don't give me what I need so that I can keep her safe. Where are you? You look like you're heading to a game or something." He squinted, scrutinizing her appearance. "Are you even trying to save her?"

A wave of guilt swept over Mari. She fought the lump in her throat and blinked back the tears threatening to spill down her cheeks. Under the cover of the sunglasses, Mari glanced over to see Anna moving her hands slowly downward. A signal that Mari needed to stay calm.

She took a deep breath. "Where is my mother?" she repeated more slowly.

"Where are my swarm algorithms?"

"I . . . I couldn't get them."

Brax shook his head and tsked. "Mari, it doesn't feel like you're properly motivated. You've had five days, and you have nothing to show for it."

Mari wanted to scream at him. In truth, she wished she could reach through the phone and poke his beady little eyes out. She focused on her story. Gesturing to the building behind her, Mari said, "I tried to get them. I even got into the building. But there were too many people. I couldn't get into her office."

Would he buy the idea that too many people could stop her from getting to her mother's computer? She obviously couldn't tell him that she'd been attacked by two coed ninjas.

"I just need a few more days. Please," Mari begged.

Brax acted as if he hadn't heard her. "Of course, you understand that I'll have to hurt your mother because of your failure," he sneered.

"Please, no!" Mari cried.

Suddenly, the camera view switched to an ornate door, one that fit in perfectly with the decor of Keating Mansion. Brax pushed a door open—the same one Mari had entered that afternoon—and stepped into the small, dark room. The phone's light switched on and illuminated her mother's small figure, huddled against the wall on the mattress, exactly where Mari had left her.

"You know I'll never give you the algorithms." Her mother's pitiful voice was quiet and weak.

"Don't hurt her!" Mari yelled.

At the sound of Mari's voice, her mother sat up and looked at the phone. She squinted in the bright camera light. Her left eye was swollen shut, and her face was covered with cuts and bruises.

"Oh, look. I guess I already did hurt her," Brax observed, drily.

Mari choked down a sob.

Brax's face appeared on the video again, his eyes staring menacingly from the screen. "I'm feeling generous. You have one more week. Get me the algorithms or you will both suffer."

The video call ended abruptly.

Mari sat, stunned. She glanced at Anna whose face was a mixture of anger and empathy.

"Mari, I'm so sorry." Her tall friend reached over and put an arm around her, pulling her into a hug. "We'll get your mom out. Don't give up hope."

The numbness in her limbs ebbed away, slowly replaced with a searing hatred for the man that hurt her mother.

And there was something else. Camaraderie. Compassion. Belonging.

Maybe even a little hope.

Chapter Eight

A S SHE PARKED TEEN Banana—the girls' compact car, which was colored a conservative forest-green this morning—in the small employee lot behind Keating Mansion and walked toward the back entrance, Mari couldn't believe she had a live animal strapped to her leg.

Before leaving for work that morning, the Banana Girls had made her practice walking normally with a sock taped above her knee.

But the sock hadn't been hairy.

And the sock didn't have a tail.

Another shiver ran down Mari's back as the security guard waved her through the employee entrance. She wondered how long she could fight off a full attack of the heebie-jeebies.

Ms. Fleishman was at her desk as usual, and Mari tried to concentrate on processing the morning's online requisitions. The best she could manage was to have the screen open on her computer and to do her best not to move her legs. She knew it was very unladylike to sit with her legs splayed apart, but the alternative was unthinkable. Fortunately, her sensible metal and fabric cubicle completely concealed everything below her waist.

She hoped that Ms. Fleishman would not be late for her morning coffee break. That was the best time for Mari to sneak in and place the sedated animal in the back of Ms. Fleishman's desk drawer.

But if the mouse's sedation started to wear off too early . . .

Mari thought she felt the mouse's tail against her leg.

She held her breath. That was just her imagination, right? Like a phantom cell phone vibration.

The leathery tail flicked against her leg again, and Mari yelped and squeezed her eyes shut.

It would be another five minutes before Ms. Fleishman took her morning break, but she hoped against hope that the woman would make an exception today and just leave early.

Another flick.

Immediately would be even better.

"You're not sleeping on the job, I hope," said a familiar voice.

Mari opened her eyes and looked up to see Chaz's dry expression.

At this point, she didn't even care if the millionaire owner of the company thought she was sleeping on the job. She just needed to get the living rodent off her body.

"No—" she squeaked. "I'm just—" another tail flick, "—aagh—trying to focus on my—" a tiny claw scratch, "—mmmm!—morning requisitions." She ended with slightly bulging eyes and clenched teeth that she hoped resembled a smile.

Chaz cocked his head and stared at her for a long time. Mari held perfectly still from the waist up, but below the desk, she did her best to squeeze the mouse into submission. The small, terrified animal wriggled and thrashed against her legs.

She twisted her chair rhythmically back and forth. She had once lulled her aunt's chihuahua to sleep that way. How far down the food chain did that technique work? Would a semi-conscious, duct-taped mouse fall for the same trick?

"I've been wondering if you might want to . . ." Chaz stared at her as she twisted and pressed her hands to her legs. "You seem distracted," he said with a thin smile. "Do you need to go to the . . ." He glanced back down the hall toward the restrooms.

Mari smiled shyly then let out a shriek as the mouse's tail slithered against her leg. She covered the shriek with a maniacal giggle.

Chaz moved around the side of her cubicle. "Is something wrong?" he asked as he prepared to look below her desk.

"Mr. Keating," Ms. Fleishman called out from her office door. "I'm glad you're here; I have something I needed to ask you about."

Chaz stopped short and looked up. "Uh, actually, I apologize, Ms. Fleishman, I have to get to a meeting. Maybe another time." Chaz's gaze lingered over Mari, one eyebrow cocked.

Mari held perfectly still, her eyes averted, until Chaz finally looked away and walked down the hall to the research wing.

"You're welcome," Ms. Fleishman said with a sly smile as she walked by Mari's cubicle.

Mari stared in surprise as her normally brisk supervisor followed Chaz into the research wing.

Sweet, strait-laced, Carol Fleishman had saved the day. She had seen a fellow working-woman in need and had come to the rescue. Mari would never resent Carol's staid manner again.

It made what she had to do next all the more reprehensible.

Once Carol was out of sight, Mari snuck into her office and crept behind her desk. She hiked up her dress and quickly tore the tape off her leg, clamping a hand over her mouth to stifle her cry of pain. She made sure to not lose her grip on the mouse, even though it squirmed for all it was worth. She wrapped a few rubber bands around the paws of the disgusting, hairy animal and placed it in the back of Carol's top drawer. She hoped it would take the little critter a few minutes to free itself.

Mari returned to her cubicle, happy to be free of the wriggling distraction. She worked for several carefree minutes until Carol returned.

Then she waited.

A bloodcurdling scream emanated from Carol's office a few minutes later. Even though she had been expecting it, Mari nearly fell out of her chair.

"Marina!" Carol wailed.

Mari rounded the corner and found her boss on top of the desk, brandishing a file folder.

"What happened?" Mari asked innocently.

Ms. Fleishman pointed to the corner behind the ficus tree. Mari moved closer, steeling herself for what would come. She lifted the tree, and the mouse scurried along the baseboard, heading for the door. Carol's scream made Mari jump more than the scurrying mouse did.

The tiny rodent scampered out the door and around the corner.

"Aaack! I hate mice!" Carol firmly declared as she slid off her desk. "Marina, call an exterminator right away."

"Yes, ma'am." Mari could hardly believe the plan had worked. The first part had worked, anyway. She hurried back to her desk. Carol slammed the office door right behind her.

Mari made a show of checking the Internet for exterminator information. She picked up the phone—holding down the receiver button while dialing the number—and animatedly described the urgent rodent situation to the dial tone.

"Make sure they know this is Charles Keating's mansion and they need to be here immediately!" Carol called through her closed door.

Suppressing a small grin, Mari relayed the information to the imaginary exterminator receptionist on the other end of the unconnected line. Two seconds later, a message from Carol popped up on her computer screen saying that she would be taking care of important business in her office until the mouse had been caught. Mari typed back a reply, assuring her boss that she would take care of everything.

Once her boss had fully accepted the ruse, Mari sent a short message to her friend "Bianca" about watching a movie later. This was the code to let the team know she had been successful and to stand by.

To make sure the fake extermination van would be admitted to the Keating Mansion grounds, Mari submitted a security request for Evergreen Extermination to enter the mansion property. Carol approved the request in under three seconds, and it was forwarded to the guard booth.

Mari winced as she considered Carol's closed door. She wished she hadn't needed to torture her boss like this, but it was for the greater good.

Once all of the arrangements were made, Mari hurried out to the parking lot, got into her car, and drove away from the mansion, checking out with security—per protocol—at the front gate. Half a mile down the road she turned onto a side lane and pulled up behind an exterminator's van—Fat Banana in disguise, sporting a virtual paint job complete with Evergreen Extermination logo on the sides and back.

Inside the vehicle, Susan helped Mari put on the coveralls of the fake extermination company, while Katie wiped off Mari's well-applied makeup and dotted her face with a few dozen freckles on her cheeks and nose. To complete the look, Mari stuffed her hair under a baseball hat with a built-in wig and a dead cockroach on the front. Now she was a frizzy-haired blonde with a dark tan. It was a lot of work to go through just to get her back in the mansion in disguise. But it was the best plan they could come up with to sneak her mother back out—having her take Mari's place in the exterminator team.

As they glanced around at each other, preparing to go, Mari swallowed against a lump in her throat. How had she been so lucky to find these women who would risk their safety for her mother?

Hannah started the van and drove them back to Chaz's mansion. Security processed them through the gate with a quick body count, a cursory look at their gear, and brief glances at their faces. Hopefully, in the same disguise, her mother would look similar enough to not arouse suspicion.

Mari suddenly realized that she would have some explaining to do at the security gate. If she stayed in the mansion while her mother snuck out in her place, she'd need to come up with a reason for how she had gotten back inside the mansion without checking in. And what about her car? She had stashed it back at the meeting spot, half a mile down the road.

She pushed those uncertainties to the back of her mind and turned her focus to getting her mother out safely. She could worry about minor details later.

Once inside the house, the girls spread out through various rooms and halls. Mari and Anna made their way to the third floor of the east wing. Mari made a show of spraying her wand along the baseboard, fighting her desire to run directly to her mother's room.

She led Anna down the short hall to her mother's cell. Approaching the door across from her mother's, Mari lightly touched her bracelet to it. They needed to know that Brax wouldn't surprise them in the middle of the rescue. As soon as her app gave the all clear, she nodded to Anna who opened the door to her mother's room. Mari dashed across the hall to join her.

The room was empty.

Mari stood looking at the bed where her mother had been just twenty-four hours earlier. Her brain refused to process that she wasn't there.

"Where is she?" Anna asked in a cutting whisper.

"I don't know," Mari shot back.

"Is this the right room?" Anna pressed.

Mari spun around. "It has to be. I'm sure it was the third floor. I'm sure it was this small side hallway." She moved back to the door. "Look, it even has the same reversed doorknob with the lock facing out. This has to be the room."

Mari turned back to the bed. The sheets were perfectly tucked under the edges of the mattress instead of crumpled in the corner where her mother had been clinging to them for dear life. There was a nightstand next to the bed. Had that been there yesterday? Would she have noticed it in the middle of the trauma of finally finding her mother?

She scanned the rest of the small room. There was a shallow wardrobe built against the wall. Could that have been there before, too? Mari couldn't remember. Her head spun, and the details were starting to sink into a hazy mess.

"What's this?" Anna pointed at the wardrobe. But it actually wasn't a wardrobe. One of the doors hung ajar a fraction of an inch. Anna pulled it open, and the shallow wardrobe folded out into a compact computer desk and workbench.

Mari moved to look at the technology packed into the tiny workstation. There was a laptop computer, though she doubted it was connected to anything outside of this room. The workbench had a binocular microscope and several bins of silicon wafers.

"Did they have your mother working in here?" Anna asked.

Mari stared, glassy-eyed, around the room. "I guess. I don't know. I didn't see this desk yesterday. I don't remember . . ."

Anna took Mari by the shoulders and shook her gently. "Mari, I need you to stay with me, girl. Look around the room. See what clues you can find."

Mari blinked and stared back at Anna's big brown eyes. She nodded.

Mari turned back to the workbench to help Anna figure out what her mother had been doing.

Picking up one of the polychromatic plates, Anna examined it closely. She flipped it over and held it out to Mari. "Is this your mother's handwriting?"

Mari took the wafer and looked at a small label on the back. It showed Monday's date in her mother's tight writing along with the words *Rejected Batch - Return to Lab 4.*

They looked through the piles of samples. They all said *Rejected Batch*.

"At least she's not helping them," Mari observed. But she didn't like the worried look on Anna's face.

"If she's only rejecting their batches to impede their efforts, they're going to figure it out eventually." Anna considered the shiny surface of the wafer in her hand. "I'm worried that they're actually producing her nano-bots."

"But without the swarm algorithms, they're useless," Mari said.

Anna lifted a shoulder. "Probably."

"I actually don't even care about the nano-bots. We need to find my mom. They must have taken her somewhere."

Anna shook her head. "She's not here, Mari. And we've already been here too long. We have a clue that leads to Lab 4, but that's all we've got right now. We'll need to come up with a new plan."

Mari felt like she'd been kicked in the gut. Her mom wouldn't be rescued today. The nightmare wasn't over. She'd have to keep working at Keating BioMed; she'd have to keep searching for her mother.

Without really thinking, she started pulling off the jumpsuit. She couldn't go back to work wearing exterminator coveralls.

Anna grabbed her wrist. "Wait. If we don't have your mother, you have to go back out through the gate with us. They counted how many of us came in. It needs to be the same going out."

She stopped and looked down at her clothes. Anna was right, of course; Mari wasn't thinking straight yet. With a sigh, she zipped the outfit back up.

The girls locked the door and made their way back to the front of the mansion. Mari had to remind herself to keep her eyes down. She barely cared if any of her coworkers recognized her. If the safety of the Banana Girls wasn't also on the line, Mari would have stormed through every hallway, shattered every window, and smashed every door until she found her mother. Instead, she was slinking away in disguise—and in defeat—with almost no hope of finding her mother.

They loaded into the fake exterminator's van and checked out through security. To Mari, everything had gone gray. Her mother was still trapped in the mansion somewhere. To make matters worse, she'd probably added to her mother's worry by telling her she was in disguise at the mansion. Of course, her mother would have good reason to worry—Mari was deep in enemy territory with no idea what she was doing.

Susan touched Mari on the arm. "We'll get her out. You have to hang in there. Things don't always go right on the first try. We've had several missions that needed a second attempt."

"Or third or fourth," Hannah added.

Mari gave her a weak smile and turned to the window.

Forcing herself to drive back to work, knowing they had failed, was like a knife in her heart. She had a good cry sitting in the car, which was fine because she had to reapply her makeup, anyway.

She walked in a sort of trance, trudging the entire length of the hall from the research wing back to her desk, barely noticing coworkers passing by. She felt like a zombie, and her entire body ached knowing that her mother remained somewhere inside the building at the mercy of a madman.

Carol's office door was still closed. Mari plodded over and knocked.

"Yes?"

"The exterminators finished a little bit ago," Mari said. "I thought you'd like to know."

"Oh, good." Carol's voice sounded relieved. "You can open the door."

Mari pushed the door open and leaned against the doorframe, doing her best to not sigh loudly.

"Bless your heart. You're probably exhausted from having to deal with this rodent problem. I'm sorry I didn't help you with the exterminators."

Mari shook her head. "It's okay. I didn't mind."

"This might help cheer you up," Carol nodded to her screen. "Mr. Brooks asked me to send you to pick up the latest batch of nano-sensors from Lab 2 and bring them up to his office."

Mari shrugged. She didn't really feel in the mood to see Trey.

"You just say the word, though, and I'll tell him he can get off his lazy butt and go pick up his own samples," Carol said.

Of course, if she sat at her desk too long, Mari was sure Chaz would saunter past. That would be so much worse than seeing Trey. She took a breath and forced a smile. "No, it's okay. I can do it."

There were, indeed, samples waiting for Mari in Lab 2. She had wondered if Trey was just looking for an excuse to send her all over the building. She knew she should be taking advantage of the time away from her desk, but it was too depressing to even consider finding her mother thirty minutes after the failed attempt to rescue her. Mari didn't think she could handle a heartbreak like that.

She traipsed up the stairs to the third floor of the research wing. She knew that's where the scientists had their offices, but it occurred to her that she'd only ever been to Trey's once, and only in passing. She found it about halfway down the hall.

She stuck her head in the open door and tried her best to smile politely.

"Hi, Marina. I was beginning to wonder if you'd be coming."

She took a few steps inside. "Why? When did you ask Carol to send me?"

"A little before lunch," he answered.

Mari tilted her head at him. "Might it have been at two minutes before noon?" She couldn't help but smile, knowing that her suspicions were about to be confirmed.

Trey clicked his mouse a few times as he searched his email outbox. "Let's see. Oh, yes, actually. It says I sent a message to Carol at 11:58 AM. Huh. Go figure." He gave her an innocent-looking grin that almost had her convinced.

"Trey, if you want to have lunch together every day, all you have to do is—"

"Will you go to lunch with me every day?" he blurted out.

A light laugh escaped Mari's lips. She helped herself to the chair in front of his desk. It felt good to be off her feet visiting with someone she could relax around. That was a dangerous thought, she knew, and Mari promised herself she would try to fight it as soon as she recovered from the day's disappointment.

"You certainly are persistent," Mari observed. "Have you always been this way? You must have driven your parents crazy."

"I'll tell you everything you need to know about how my parents felt—I'm an only child."

Before she had a chance to stop herself, Mari added. "Me too." She quickly ran a hand across her brow to hide her eyes bugging out. What was she doing? What was it about this guy that tricked her into letting her guard down?

"My parents were both really into their work," Trey continued. "I guess once they had me, they checked off that box on their life to-do list and went back to their work."

Mari didn't know exactly what to say to that, so she nodded. A split second before he spoke again, Mari realized what was coming.

"How about you?" he asked.

She hadn't made up a fake story about her family dynamic. She hadn't thought she'd ever need to talk about them. She didn't think she could pull off a credible story on the spot, so she went with a vague approximation of the truth. "Oh . . . uh, my dad left when I was really young, and my mom never remarried. She sort of threw herself into her work. Kinda like your parents."

"Yeah," Trey agreed, nodding.

Several seconds passed in silence.

Getting comfortable with Trey was dangerous. She would need to figure out a way to put some distance between them before she accidentally let something important slip.

Had she already said yes to lunch every day? That might be a mistake.

Trey leaned forward and rested his elbows on his desk, looking at her intently. His casual tone belied the earnest expression on his face. "So, besides her big brown eyes, did you inherit anything else from your mother?"

Mari froze. Trey's gaze grew more intense, as if he wanted to communicate something through his look. He gave an almost imperceptible nod.

Her heart pounded in her chest. Did Trey know about her mother? How could that be possible?

Mari tried to think, but the blood pulsing in her ears made it hard to concentrate. Trey was a scientist here at Keating BioMed. And he was working on nanotechnology. Was it possible that he knew that her mother was being held hostage somewhere in the mansion? If so, was he an accomplice, or was he trying to help her? She didn't dare say anything. It would completely blow her cover.

Her eyes wandered the room without really focusing on anything. Pushing herself abruptly out of the chair, Mari fumbled for an excuse, "I . . . uh . . . I have to get back to my desk."

"Marina? I'm sorry if I—"

She held up a hand as she fled the room.

Halfway down the stairs, Mari stopped on the landing and leaned against the wall. Her lungs heaved with shuddering breaths. How could her mother be so close yet so completely out of reach? She'd held Mari in her arms just the day before, and now she had vanished into thin air. Mari didn't know who, beyond Brax, was part of the scheme, but it didn't really matter. Only her mother mattered.

As her breathing returned to normal, her hands slowly clenched into fists. She didn't care if she found her mother on the same day as their failed rescue; she just wanted to find her.

She refused to go straight back to her desk and mope. This was the perfect opportunity to check the research wing. That must be where they had moved her mother.

She exited the stairs on the second floor and headed for an area she hadn't checked. She passed workrooms and utility closets, keeping her eye out for places where a hostage could be hidden. Unfortunately, there were too many employees moving around the halls for Mari to stop and check every door. Twice, she was able to duck around a corner and hold her bracelet to a locked door. Empty both times.

She tried to think like a criminal mastermind. She tried to think like Brax. Where would he put a hostage? It would need to be somewhere accessible but also secure.

In the hall on the way back to her desk, she decided she'd need to go back and talk to Trey at some point. She really wanted to march up there and interrogate him over what he knew about her mother—it might not be smart, but she was sure it would make her feel better. Whatever she did, she knew she shouldn't—or couldn't—leave things with him the way she had. If he knew anything about her mother, she needed his help. Whether he gave that help willingly or not was a different question.

After thirty minutes of staring at her screen, not really doing anything but stewing over her next move with Trey, Mari stood and went to Carol's door. She held her phone as if she was just reading a message. "Trey needs me for something," she fibbed.

Carol nodded. "Tell him I'm going to start billing his department for your hours." Unlike the first time her boss had threatened that, Mari could see through her gruff exterior to the kind soul underneath.

On the way up the stairs, Mari decided she should probably start with an apology, not that she had done anything wrong. Trey was the one making weird comments about her mother's brown eyes. Maybe she really should yell at him—put him on the defensive.

As she approached Trey's office, Mari heard voices spilling out into the hall. She slowed a few feet from the door.

"I can see how it's going; you two are obviously getting along well."

That was Chaz's voice. He sounded upset.

"Chaz, you know, you're the one who asked me to do this." Trey's voice was calm but defensive. "You asked me to keep an eye on her. That's what I'm doing."

Mari's limbs went cold. Trey had been keeping an eye on her the entire time? On Chaz's orders? The floor threatened to tip underneath her. She placed a hand on the wall for its steadying strength.

She glanced around the hall. This was no time to get caught eavesdropping, but she needed to hear the rest of this conversation. The Executive VP of Supply Chain had an office across the hall, and Mari knew she was at a conference in San Francisco all week. In a blurry haze, she tiptoed across the hall and hid inside the door of the VP's empty office.

As her breathing steadied and her vision sharpened, a fire quickly replaced the coldness in her limbs. Her resentment bristled and burned. How dare these men talk about her as if she needed watching or like she was a project that could be passed from one to the other?

She strained to hear the conversation. The tone of Chaz's reply was curt. "Well, I didn't think you'd need to be quite so friendly doing it."

"Being friends is a necessary part." Trey paused. "I'm sure you know what I mean." The implication in Trey's tone hung heavy in the air.

Mari wanted to walk across the hall and punch both of them. Unfortunately, that might get her fired—or worse.

"Well, just watch yourself. I didn't give you this assignment so you could flirt with her," Chaz replied.

If Mari didn't know better, she would've thought Chaz sounded jealous.

"I'll keep it professional," Trey replied.

"Fine. And get back to work on the project." Chaz's voice suddenly sounded closer.

Mari flattened herself against the wall of the vacant office and held her breath. Chaz's footsteps quickly receded down the hallway back toward his office. Mari quietly let her breath out.

The Project. Mari wondered what that could be.

Was she the project? Or her mother?

Or both?

Chapter Nine

YOU CAN'T SUCCEED AT the mission if you can't keep the job.

The Banana Girls had given her that piece of advice when she'd come home the night before, distraught over the failed rescue. They had done their best to cheer her up, but Mari knew they were just being polite.

She had let her mother down.

She had let everyone down.

Initially, Mari had wanted to come back into work that morning and yell at Trey for half an hour and then go insult Chaz's parentage. The Anna had talked her down from that ledge—mostly.

She knew that working undercover at Keating BioMed was the best bet for figuring out a way to get her mother out. It's probably what the professionals would have done if she hadn't been forbidden by Brax from contacting them.

But it was Friday again, which meant Brax had had her mother for a whole week, which meant that despite all her efforts, her mother was still trapped somewhere, hopefully nearby.

She knew even if she found her mother that morning, it would be impossible to pull off a same-day rescue. But she hated the idea of spending a weekend in high-life luxury—even if she was using every waking moment getting caught up on homework and feeling guilty—while her mother was a hostage for three more days.

Maybe if she could find her mother before the end of the day, the team could figure out a way to sneak into the house over the weekend while no one was at work.

You can't succeed at the mission if you can't keep the job.

The mantra repeated itself over and over in her mind that morning as she was forced to tabulate the week's requisition numbers instead of scouring the mansion for her mother. Her brain echoed with the phrase each time she had to smile sweetly as various scientists stopped by with new orders or asked how her day was going. And the saying burned hot in her gut as she came to a momentous realization—not only did she need to not lose her job, but eventually she'd have to exploit Trey or Chaz's interest in her in order to complete the mission.

Trey or Chaz.

Chaz obviously had more to offer: power, position, full access to the mansion. But she had never really trusted him.

Of course, her trust in Trey wasn't at record high levels either.

She had already been a little weirded-out by Trey's comment about having her mother's brown eyes, but after learning he was keeping tabs on her at Chaz's request, she just couldn't be near him without wanting to wring his neck.

So maybe she should go find Chaz—casually, if possible—and take him up on the offer of another dinner at the Corinthian Club. She could flirt with him, tell him how interested she was in him, and see where things went.

The idea made her want to puke on his expensive leather shoes.

That pretty much made the decision for her.

Trey it was.

At five minutes till noon, she left her desk and headed up to Trey's office. She tried to time it so that she'd be walking in right at 11:58. Hopefully, he would appreciate the gesture.

She ended up pretty near the mark.

"Hi," she said, peeking through the door in what she hoped was a light, playful way.

Trey looked up. "Hey," he said, before returning his attention to his work.

Was he really blowing her off that easily? She'd have to level up her allure factor.

Did she even have an allure factor?

Act like Katie, she thought.

"Hey. Didn't we have a standing lunch date? Are you backing out on our arrangement?" She gave him what felt like a way-too-cheerful smile.

He considered her with a skeptical expression. "You stormed out of here pretty upset yesterday."

"Pshh." Mari waved her hands downward, dismissing his concern. She lowered herself coyly into the chair. She hoped he didn't want to delve into a genuine conversation; she wouldn't be able to hang on to this bubbly persona for much longer.

He stared at her a moment before returning his attention to his computer. "You really don't have to have lunch with me. I know you've got that important project you're working on. And truth is, I've got projects myself—more than the ones here." He gestured to his office.

Mari's brow furrowed. Could this guy be any more obtuse?

"What are you talking about?" she asked.

Trey rolled his eyes. "You know . . . all of that wishing you had more time away from your desk?" He nodded his head and spoke each phrase slowly, as if she should be able to catch his meaning. "All of the behind-the-scenes scheming I had to do so you could . . . you know." He waved his hand vaguely. "Haven't your meanderings ever taken you up the stairs?" He jabbed his thumb in the direction of the old mansion. In the direction of Brax's wing on the third floor.

Mari's jaw went slack.

Trey knew what she was doing.

He must know about her mother being held captive.

Was he in on it?

His office probably wasn't the best place to grab him by the neck and flip him onto the ground. To say nothing of pinning him there and individually breaking each and every one of his fingers until he talked.

But she really wanted to.

The sound of approaching footsteps echoed in the hall. Mari shook herself from the fantasy of hurting Trey and looked up in time to see Brax stride into the office.

It felt as if a pit had opened beneath her, and she was falling into it. Her world spun, and she fought the urge to grip the arms of the chair to keep from tipping.

Brax only gave her a cursory glance before stepping toward Trey's desk. "Trey, I wanted to ask you about those private-industry sectors we discussed. We can find a much larger market for the nano-bots if we include foreign companies as well. I sent you a list that I want you to review as soon as possible."

Trey nodded. "I'll get right on it." He cast a furtive look at Mari.

"And while I'm thinking about it, we'll probably need you to help out with the presentation next week. If Chaz is going to have that idiotic social gala, we might as well do some selling while all of those important people are here."

"I've already got my tux," Trey replied drily.

Brax barked out a short laugh and walked from the office.

Mari broke into a cold sweat. Fortunately, it seemed that Brax hadn't recognized her. Katie and Susan really had worked miracles with her hair and makeup.

Forcing herself to breathe normally, she stole a glance at Trey who responded with a simple raise of his eyebrows.

By running errands for Trey, had she unknowingly been helping Keating BioMedical create a new product from her mother's stolen work? Trey seemed to be pretty chummy with Brax. How much did he know?

And what was with those gestures toward the third floor? Was he taunting her?

Projecting every bit of confidence she could muster, Mari glared at him. "So, you know Brax?"

"Well, he *is* Chaz's cousin. And he sort of launched the project. So, yeah." He cocked his head to the side in a look of bewilderment. "Marina, you're a smart woman. I'm sure you've figured it out by now." He stared back at her with a little quirk at the corner of his lips. "Brax. The company. My work." He gestured to the stack of lab samples in front of him. "This is pretty much why I'm here." His smile broadened to a leer. "I'm sure you can put two and two together."

With a quick wink, he turned back to his computer.

Mari sat stunned.

Had Trey been working with them all along? Were they all simply toying with her?

The edges of her vision started to dim. She had to get out. She had to get away from this den of villains.

Mari abruptly stood. She fled the office, ran down the back stairwell, and burst out into the parking lot. Her hands shook as she fumbled with her car keys. She wanted to sit in the car and cry, but she couldn't. With gritted teeth, she forced herself to drive out the front gate and onto the quiet suburban road.

Without really knowing where she was headed, Mari drove. The road blurred as silent tears filled her eyes and splashed into her lap. What was she doing? How could she possibly succeed in the mission to free her mother? The Banana Girls had been kind enough to help, but she was an eighteen-year-old college freshman. She was in way over her head. She didn't know anything about secret identities or covert hostage rescue operations.

And to add insult to injury, she was being forced to sit at a cubicle, day after day, knowing that her mother was trapped in a small room nearby, while the perpetrator walked freely around the mansion, and yet Mari was unable to stop him.

It was probably fortunate that she'd been so shocked at Brax's entrance. If she'd known he was coming, she would have throttled him.

Several hours later, when she had finally found her way back to the penthouse garage, Mari resolved to tell the girls that she was very grateful for all their help, but that she had decided to just go to the authorities and hope they could get her mother out safely. Maybe the FBI had an expert team of agents that could do the job.

On the fifty-three-floor elevator ride up to the penthouse, she wavered a little in her decision. She didn't want to hurt their feelings, considering how much they'd done for her already. Actually, the problem wasn't them at all; it was her. She was the weak link. She would just have to tell them that she wasn't cut out for it.

As she strode confidently into Club Banana, the girls looked up from their books and computers.

"You're home early," Susan said.

Mari squared her shoulders and took a deep breath. "I have to quit. I'm sorry. I just can't do this anymore. I think we should turn it over to the CIA or the FBI or whatever."

Sitting on her favorite plush chair in the corner, Hannah rolled her eyes and muttered something that sounded like "drama" before going back to her tablet.

"Come over here," Anna said, patting the spot next to her on the sofa.

Mari paced the room. "No, I'm not going to let you talk me out of this." Her hands were balled into fists. She wanted to hit something. "I'm the reason my mom is still a hostage to that vile piece of low-life and his slimy minions. It was crazy to think that we could pretend to do what real spies do. It's not going to work."

"Mari, you just need to . . ." From her favorite spot on the sofa, Susan took several deep breaths, making rising and falling motions with her arms and hands.

"I think we should talk about it," Anna added calmly.

Mari didn't want to calm down, and she didn't want to talk about it. She didn't want to risk that the Banana Girls would convince her to try again.

Although part of her did want to wipe the smug look off Hannah's face. She hated that Hannah had been right.

"We just need to call the authorities so they can send in their crack shot team of agents to get my mother out," Mari said.

The ladies shared a knowing look.

"What?" Mari asked.

"We're the team," Katie said.

"What team?" Mari demanded.

"The team that the FBI sends in to get the job done. We're the ones they call," Anna said.

Mari gaped at them. "Seriously? You really are secret agents?"

Susan nodded vigorously. Katie smiled. Anna just lifted her brows and shrugged.

Mari paced again, flustered by this new information. "Well, it doesn't matter; I haven't got what it takes to be a spy. I can't even get my own mother out of a hostage situation."

There was a short knock at the door. Before Mari even thought twice, she stepped through the entryway hall and opened it.

Trey stared back at her from the doorway, a wry smile on his lips. "Hey."

Adrenaline surged through Mari's body. How had he found her? Instinctively, she planted her foot, swung her leg forward, and kicked him square in the sternum. Trey flew backward across the hall, and Mari slammed the door.

"Security breach! Emergency! Code Red!" She ran back into the living room. "There's a bad guy right outside. We've been compromised!" She stared at the other girls. "Do something!"

Hannah sighed and stood from her spot. "Calm down. The building is completely secure. No one can get on this floor without authorization."

"But, wow!" Susan said with a giggle. "Tell us again how you're *not* spy material. That was awesome!"

Mari ignored her. "How could he have found Club Banana?" she asked Hannah.

"Let's figure out who you assaulted first." Hannah opened the door.

Trey had gotten back up, but he stood several feet back from the door, rubbing his chest where Mari was sure she'd left a deep imprint of her shoe.

"Trey Brooks?" Hannah asked.

Trey nodded.

Hannah stepped to the side. "Come on in."

He entered with some obvious—and understandable—trepidation.

"You know this guy?!" Mari asked in disbelief.

"Not officially." She turned to Trey and held out her hand. "I'm Hannah." Then turning back to Mari. "How do you know him?"

Mari's eyes bulged. "This is the creep at work who's in league with Brax and makes weird comments about my mom and the third floor of the mansion."

Hannah shook her head as she closed the door. "You're not making any sense," she said as she walked past Trey and Mari on her way back to her favorite seat.

That left Mari as the only one to block the rest of the secret penthouse from her coworker-turned-nemesis. She glared at him.

"I thought I should stop by and clear things up," Trey said as he held Mari's gaze. He moved toward her but stopped as his hand went absently to his chest.

Mari folded her arms and eyed him warily. "You can start by explaining why you followed me here."

Trey held up his hands in defense. "I didn't follow you. I put in a contact request through my superiors. They gave me the address and clearance." He nodded toward Hannah.

Mari shot a glare at Hannah over her shoulder. "You could have mentioned that earlier."

"And miss all the drama?" Hannah muttered without looking up.

Turning back to Trey, Mari put up a hand. "Wait. What do you mean your superiors? Are you a spy, too?"

Trey smiled. "Agent. Yeah. I was assigned to infiltrate Brax's operation by going through Keating BioMed."

"So you really aren't a brilliant scientist," Mari observed.

Trey laughed at her use of his earlier joke. "No. Well, sort of. Part of what I told you was true; I really did graduate from UCLA. But I've definitely been faking my way through the nanotech stuff. I majored in materials science."

"And why didn't you tell me you were on the case?" Mari asked.

"I tried!" Under Mari's continued glare, he hastily added, "What do you think I was trying to say when I mentioned your mother's eyes and you wandering around the mansion?"

"I thought you were being creepy!" Mari shot back. "Why didn't you just say it?"

"Agents aren't supposed to make contact with other operatives outside their team," Anna said. "It avoids dangerous misunderstandings. Obviously."

Mari threw up her hands and walked over to the couches. "So, you couldn't come out and say you were trying to help, but you could totally freak me out about my mother and Brax?"

Trey moved around the other side of the sofa, running a hand through his wavy brown hair. "I thought for sure you would understand what I was trying to say. I mean, why would an employee at Keating BioMed make random comments about your mother's eyes or the residence wing on the third floor?"

Mari rounded on him. "Because he was part of the kidnapping team, and he wanted to torment me!"

Trey opened his mouth, but he must have seen his actions in a different light, because he paused then snapped his mouth shut. As the silence stretched out, he looked awkwardly around the room for help from the other girls.

Anna gave Trey a patronizing smile. "Don't feel bad, Trey. Even smart guys can act like dumb boys sometimes."

Katie decided to join the fray. She stood and walked toward Trey. "Let me get this straight, you knew you weren't supposed to make contact with an undercover operative from another division, so you decided to subvert the rules and *hint* at her identity? Do you have any idea how much trouble you could be in for this?"

Inching away from Katie's impending assault, Trey held up his hands to defend himself. "Hold on. Those regs are there to make sure we don't accidentally make contact with the wrong person. It only took me a few minutes to figure out she was Dr. Sandoval's daughter. So technically, I didn't have to worry about contacting the wrong person."

Susan picked up the attack next, flailing her arms in Trey's direction as she approached. "That's your defense? That you knew you weren't making a mistake? Do you realize how risky your attempt was, not just for the mission, but for Mari's emotional well-being?"

Trey was backing himself into a corner, both figuratively and literally. "I . . . I'm sorry," He offered his assailants the feeble apology, then he peeked around them and looked straight at Mari. "I really am sorry, Marina. I thought you understood my hints. I swear. I just thought you were being shy. As soon as I realized you'd misunderstood—" he glanced quickly at Katie and Susan. "—uh, that I had screwed up, I submitted a top-priority contact request. I came over as soon as I could."

Susan and Katie continued to stare him down. Trey obviously didn't know what to do with Mari's self-appointed bodyguards. They weren't backing down. It was touching, really. Mari had never had friends like this—ones that would stand up and defend her when she really needed it. It made her feel . . . safe.

"Katie, Susan, it's okay." The girls relented at Mari's insistence. Mari walked around the sofa to stand in front of Trey. She considered him for several moments. He had always been kind to her. And despite the weird comments about her mother and the case, she trusted that he had good intentions.

An expression of relief crossed his face. "Thanks, Marina."

"Actually, it's Mari," she said, her arms still crossed defensively.

"Mari." Trey smiled. The look in those green eyes would melt Mari's resolve if she wasn't careful. "I like that."

"You're really an operative sent to help me save my mother?" she asked.

Trey rubbed the back of his neck and frowned. "Well, technically not sent to help you—" He must have caught the flash of disappointment on Mari's face, because he straightened and smiled. "Yes. I am."

Looking around at the determined expressions of her friends, Mari took a deep breath and extended her hand to Trey. "Then welcome to the team."

She still wasn't sure if she could save her mother, but she knew she wasn't doing it alone.

Chapter Ten

"I'M SO SICK OF homework," Mari said as she pushed her laptop away. She turned to Anna who was in the kitchen preparing a Saturday afternoon snack, as she called it. "How do you girls keep up with school? I've missed one week of classes, and I feel like I'll never recover. In fact, if it weren't for Katie going to my linear algebra class and taking notes for me, I'd probably just fail that one."

Katie twisted around in her spot on the couch and put her arms over the back so she could see Mari better. "By the way, there is this amazingly hot guy who sits in the middle on the left side. He looks and acts like a total California boy." Katie heaved a deep sigh and flopped back onto the couch. She popped up a second later. "On an unrelated topic, I might need to visit you after that class one of these days, you know, just to say hi."

Mari glanced back at Anna, and they shared a knowing smile.

"Well, luckily you won't have to study for much longer," Anna said.

"Why not?" Mari felt a wave of concern. If she didn't get caught up in the assignments she'd missed, it would be very difficult to get the grades she wanted.

Anna dumped a can of minced pineapple into a bowl and stirred. "Because I invited Trey over to do some mission planning with you."

Mari's cheeks heated. "Sure, I guess I can take a study break."

By the time Trey arrived, Anna had the table spread with snacks worthy of an evening mixer. He was friendly and charming as he visited with the Banana Girls. They all took their food out on the balcony and relaxed in the afternoon sun. After several minutes of visiting, one by one the other girls went back inside—though Anna very nearly had to drag Katie from Trey's side—leaving Mari alone with her very handsome coworker and, she now realized, co-spy.

"So, we should probably talk about the mission," Trey said with a crooked grin that brought out his dimple.

"Why did Chaz ask you to keep an eye on me?" Mari had been wondering that for two days but had forgotten to ask.

"Well, you are sort of a handful, so . . ."

Mari glared at him. "I'm serious, Trey."

"Oh, you're serious. I guess that means I have to come up with a good reason."

"The real reason, please."

Trey rubbed the back of his neck. "Well, let's just say that Chaz is super paranoid about corporate espionage. He's absolutely convinced that his competition will figure out a way to get a mole inside his organization and steal all of the company's technology."

"And he suspects me?" Mari wasn't excited about having drawn additional attention to herself.

"Not necessarily. But you were hired so fast, and without his approval. He told me to make sure you weren't snooping around anywhere."

"But you did catch me snooping around. On my first day." Mari felt like her first day at Keating BioMed had been months ago, not five days.

"True. But that was actually before he told me to keep an eye on you."

Mari looked straight at him. "Wait. All of that attention on my first day, that wasn't because Chaz told you to?"

"No. You earned that attention all on your own," Trey said with a broad grin.

"With help from the Banana Girls," Mari added.

Trey shrugged. He didn't look convinced.

They sat in friendly silence for several moments.

"You wanna go on a walk?" Mari asked.

"Definitely."

On the way down in the elevator, Mari picked up the previous topic. "You don't think Chaz knows that I'm Dr. Sandoval's daughter, do you?"

"Truthfully, I'm not sure Chaz knows much about your mother. Almost all of Keating BioMedical's business operations are legal and above-board. But, as far as I can tell, Chaz leaves the questionable stuff almost entirely to his cousin. I doubt Chaz even knows your mother is in his mansion."

Mari's smile tightened. "So, Chaz is a creepy, conceited, spoiled, rich boy, but he's not a kidnapper?"

Trey laughed. "More or less."

Out on the street, they walked casually south, zigzagging block to block with no particular destination in mind. The sounds of a Saturday afternoon in Midtown echoed against the surrounding buildings—cars driving past, music from a nearby event, and leaves fluttering in the breeze. Mari loved the life and vibrancy all around her.

"So why did Chaz ask you specifically? Why not ask Carol?" Mari asked.

"Well, Carol's the one who hired you so suddenly, so he might think she can't be trusted."

"Oh. I hope Carol doesn't get into trouble for hiring me. It really has been the perfect chance to—" Mari grabbed Trey's arm. "Wait! You don't think Carol's a sp—I mean agent, too, do you?"

Trey patted her hand. "Not everyone can be a spy. Some people are just good citizens willing to help when they know it's the right thing." His hand lingered on hers for a second before she released him and they continued their walk.

After they turned the corner on the next street, Trey pointed down the road. "Look. It's Cafe Agora. Where we had our first . . . where we met for dinner after your first day of work."

Mari was glad Trey wasn't quite sure how to quantify their relationship, either. "You know, we're halfway to my apartment. You wanna see where I live? I mean, where I used to live? Or where I'll be living again, someday, hopefully . . ." She let her clumsy invitation trail off.

Trey turned his adorable grin on her. "Lead the way."

About a block later, Mari regained a small bit of composure and was anxious for something to break the silence. "So why does Chaz trust you with keeping an eye on me?"

"We're actually friends. Sort of."

Mari glanced at him. "Sounds like there's a story there."

Trey lifted a shoulder. "Yeah. We met a few years ago at a car collectors' show. I had just picked up my third classic car. He was looking for one just like it. Apparently, he thought waving wads of cash would convince me to sell. But he's not the only one who came from a well-off family."

Mari's eyes grew. "You mean you're rich, too?"

"Nowhere near as rich as Chaz," Trey said with a laugh. He glanced around and lowered his voice. "And don't tell anyone. It's supposed to be a secret."

"Why does it need to be a secret?"

Trey rubbed his chin. "Well, that's sort of how I got Chaz to give me a job. I told him my parents had cut me off from my trust fund."

"Wow. I guess you're just full of secrets," Mari observed.

Trey grinned. "It sort of comes with the territory."

They walked another half a block in silence while Mari mulled over what Trey had told her.

"So let me get this straight," she finally said. "Chaz suspects the two women who are either amateurs or blissfully ignorant of the whole espionage thing, while the whole time completely trusting the legitimate infiltrator because they both like classic cars?"

A wide grin spread on Trey's face. "Human nature can be funny sometimes, can't it?"

"And a little bit ironic," Mari added.

Mari wondered how she had gotten herself into a situation where she was taking a casual walk down the street with a spy. A rich spy, at that. Pedestrians passing them on the wide sidewalk had no idea they had just walked by a spy—or two.

A guy coming out of a burger joint across the street caught her eye. He didn't really look out of place, per se, but something was weird about him. She wondered if someone trained as a spy would be able to pick out why.

Could spies recognize other spies just by looking at them?

"Here's my street." She and Trey turned left a few blocks up from her condo.

Seeing the cars lining her street brought back the memory of the last time she'd been there—when she and Anna had lost the stakeout guys in a high-speed chase.

She really shouldn't be waltzing straight up to her apartment with a spy from Keating BioMed. The goons might still be there.

Goons.

Mari glanced nervously over her shoulder. The guy from the burger joint had just crossed the street to follow them. She was pretty sure he had looked a little familiar. Now she knew why.

Clueless—the thug from her walk home the week before.

Had he recognized her?

Maybe he and Lost were still on the stakeout, and Clueless was just picking them up a late lunch.

Mari needed a way to figure out if he was following them. "I think I parked over this way," she said, steering Trey across the narrow street to a small parking lot.

"Parked? Are we coming to pick up your car?" he asked.

Mari shook her head and hazarded a glance toward Clueless under the pretense of checking for traffic.

He looked straight at her.

As a perplexed expression spread across his face, Mari's stomach dropped. He might be clueless, but it wouldn't take him that long to figure out where he recognized her from—blonde highlights or not. He was staking out her apartment, after all.

Taking Trey's hand, she led him across the parking lot, crisscrossing through several rows of parked cars.

His muscles tensed in response to her sudden change in behavior. "What's going on?" he whispered.

"Brax's goons are probably still staking out my place," Mari said as they made a sharp turn on a narrow access street that bisected the block and used the cover of an overgrown hedge to hide their escape.

"So, we're running through back alleys because someone might be watching your apartment?"

"No. We're running because one of them is following us." She turned to look at Trey. "Unless you think we should stop and fight him. I'm not sure if he got a good look at you."

"As much as I'd love to show off my fighting skills, running is usually a better idea." Trey glanced around for a way out of the access road than the obvious way back onto Mari's street.

Pointing to a set of dumpsters behind an old house-turned-restaurant, Mari pulled him across the narrow road. "This way might work." She scaled the first dumpster and hopped onto the second. Trey followed. She reached up to the railing of an exterior balcony half a story off the ground that ran around the house. She realized that from her new vantage point, she could see above the overgrown fence separating them from the parking lot.

Unfortunately, that meant Brax's thug could see her, too.

Swinging her leg quickly over the railing, she rolled onto the raised porch. "Hurry, Trey; he saw us."

Trey followed Mari's lead, landing lightly next to her. Crouching low, they ran the length of the balcony until it met a mismatched patio that wrapped around from the front of the building. A few small groups sat at the scattered tables finishing their lunch meals. Mari slid casually over the rail and pretended that was the normal way to get up to the dining patio. She glanced back and saw Trey looking a little nervous as well.

Grabbing Trey's hand, Mari turned back to the curious diners. "We've just been so excited to finally eat here."

Her lighthearted humor earned a few chuckles, and the patrons returned to their conversations. As they weaved through the tables, Mari glanced back and saw Brax's goon coming around the building onto the balcony—he had chosen to use the ramp instead of climbing up the dumpsters. She pulled Trey forward to increase his pace.

Hustling down the steps from the balcony at the front of the restaurant, Mari looked both ways down the busy street. To the right, the buildings got smaller—more individual houses, fewer business and high-rise condos.

She pulled Trey the other way toward the larger buildings and started a casual jog. Where was the line between getting away and drawing too much attention?

When Mari heard hard footfalls behind them coming down the balcony steps, she broke into a full run, pulling Trey along with her.

They scampered across an intersection without waiting for the light. "Where are we going?" Trey asked between breaths.

"I have no idea," Mari replied. "You wanna lead?"

Trey shook his head. "You know the area better. Just find us somewhere to hide."

Half a block past the intersection, Mari grabbed Trey's hand again and pulled him into the wide entrance of a three-story parking garage.

"A parking garage?" Trey said as they flew past a line of cars waiting to exit. "Don't you ever watch movies? The bad guys always catch them in the parking garages!"

"Do you have any better ideas?!"

"Sure. Anything but a parking garage."

They ran up the spiral ramp to the second floor. Trey's speed started to fade halfway up, so Mari pulled harder on his hand. That sprint interval training was finally paying off.

Before she could continue up the ramp to the third level, Trey steered them out onto the second deck and behind a large, black pickup truck.

"He's definitely going to catch us if we stop," Mari whispered.

"Let's hope he goes up to Level Three. Then we'll quietly slip out," Trey said.

"And if he comes straight to this floor?" Mari asked.

Trey frowned. "We should probably have a backup plan. Can't you think of a better place to hide?"

Mari racked her brain for the alleys and streets and business within a few blocks of her apartment. "I've got it," she declared.

Trey held up a hand as the sound of footsteps echoed up the spiral ramp. Mari wished they had hidden a little farther from the ramp. This position didn't give them much chance to avoid being seen.

Mari held her breath as the steps slowed. If the goon came out of the ramp and past the first few cars, he'd see them for sure. Mari shifted into a low crouch, preparing to move around the front of the car to stay hidden or run, if necessary.

Ducking low, Mari could see Clueless' scuffed leather dress shoes. He stepped slowly out into the main parking lane and moved up the row. Mari looked up at Trey and tilted her head toward the other end of the pickup truck. Silently, they inched their way along the side of the vehicle until they reached the front bumper.

Mari peeked below the undercarriage again. Five more steps and the goon would see them. She scooted to the front of the car, wedging herself between the bumper and the smooth cement wall of the garage. Trey followed her, leaning his body against her back to keep their heads ducked low.

This wasn't what she had in mind when she'd suggested a walk, but she had to admit that if it weren't for the threat of imminent capture by the bad guys, she would be enjoying the feeling of his broad arms draped around her, protecting her from danger.

Mari wriggled to the side a bit so that she could look directly at Trey. Though she could see the apprehension in his expression, his face still had the same crooked grin. With a slight tilt of her head, she motioned back toward the ramp with a questioning look.

Trey craned his neck, trying to track their assailant's progress deeper into the garage. He turned back and gave Mari a quick nod. She crawled forward until they were free of the truck's bumper. Hunched behind another car, she ran quickly and quietly for the ramp, Trey close on her heels. As they made their escape, Mari looked back and caught a glimpse of Clueless. He had reached the end of the row of parked cars and had barely turned around.

He saw them the moment before they disappeared down the ramp. "Hey!" he yelled after them.

They just couldn't catch a break with this guy.

"Run!" Mari said.

"Of course," Trey sounded resigned.

Was this something that happened to him regularly?

They wound down the ramp and ran past the cars still waiting at the automatic pay booth. Out on the street, they turned away from Mari's apartment and sprinted along the sidewalk. Watching for a break in oncoming traffic, Mari darted across the street at the first chance she got, pulling Trey behind her. They dodged pedestrians and trees, weaving back and forth on and off the sidewalk and curb.

Up ahead, Mari saw the entrance to the small bookshop they could hide in. She hoped they could make it through the door before being spotted again. Maybe Clueless had lost them in the shuffle of the Saturday afternoon shoppers.

The shop bell rang as they burst through the door. Frank, the owner, was not sitting at his normal perch at the front counter. Perhaps he was in the back room.

Mari led Trey past tables stacked with new books that adorned the front of the shop to the rows of tall bookcases in the back. This was the perfect place to go if a person wanted to find some solitude in a book.

Or if a person was pretending to be a spy and needed to hide from a pursuer.

With an amazingly handsome co-spy.

Theoretically.

Beyond the last row of books, there was one more short, stubby aisle tucked in the back corner of the shop. Mari pushed Trey down the tiny aisle, casting one last look toward the front of the empty shop. No Frank. No Clueless.

Mari remembered a little too late that this aisle was very short, and rather narrow. It had been perfectly comfortable when she had hidden herself there a few weeks ago with a good book. No one came to that aisle, and she wasn't in anyone's way.

Now, with two people, it was a much smaller space. Particularly with the need to stay absolutely unseen. Mari inched toward Trey until she was fairly confident that none of her could be seen from the front of the store.

She could have squeezed in closer to him, but as long as Clueless hadn't seen them come in, it wasn't really necessary. Besides, the smirk Trey was giving her at the moment made her second-guess her choice of backup options.

"Have you scouted out all the best hiding places in this part of town? I mean, this is an amazing spot you've found here." He made a show of inspecting the tiny space. "Definitely prime real estate." He finished with a wink.

As she opened her mouth to deliver a witty reply, the shop bell rang. Knowing their little nook was not easily visible from the front, Mari hazarded a quick peek around the side of the last bookshelf.

Her favorite goon, still carrying his bag from the burger joint, stood gazing around the small shop.

Mari pressed herself against Trey's body, the desire to stay hidden winning out over any inclination to keep a respectable distance. Trey's breath tickled her cheek, and she really wasn't sure where to put her hands. She finally let them rest against his upper arms. Two new desires were now warring within her. The first was to keep her hands there as a defense against any attempt he might make to pull her closer. The second was to snake them around his back and see how little space they could take up behind the bookcase.

Trey gazed down at her, an irresistible grin on his lips. "Isn't this the part where the sinister temptress says to the brave, young hero, 'You've fallen for my evil plan'?" he whispered.

Mari shook her head and glared at him.

How could he make jokes at a time like this?

With so little distance between them, Mari realized that he didn't only have the dimple in his left cheek, there was a much smaller matching one in his right cheek, too. Heat crept up her neck as she realized she was staring at his face, mostly his lips.

His expression slowly turned from playful to earnest as his glance darted to her lips as well. Ever so slowly, he leaned down towards her. Mari's eyes went wide, and she glared her astonishment at him. Unfortunately, he seemed undeterred by her silent reprimand.

Footsteps echoed through the bookshop.

Footsteps that were growing closer.

After realizing that the front of the shop held no hiding spots, Clueless must have been making his way around the display tables toward the bookshelves in the back.

Three steps.

Pause.

Three more steps.

Pause.

Mari imagined him moving methodically forward along the aisle, stopping to check every bookcase. She turned a panicked expression to Trey. His smile was gone, replaced by his own look of concern. Very quietly, he squeezed sideways past Mari and placed his body between her and their stalker, facing the aisle. She wrapped her arms around his middle and pulled herself close against his back.

Three steps.

Pause.

Three more steps.

Pause.

Her heart pounded out an SOS signal that should have been detectable by nearby seismographs. She wasn't sure how the goon creeping down the center aisle hadn't discovered them already. Trey's arms tensed over hers.

Three steps.

Pause.

Three more steps.

Pause.

The sound of the brute's footfalls had come so close now that Mari could hear the slight squeak of his rubber sole against the hardwood. She squeezed her eyes shut and held her breath.

"Hey! No food allowed in here. Didn't you see the signs?" That was Frank's voice. Wonderful, robust Frank.

Clueless took one more step toward their hiding place.

Louder, heavier footfalls moved toward them.

"Listen, buddy. If you don't take your food out of here, then I'll be forced to do it for you."

A grunt of acknowledgment came from just around the bookshelf. Begrudging footsteps receded slowly down the aisle and, with a jingle of the bell, the front door slammed closed.

Mari let out a long breath and released her grip on Trey's middle. "I think it's safe."

Trey shook his head. "We can't be sure yet."

Mari waited a few more seconds, pressed up against Trey's back, before speaking again, "Really, Trey, I think it's fine."

He turned around to face her, a broad smile on his face. "Hey, who's the secret agent here, me or you?"

Some of the tension in Mari's shoulders relaxed. He was clearly teasing her. She poked his muscled chest. "Okay, Mister Super-Spy, what's the best course of action when you have a claustrophobic ninja trapped in a corner?" She pushed a little harder against him with her palms, not disliking the feeling.

With one last smirk, he backed out into the aisle, freeing her from their hiding place. Mari looked up and saw Frank lumbering toward them.

"Can I help you two find any—" Frank's smile broadened as a look of recognition spread across his weathered face. "Steampunk-romance girl. You back for more clockwork and corsets?"

Mari glanced at Trey, who had moved a hand to his mouth, likely trying to smother a grin. His brows went up in a questioning expression.

She put her hands on her hips, glaring at him. "It's a guilty pleasure of mine. Don't tell me you don't have any of those."

Trey held up his hands, a broad grin on his face. "Hey, I'm not judging. I buy stupid old cars in a vain attempt to impress women."

With a huff, Mari turned her attention back to the shop owner. "Thanks, Frank, but not today. Do you have another exit besides the front door? We're hoping to avoid that burger-and-fries guy you so kindly got rid of for us."

Frank's brow ticked up. He considered her for a moment then nodded. "Follow me. You can go out through the stockroom."

After a few turns through narrow alleys and side roads, Trey and Mari were safely on their way back to Club Banana.

"That was a close one," Mari finally said. "I can't believe we made it out of there without getting caught."

Trey chuckled. "I can't believe that guy still had the food bag in his hands. What a rookie mistake."

"Can you blame him, though? Those guys do make good burgers."

Trey picked up the thread of the joke. "And fries."

CHAPTER ELEVEN

FIRST THING MONDAY MORNING, Carol called Mari into her office.

"You disappeared Friday afternoon."

"I . . . uh . . . didn't feel well," Mari replied.

"I can appreciate that. Just give me a little warning next time." Carol considered her for a moment and gave a single nod, as if that closed the matter. "We actually have a bigger issue, though. I didn't think Mr. Brooks would take my joke so seriously, but it seems that he's requested that you do double duty for his department."

"Oh?" Mari tried to act like the idea surprised her.

In reality, this was the plan she and Trey had devised over the weekend. They knew they needed to come up with a way to free up Mari for more focused searching. Having Trey along to stand as lookout would make it easier for Mari to check every single room.

After their adventure walk in Mari's neighborhood on Saturday, they'd stayed a little closer to Club Banana. To aid their brainstorming efforts, they'd eaten ice cream on the rooftop terrace, soaked in the hot tub together—twice—and spent an entire afternoon walking through nearby Piedmont Park. The idea of asking Carol to let Trey borrow her for other work had actually occurred to Mari during their first dip in the hot tub.

But that information was on a need-to-know basis.

And Trey hadn't needed to know yet.

Carol continued her explanation, bringing Mari back to the present. "Apparently the arrangement would be that anytime you can be spared from your work for me, he would put you to work on a project he needs help with."

Carol glanced up to see Mari's reaction. Mari wasn't sure how her boss was feeling about it, so she didn't know exactly how to act. She gave a half-hearted shrug.

Carol's mouth pinched as she leveled a stern gaze at Mari. "If you want, I can fight him on this."

"That's okay. I don't mind." Mari tried to sound accommodating. She hoped she didn't sound too eager.

Carol considered her for a moment, a wry smile on her face. "I figured that's how you would feel."

In an attempt to deflect, Mari said, "I'm sorry I won't be your assistant—full-time, anyway. You've been so kind and understanding. I've enjoyed working for you."

Carol waved off Mari's overly-sweet sentimentality and glanced out her office window. "I guess I should be grateful he didn't try and steal you completely."

"Does that happen often?"

Carol leaned back in her chair and sighed. "It's the story of my life here. My assistants never seem to last long. Either they're incompetent, and I'm forced to fire them. Or they're exceptional, and someone else notices and steals them away." Carol paused and raised a brow. "Of course, catching the eye of our young VP of product development meant you were pretty much a goner from the start."

Carol's astute observation caused Mari's cheeks to heat. She cast about for some way to steer the discussion into safer waters. "So, do I wait to be summoned upstairs, or do I check with you when I'm finished with my work? Or do we set up a joint-custody calendar?"

Carol laughed. "Just get to work. Mr. Brooks and I will sort out the details." She shooed Mari out of her office with a smile.

Hoping to make sure she was available when the opportunity arose, Mari set to work on her standard daily assignments. Knowing every second she could free up would be an extra second she could spend searching for her mother was all the motivation she needed.

Of course, getting a chance to spend more time with Trey didn't hurt either.

Apparently, sorting out the custody details didn't take long, because half an hour later Carol told her she could go help Trey for the rest of the morning.

Over the weekend, they had talked about needing to act normal and avoid talking about the mission, knowing that his office might be bugged. So, when Mari knocked on his door, she tried to make it sound official. "You wanted to see me?"

"Yes, please come in," Trey replied, equally business-like.

As she moved to sit in front of his desk, he very purposely winked at her.

She smiled back, trying not to give him the satisfaction of any further reaction.

She cleared her throat. "You did mention earlier that there were a few potential pitfalls on this project, things we might need to *avoid*." Mari put special emphasis on the last word and gave Trey a wide-eyed look of warning.

He smiled and gazed across the desk at her. "That's true. The public-facing aspect is very important." That probably meant that he knew things could be overheard. "But it's okay if there are behind-the-scenes issues at the lab that they don't ever know about."

Did that mean it didn't matter if he winked at her because no one could see it?

He arched a single brow, inviting her to contradict him. Mari glanced around the room and decided that, aside from the window to the hall, there was no way anyone could have seen his wink, or presumably any other silent action or body language. Mari shook her head in exasperation.

Somehow, their shared secret had made him even more flirtatious, if that was possible.

She laughed and relaxed back into the chair.

Did he plan to silently tease her as they worked together?

Two could play at that game.

It had always been a little too easy—and dangerous—to let her guard down around him. Now that she was finally allowed to, she gave herself permission to enjoy it.

Of course, this arrangement—their secret relationship superimposed on a business one—made it all the more difficult to pretend he was just a coworker.

Mari bit her bottom lip as she raised a brow suggestively at him. Trey's initial reaction was one of surprise, but he quickly recovered. After several moments of staring at each other, trading grins and smirks, Trey nodded toward his computer. "Take a look at the results here from Lab 2."

Mari moved to his computer. Instead of pointing at the window with the lab results, Trey indicated a small corner of the screen where he had typed the message:

— Where should we start our search?

Mari grinned and leaned over to type on his keyboard. Trey didn't move completely out of the way, so Mari's side pressed against his shoulder. He smelled good, but Mari tried not to notice. In the same text box, she replied:

— I'll be checking the second floor of the research wing next. Do I have to take you with me? ;)

He chuckled softly. "That's an interesting idea," he said, clearly continuing their fake conversation for any eavesdroppers. Mari absently moved her hand to his shoulder when he leaned in and typed:

— Yes, I have to come with you. That was the plan. Plus, Chaz will be less suspicious if I'm with you.

Mari leaned over Trey and typed again:

— Fine. Let's go. :P

She didn't immediately pull back, enjoying leaning against him for a few extra seconds. Being near him was calming—as if she could shut out the reality of her mother's imprisonment and her own looming, impossible deadline.

This was hopeless. How was she ever going to find her mother again? And in time to rescue her before Brax called? Or worse?

As Trey stood to leave, he glanced down at her. He must have seen something in her expression because he reached for her, pulling her protectively close to him. Mari melted into his arms, her head against his shoulder. She could feel his strong hands against her back. The light scent of his skin drifted around her.

Mari could have held the embrace forever.

She willed the clock on the wall to stop ticking. She needed more time to find her mother. She needed more time in Trey's arms.

At the sound of approaching footsteps, Trey slowly released her, letting his hands drop reluctantly to his sides. "Well, let's get started," he said. The phrase sounded innocent enough, but his expression overflowed with concern.

Mari took a fortifying breath, staring into his deep green eyes, and nodded.

She could do this.

She had to.

They walked into the hall, and Trey motioned toward the far end of the office wing. Mari had come to this floor several times before—it even reminded her a little of the halls and offices in her mother's research department—but she'd never been able to really search it because she couldn't risk being caught snooping around where she shouldn't be.

With Trey's help, they were able to do a full search. Trey walked slightly ahead of her. If an office door was open, he would wave or nod at the occupant. If it was empty, he would point to the room, and Mari would check it while Trey watched the hall. On closed doors, Mari would hold the bracelet against the surface to listen for breathing inside.

Three times, her watch indicated breathing in the room. Trey knocked on each door to make sure the person inside wasn't her mother. He was forced to be creative in his excuses.

Using this process, they swept the entire top floor of offices in less than an hour. Of course, they were assuming Mari's mother wasn't tied up in the closet of someone sitting peacefully at their desk. It seemed like a reasonable assumption.

Right after lunch, Mari spent an hour back at her desk, catching up on her responsibilities. Then she rejoined Trey as they searched the second floor of labs. Their reconnaissance of that particular floor required a slight change to their routine. The labs almost all had people working inside, so a breathing scan from her bracelet wouldn't have done any good. However, they all had large safety glass windows. So, Mari and Trey positioned themselves on each side of the windows, barely out of sight of the workers, so they could visually check that nothing suspicious was going on.

Mari hoped that if any of the workers did notice their strange, voyeuristic behavior, that they wouldn't mention it to anyone.

Her bracelet indicated breathing inside a handful of smaller workrooms. Rather than intrude on each one—and call unwanted attention to themselves—they alternated between Trey standing guard as Mari snaked the small camera under the door and Trey walking in and pretending to be looking for someone who might normally be in a workroom like that. Using the camera snake made Mari nervous. Watching Trey bumble out of a room with a confused look on his face made Mari giggle.

As the afternoon went on and their search progressed downward through the floors of the research wing, Mari's hope of finding her mother before the deadline was on a similar downward trend. By the time they finished checking the labs and workrooms on the main floor, Mari's optimism was particularly low.

Walking along the corridor from the labs back to her cubicle, she let out a soft sigh.

Trey nudged her gently in the shoulder. "Three down, one to go," he said.

Mari frowned. They had done all three floors of the research wing. "One more?"

Trey discretely pointed downward.

Mari inhaled sharply. "That's right. I forgot about the basement," she said.

Trey smiled, his eyes bright. He leaned closer and whispered. "It's mostly storage rooms with boxes of old experiments. But it's definitely worth a shot."

The crushing weight on her soul felt just a tiny bit lighter. Trey had been a lifesaver on this mission. She was lucky he'd been assigned to infiltrate Keating BioMedical right before her mother was abducted.

Not for the first time, Mari wondered what Trey's assignment had really been.

"Trey? Are you sure this isn't keeping you from your other *projects*?" She hoped that her emphasis on the last word would help him to know she wasn't talking about his regular job.

Trey's lips tilted in a crooked grin. "Don't worry about that. I still have ways to get those things done, too."

Mari bit her lip. "Really, Trey. I don't want you to get in trouble."

Glancing over at her, he slowed his pace. "First off, you're absolutely adorable when you do that." He raised a brow and looked down at her lips. As his gaze moved back up to her eyes, his playful smirk faded.

"And second, this"—he gestured between them—"is more important than those other projects."

Was he talking about them working together to find her mother?

Or just them . . . together?

Mari gave a small, nervous nod.

Mari's heart warmed at the thought of Trey risking the disapproval of his spy boss because he thought saving her mother was more important. Either that, or he thought their relationship was more important, which was almost as good.

CHAPTER TWELVE

THE NEXT MORNING, MARI channeled Susan's nervous leg-bouncing as she waited at her desk for Trey to message her that he was ready. She wondered if perhaps he knew that she was anxious to search the basement and he was intentionally making her wait. She glanced at her jittery leg and pressed down on it with her hands.

The next second, Trey was standing at her cubicle. "Hi, Mari—"

Mari's eyes shot wide.

"—na. Mari-na. Hi, Marina."

Mari cocked her head sideways and glared at him. She had worked so hard not to blow her cover; it would be just her luck if Trey did it for her. She glanced both ways, but didn't see anyone. Carol was the only one who could have been within earshot, and hopefully she didn't notice.

With a quick wink, he sauntered over to her boss' door. "Good morning, Carol. How are you this beautiful morning?"

"I'm fine, you sweet-talker. If you're here for Marina, you don't have to ask my permission. She knows when she's free. You keep this up, and I'll start charging a transaction fee for your jabbering."

Trey laughed, executed a deep bow, and backed away from the door. As they walked away from her cubicle, Mari could have sworn she heard giggling coming from Carol's office.

Trey and Mari walked toward the in-house bistro at the far end of the research wing. As they approached the end of the corridor, Trey led them down a side hall to a small staircase she'd never noticed before.

They carefully descended the flight of stairs to the basement. The door creaked open onto a deserted hallway. Mari checked both ways. No fancy carpet or spacious offices here. Just a long stretch of closed doors—storage rooms, if Trey knew what he was talking about.

This would be the ideal place to keep a hostage.

With Trey acting as lookout near the stairs, Mari moved quickly from door to door, pressing her high-tech bracelet against each one and waiting for the readout on her watch to declare it empty.

Mari wasn't sure if she expected to easily find her mother—her hopes had soared after Trey had reminded her about the basement—but after the first five doors, her confidence ebbed. And by the time she had checked to the end of the hall on one side and was halfway back on the other, she was an emotional wreck.

They had checked everywhere.

Would they ever find her mother?

What if Brax had made good on his threat?

At the doorway to the stairwell—without really thinking about it—she fell into Trey's arms. He pulled her close and just held her while she sobbed into his chest.

Trey softly stroked her hair. "Shhh, it's okay. Hang in there."

Once she had steadied her breathing, Mari pulled back and wiped a hand across her cheek. "Sorry. I'm not usually like this."

Trey gazed down at her with such kindness and concern, it was nearly her undoing again. He shook his head. "I don't mind. Hopefully, better than crying into a pillow."

She looked up at him with a watery smile. "Not quite as comfortable, but way more enjoyable."

He gave her one more quick squeeze before saying, "We should probably head back."

As the sounds of their coworkers at the bistro filtered down the stairwell from the hallway above, Mari realized he was probably right. But she hated to lose this closeness.

"What am I going to do, Trey?"

"Not give up," he replied immediately. "And lean on me whenever you need to."

She leaned into him. "I think I need to right now."

His arms closed tightly around her. They stood there for what must have been five minutes but felt like only two seconds. He didn't insist that she stop crying, and he didn't seem uncomfortable with her being overly emotional.

Though she did feel a little better, she still missed his embrace when he released her.

Halfway up the stairs back to the main hall, he stopped and turned to her. "Assuming she's still here at Keating Mansion—"

Mari felt her heart drop. "Don't even say that," she said.

He gave her an apologetic grimace. "Sorry. I'm sure she's still here. This is where the research is happening. This is where the nano-bots are being produced."

Even though her stomach hadn't quite recovered, Mari nodded her acknowledgment. "You were saying?"

"The only other place she could be is back in the original mansion." When Mari didn't say anything, he continued. "In fact, it sort of makes sense. Even though all the production is happening here in the research wing, there are so many scientists and technicians coming and going, it would be almost impossible to keep a hostage a secret. They would have more control over who wanders around the old mansion."

"They?" Mari asked. "Do you think . . . could Chaz be involved?"

Trey shrugged as he blew out a long breath. "Maybe. It's hard to say for sure at this point."

Mari gazed up the stairs, off in the general direction of the old mansion. She turned to Trey and squared her shoulders. "Okay. What's the plan?"

"We need to think of an excuse to be wandering around in the old mansion."

"Does it need to be an excuse for both of us? Because there's a certain millionaire who happens to live in the mansion in question, and he's invited me to come visit him in the residential wing anytime I want. So . . ." She intentionally left the end of her statement hanging.

Trey's brow furrowed. "Hold on. Weren't you the one who was concerned that Chaz might be involved?"

"Well, of course. I wouldn't want to drop in on him for a friendly visit unless I was sure about his character." Her lips cracked into the smallest of smiles.

"Mari, I really don't think you should be . . ." He considered her more deliberately. "You're teasing me, aren't you? Trying to make me jealous?"

"Maybe." Mari shrugged, but her smile grew. "Is it working?"

"That depends."

"Depends on what?"

"Whether you'll go out to dinner with me again."

Mari smiled. "So . . . you're holding your jealousy hostage until I agree to go on a date with you?"

A dimpled grin spread across his face. "Something like that."

They continued up the stairs and down the main hall of the research wing.

Trey stopped at the door to the stairwell. He nodded toward Mari's desk. "I guess I can share nicely with Carol. I'll meet you for lunch."

After a few hours of mundane tasks at her desk and the fastest lunch they'd had together so far, they walked past Mari's cubicle, through the parlor into the old mansion.

"So, do we have an excuse for being in the mansion?" Mari asked quietly. "Or do we even care about that at this point?"

"One of the hardest things about being a you-know-what is not getting sloppy in the middle of a project."

That was plenty of advice without actually answering her question. Mari raised an eyebrow in his direction.

"In this case, we don't have a good excuse, but Chaz's assistant told me he's out of the office for the rest of the day."

Dodging the butler, they worked their way through the various sitting rooms and gathering areas, including the grand ballroom, though Mari had no idea what Chaz would use that particular room for. They didn't dare go into the kitchen, even though it was obvious that there were people inside. Trey figured it was safe to assume her mother wasn't being asked to prepare a chicken marsala for dinner.

After a quick check for additional work at Mari's desk, they mounted the back staircase of the old mansion.

Together, they worked their way around the second floor, including the residential wing, checking every open room and every locked door. Mari had already gotten her hopes up once that day, so she was grimly pessimistic about their chances.

Unfortunately, even after an hour of exploration, they had nothing to show for their search of the second floor. They moved to the third floor and searched the west wing. Not a single occupied room to be found.

As they stood on the landing of the grand staircase in the center of the third floor, Mari stared down the dark hallway to Brax's wing. She shook her head and glanced at Trey. "Where else could she be?" she whispered.

Trey nodded slowly. "Yep." He turned toward Mari, apparently appraising her. "You ready to do this?"

With one last fortifying breath, Mari nodded and took a tentative step into the hallway, then two. A dozen steps into the dark, she pressed her bracelet against the first door. Nothing.

She glanced over her shoulder at Trey standing guard on the landing. He nodded his encouragement. Mari crossed the hall and checked the facing door. Again nothing.

Hesitantly, she crept farther into the darkness.

She had nearly reached the door to the next room when a faint metallic sound creaked from somewhere down the hall.

Mari froze.

Her hammering heart threatened to beat its way out of her chest.

Glancing over her shoulder, her eyes locked with Trey's. The surprise and fear in his wide eyes matched her own.

BANG.

The slam of a door reverberated along the silent corridor.

Mari whirled around and hurtled down the hall. Trey waited with an outstretched hand at the landing. She took it, and they flung themselves down the curving staircase three steps at a time.

Halfway down, Mari stumbled awkwardly. Trey tightened his grip on her wrist and saved her from face-planting on the last step. The effort cost him his own balance, however, and he tumbled over Mari, bringing them both down into a sprawling mass of arms and legs on the second-floor landing.

Despite the flailing limbs, Trey's face came to rest inches away from Mari's. She stared into his deep green eyes for a few seconds before the sound of footsteps on the floor above jolted them into action. Mari extricated herself and pulled Trey to stand next to her. With several furtive glances at the stairs behind them, Mari and Trey casually moved to the rear staircase and descended to the parlor and Mari's cubicle.

As she sat down, Mari let out a small sigh of relief.

"Close one." Trey whispered with a wry grin. "We might be forced to wait until you-know-who is away for the day." He tipped his head toward Brax's wing.

Mari nodded through her disappointment.

Tomorrow was the deadline. Even if they did find her mother, what could they do to rescue her? She'd have to beg Brax for more time. Would he agree?

For the remainder of the afternoon, she worked through a few tedious assignments until it was time to leave. She said goodnight to Carol and trudged out to the parking lot. She got into her car and drove around the mansion and along the curving road toward the gates.

Without really paying much attention, she strayed slightly into the middle of the narrow, winding lane. A blaring honk startled her back to focus. She swerved slightly to give the oncoming vehicle—a deep orange car—enough space to get by. As the two cars slowly passed each other, Mari looked over at the other driver, hoping to convey her apology for the poor driving.

The driver's diamond nose ring glinted in the late-afternoon sun. It was the thug from the alley, Nose-Stud.

He froze in the middle of making a rude gesture, his jaw going slack.

Mari immediately riveted her attention back to the road in front of her. She was forced to slow at the security gate, where a familiar security guard smiled and waved her through.

Maybe Nose-Stud hadn't recognized her.

Maybe he had been fooled by her disguise.

Maybe he had been mesmerized by her beauty.

The screeching of tires behind her said otherwise.

Glancing in the rearview mirror, she saw Nose-Stud pull his car in a wild U-turn on the too-narrow drive, skidding through several car lengths of well-manicured lawn.

Mari mashed the accelerator as she pulled a hard left onto the suburban street that wound past Keating Mansion, instinctively heading in the opposite direction than her normal drive home.

How fast did she dare go on such a small road?

How fast *could* she go in the small car?

She hit 55 mph after a few seconds. Though it didn't look like much more than a sensible compact car, Teen Banana was no slouch under the hood. She slowed as she caught up to a minivan going much closer to the speed limit. She hesitated for a split second, debating whether to pass the car in a no-passing zone.

The fact that she was even considering it felt like a sign that she might eventually get the hang of this spy stuff.

She checked her mirror again. Nose-Stud was gaining on her.

She gunned the engine and pulled out into the other lane, quickly passing the minivan before successfully veering back onto her side of the road. It hadn't been a picture-perfect pass, but the honking and swerving by the oncoming food truck had seemed unnecessary.

Accelerating again, Mari put some distance between her and Nose-Stud. She glanced around, trying to get her bearings. It might have been smart to throw the guy off by not taking her normal route away from the mansion, but she wasn't as familiar with the roads in this direction. That put her at a disadvantage.

How was she going to lose him without getting lost herself?

She considered turning onto one of the many residential streets blurring past. But if she ended up trapped on a dead-end road, then what?

In the rearview mirror, she saw Nose-Stud swerve around the minivan. She needed to come up with a plan, and fast. If only the Banana Girls had left her something useful somewhere in the car.

While doing her best to watch the road, Mari opened the center console and dug around blindly with her hand. Unless a pack of licorice bites was going to save the day, she was out of luck. She popped open the glove box next. Nothing but maintenance receipts and emergency flares.

She glanced up at the road just in time to see a pair of tail lights coming up fast. She slammed on the brakes and steered out of a wicked fishtail by diverting to the narrow shoulder. Mari hadn't intended to do anything crazy, but now that she was already fully committed, she floored it and swung past the SUV back into the regular lane.

The sparse suburban landscape progressively morphed into industrial buildings with wide loading ramps and large parking lots. Suddenly there was too much traffic to safely pass the slowing cars—not that she had done either of her previous passes safely.

She eased off the gas and checked the rearview mirror for her pursuer. Remembering her plan, she stole a quick glance at the back seat.

Perfect.

One of the girls had left a black knit beanie and sunglasses back there. She'd need to remember to congratulate them on their excellent placement of emergency disguise kits. She hastily pulled the items into her lap as she scrutinized the nearby manufacturing businesses for a way to execute her plan.

On her right, cars poured out of the parking lot of a bottling plant. It was quitting time, after all. She slammed on the brakes and turned hard. Getting into the parking lot was no problem, but hopefully that would work in her favor.

Mari was pretty sure that Nose-Stud would have seen her turn in. She'd only have a few seconds to get this right. As she passed dozens of cars lined up to leave the lot, she watched for a small gap toward the end of the line. Politely putting on her blinker, she pulled into an empty parking space. She jabbed a finger at the color control console and swiped through half a dozen options until she found a sky blue that would work—she didn't have time to find Anna's nondescript silver-gray. As the exterior paint job slowly morphed from forest-green to light blue, Mari pulled the beanie over her head and hastily stuffed her hair into it. She donned the large sunglasses and did a quick check in the mirror.

This might work.

She took a deep breath and put the engine in reverse. When a kind would-be coworker left a gap for her, she pulled into the line of cars. She straightened her sunglasses and leaned forward for a peek at the hood—just to make sure it had indeed changed colors.

Way at the front of the line, an orange muscle car inched slowly toward her. Mari forced herself to breathe normally. She tugged slightly at the corner of the beanie. Nose-Stud continued creeping forward, looking at the cars in the line and others parked nearby.

Would he be looking for a young Latina driver in a Ford Focus?

Or would he be looking for a driver with long brown hair in a green compact car?

He was just a few cars ahead of her now. Mari watched his eyes dart left and right as he edged forward. The other drivers in line didn't seem overly concerned, so she tried to match their indifference.

As he glanced her way, she remained perfectly motionless except for her pounding heart. He looked the other way at a row of cars parked nearby. Mari let out a slow, shaky breath. Her itchy pedal foot wanted to lift off the brake, slam on the gas, and literally burn rubber out of the parking lot. She forced her foot to stay where it was.

With a quick check in her side mirror, she caught a glimpse of orange as Nose-Stud did a U-turn at the end of the parking lot. As her predator moved up the line of cars—in the wrong lane this time—a chorus of honks from law-abiding citizens followed him. She watched in the mirror as the growing medley of disapproving honks made the poor guy more and more agitated. Nose-Stud didn't even spare her a glance as he sped past.

Mari laughed and laid into her horn with the others. "You jerk!" She shook her fist at the retreating vehicle—with probably more justified gusto than any of the others. "That's right! Get out of here, moron!"

CHAPTER THIRTEEN

MARI COULDN'T BRING HERSELF to mention the Nose-Stud car chase to the team. She figured she was already on thin ice because of the failed rescue attempt. She didn't want to risk them cancelling the mission.

Not that it mattered. She had twenty-four hours to find her mother before her already renegotiated deadline. She didn't know if Brax would give her more time. She didn't even want to consider what he would do if he lost patience with her.

She was sure they didn't call it a deadline for nothing.

By the time she made it to work the next morning, her lack of sleep had combined with the unrelenting anxiety over her mother to make Mari a nervous wreck.

"Dear, could you—"

Mari jumped nearly a foot in the air when Carol snuck up and touched her shoulder.

"Sorry." Mari said quickly.

Carol gave her a look that was part scolding and part sympathy. "Is that man just running you ragged?"

For a second, Mari had to remind herself that Carol wasn't talking about the unnerving car chase with Brax's henchman, so she must be talking about Mari's work with Trey. She forced a smile. "No. He's not overworking me. I just . . . didn't sleep well last night."

One of Carol's eyebrows went up, as if she knew Mari wasn't telling the truth, but she wasn't sure if it mattered. "Well, I was about to say that there were so few requisitions yesterday that you could probably get an early start helping Mr. Brooks today. But I think maybe—"

Mari shot up out of her seat a little too quickly. "It's okay. I don't mind. Thanks." And before Carol had a chance to object, Mari was halfway to the stairwell. Let Carol think what she would, Mari couldn't pass up the opportunity to continue the search for her mother.

Spending more time with Trey wasn't all bad, either.

She knew she couldn't unburden herself of everything, not in his office anyway. But just being near him would improve her mood.

Without even bothering to knock, she walked confidently into Trey's office and settled herself in the chair next to him. Trey turned to her with a warm smile and a happy expression. She knew that look. He wanted to tell her something.

"We might be going about this project the wrong way," he said.

Mari shot a warning glance at him but then realized anyone listening would think he was simply referring to the pretend project they'd been working on.

With a tilt of his head, he motioned Mari closer. "Check this out."

On their customary document in the corner of his screen, he'd written:
— *We need to talk.*

Mari looked at him with questioning eyes and a lift of her shoulders.

"Do you mind if I turn on something upbeat to keep us motivated?" he asked.

This was new. He was going to play music for them. "Sure," she replied.

Trey activated the music player on his computer and clicked a playlist. The sounds of smooth jazz softly emanated from the small speakers. He nodded his satisfaction and slid his chair closer to Mari—much closer.

Taking her face in his hands, he brought his mouth up to her cheek. Mari's stomach fluttered wildly, threatening to fly away.

"This way we can talk a little more freely," he whispered in her ear. The stubble on his chin brushed past her skin.

Mari glanced through the open window into the hall. Satisfied they wouldn't be seen by any casual passersby, she touched his cheek and leaned in to whisper, "The first thing we need to talk about is your description of smooth jazz as motivational and upbeat." She grinned at him.

They switched positions of lips and ears again. "Are you mocking the smooth jazz?" he asked.

"Only when you describe it as upbeat," she replied in a soft whisper. "In my house, this was sleeping music."

He suddenly pulled back, and Mari nearly laughed out loud at the look of feigned shock and disbelief on his face. His expression quickly turned playful. He crooked a finger at her, and she leaned in for another exchange. "If you're finished insulting my music, shall we get down to business?" he asked.

She nodded but didn't move her cheek away from his lips.

"After we searched the basement of the research wing yesterday, it made me wonder whether the old mansion has a basement." His rumbling, soft voice tickled her ear.

Mari shrugged but stayed close to him. The smell drifting off his skin was intoxicating, but she couldn't will herself to be strong enough to pull away from him just yet.

"I could check the plans on file with the county." He slid back toward his computer.

Mari had to shake her head to clear the spell he had over her. And just in time, too. She dove for his arm right as he began to type. That got his attention. She shook her head and leaned close to him. "What if they're monitoring your Internet connection and search history?" She pulled out her mission phone and began typing a text message.

— Bianca, I think I left my watch at Diana's house in the downstairs, downstairs. You know, by the grandfather clock. Can you check for me?

She pressed send then showed the message to Trey.

His brows furrowed. "What?"

She whispered, "I'm asking the Banana Girls if they can check whether Keating Mansion has a basement." At Trey's puzzled expression, Mari added. "It's in code."

"Obviously. But how could that possibly mean you're asking them to find out if there's a basement?"

Mari held out the phone for him to see as she whispered, "'Bianca' is the Banana Girls. And 'Diana' is the name for anything having to do with Chaz."

Trey shook his head in confusion.

That would be a tough one for him to figure out. It was in code for a reason, after all.

"It's an association code. Who's the most famous Charles you can think of?"

Trey's brow furrowed in concentration. "Charlie Brown?"

"Prince Charles," Mari answered for him. "Who was married to Princess Diana. So Diana means Chaz," she explained in a low whisper.

Trey rolled his eyes. Clearly, he understood, so she continued. "Watch is the item we decided would mean to look or check something. Then I said 'the downstairs, downstairs.' That obviously means basement." Trey tilted his head as if he wasn't quite sure he agreed. "And I added the 'grandfather clock' part, just in case they were wondering whether I meant the old or the new building."

When she leaned back, Trey considered her with something akin to awe on his face. Or maybe it was disbelief. Mari hadn't completely mastered his facial expressions yet.

"Are you still going to let me take you to dinner tonight?" he asked in full voice.

After whispering for so long, speaking at regular volume caught her off guard. Mari supposed it wouldn't hurt if someone overheard them talking about dinner plans. Forcing her shoulders to relax, she shifted in her seat—grateful to give her insides a break from being so close to him—and nodded.

"Where should we go?" he asked.

Mari smiled. "Anywhere but Mexican food is fine."

"Why not Mexican?"

"Because just about every guy who's asked me out thinks because I'm Latina, I want Mexican food."

Trey furrowed his brow. "Hmm."

He clearly didn't understand, so Mari tried again. "It would be like if people thought you were Italian and only ever took you out for pizza."

"I love pizza," he said.

Mari glared at him. Was he trying to misunderstand?

"Fine. But imagine that your mom makes the best pizza ever, but you don't get to eat that pizza, you have to eat some sad, droopy, cardboard pizza."

Trey winked. "Got it. No Mexican food then." He'd probably understood her the whole time.

"So, which of your fancy cars are you picking me up in?"

His smirk answered before he spoke. "You'll see."

Mari opened her mouth to reply when her phone buzzed. She held it up for them to read.

— Diana has a modern clock in the downstairs. Her grandfather clock is on the main floor. You must have been mixed up about that. But I just checked and found it on the shelf next to The Wizard of Oz, *on the side by* Meet Me in St. Louis. *You left it the night we watched* The Secret Garden, *if that helps.*

Mari frowned as she puzzled through it. She nodded her head and smiled as she realized what some of the parts meant.

"Have you decoded it yet?" Trey asked in her ear.

His return to sudden closeness made her stomach flip. She fought the urge to lean against his shoulder.

"Partly."

"Care to share?"

Mari glanced at him. They were so close that she could see the individual lines near his eyes when he smiled. She really should lean back to put some distance between them so she could think clearly.

But she didn't want to.

"I think the first part means that the research wing has a basement, but the old mansion doesn't. But then there must be more because . . . " Mari puzzled over it for a moment before Trey nudged her to continue. "They must have looked it up and found out . . . something. And then the clues are three different movies."

"Obviously. But how is that helpful?" Trey asked.

"Well, we have to figure out what each movie means," she whispered

Trey scratched his chin theatrically. "So, *Wizard of Oz* . . . Chaz gets smashed by the mansion falling on him, and your mother takes his ruby slippers to get home."

Mari clapped a hand to her mouth to keep from laughing out loud. Just the image of Chaz wearing ruby slippers was too much. Trey's shoulders shook with repressed laughter, too.

When they'd regained some composure, Mari leaned in again. "As nice as that might be, I don't think that's it." She thought for a moment. "What does *The Wizard of Oz* have to do with a basement?"

"They went into a cellar during the tornado," Trey offered.

"Oh, I bet that's it. When they mention finding it by *The Wizard of Oz*, that could mean there's a cellar instead of a basement." She looked at Trey for confirmation.

He shrugged. "Don't look at me. It's your secret code."

"On the side by *Meet Me in St. Louis* . . . it seems like St. Louis has something to do with it," Mari said quietly.

Trey leaned close to Mari's ear. "Maybe we need to go to St. Louis. Or maybe there's a St. Louis street nearby somewhere."

She cocked her head at him. "You're not very good at this," she said with a teasing grin. "Do you have a backup plan for your career if this doesn't work out?"

He scowled and whispered again, "You've got something better?"

"Why would she say 'on the side'? That doesn't make sense." Mari paused, and then it hit her. "What if she meant the side of the house? If we're right about the cellar part, then we'd need to know which side it's on."

"Is there a St. Louis side?" Trey asked.

"Hmm. St. Louis is northwest of here. I wonder if it's on the northwest side of the mansion."

Trey glanced around for a second, like he was getting his bearings then shook his head. "I don't think so. That's the side with the driveway leading to the employee parking lot."

"Let's go find out." Mari stood and walked toward the hall. She stopped at the door when he didn't follow her. She gave him a playful glare.

He responded with a series of hand gestures that left Mari very doubtful about his future as a covert agent. She scowled at him in confusion.

Trey simplified the gestures.

He pointed to her with one hand—'you.'

He pointed to himself with the other hand—'me.'

He jerked his head in the direction of the employee parking lot—that must mean 'out back.'

He touched his fingers together—'kiss?'

Mari blinked as heat rushed to her cheeks. Then she realized he must have meant 'meet.'

Clearly frustrated with her lack of comprehension, Trey stood and closed the gap between them. His fingers brushed against her neck as his hand threaded through her hair. He tilted his face down toward her, his intense green eyes gazing into hers. Mari held her breath. Just as she closed her eyes and tilted her face up, she felt the scruff of his cheek against her ear.

"We shouldn't be seen walking out onto the grounds together. You wait here for a few minutes, then meet me out on the northwest side of the mansion."

His whisper sent chills down her back. He walked out the door and disappeared down the hall, but the shiver lingered. Mari wasn't sure how many minutes passed before she was capable of rational thought again. She took a deep breath and proceeded out into the hall after him. She took the longer way to the exit at the end of the research wing, just in case Trey had gone out the closer exit.

Out in the parking lot, Mari made her way along the drive leading to the front. Halfway around the side, she caught a glimpse of Trey standing next to the weathered northwest wall of the mansion. Mari stepped up next to him.

"I don't think there's any cellar on this side of the mansion. Could we have been wrong about the northwest direction? I mean, if they had wanted to use a movie to tell you it was on the northwest side, why not *North by Northwest*?"

Mari rolled her eyes. "It's a code, Trey. It's not supposed to just say it; that sort of defeats the purpose."

"If the purpose was for us to not know what they were talking about," he motioned to the empty ground around the wall of the mansion, "then they succeeded."

Pulling out her phone again, Mari reread the message. "You left it the night we watched *The Secret Garden*, if that helps."

"Tell them it doesn't help. That's not giving away the code, right?"

Mari laughed. "We have to think about the clue. Why would they mention *The Secret Garden*?"

"Should we check the ornamental gardens? They're behind the tennis courts."

"Why would they send us to this side of the mansion only to have us go somewhere else?"

They stared at each other for several moments. Mari was tempted to just keep staring at him, but she had a job to do. She looked down at the ground around them. Then, almost simultaneously, she and Trey looked across the small lane, farther northwest of the mansion, and saw a large shed—more like a small cottage—nestled among the trees that formed the edge of Keating Mansion property.

It was the gardener's shed. Mari had been there earlier on one of Ms. Fleishman's errands. How could she have forgotten?

Without a word, they snuck across the road and ducked behind the shed. Mari's heart pounded a furiously increasing rhythm as she fumbled with her bracelet against the cottage door. She scrutinized the readout on her watch as the seconds slowly ticked by.

ROOM EMPTY

She slumped forward and thumped her head repeatedly against the surface.

Trey placed a large hand between her head and the door, halting her momentum. "Don't do that. We're still going to need that resourceful mind of yours."

Mari sighed and stood. He was right; she had to stay smart. She glanced around the base of the shed. "What about the cellar?"

Trey walked around the corner of the small building, searching the ground. "Here it is," he called.

Mari raced to his side and saw the brown double doors angled against the foundation. She wasn't sure she could handle any more of this emotional rollercoaster. She just wanted her mother back safe and sound. Was that too much to ask?

She stood there for several seconds until Trey prodded her forward. She knelt next to the door and firmly pressed the bracelet against the surface.

Would her mother be in there? She held her breath as she waited for the verdict.

ROOM EMPTY

Mari was too emotionally exhausted to even stand back up. Her limbs felt numb. She would have slumped down into the grass against the side of the cellar doors, but Trey was there too quickly, catching her in his arms and lifting her to him.

She shook her head. "I can't do it. Please don't make me look anymore," she whispered. "It hurts too much." She felt tears welling up in her eyes, and she didn't even bother trying to stop them.

With his thumb, Trey brushed away a tear running down her cheek. Mari couldn't bring herself to look at his face. She was afraid to see disappointment. His arms squeezed even tighter around her shoulders.

"I would say I'm not normally like this," Mari murmured into his collar. "But I think I'm starting to make a habit of it."

She felt the deep chuckle rumble in his chest. "After we rescue your mother, if you're not too busy, I think I'd like to spend time with you during your regular life."

Mari wrapped her arms around his middle. For the briefest moment, the anguish melted away. All she could feel was his chest beneath her cheek. She knew the despair would come back, and with a vengeance, but she reveled in the blissful abandon of his embrace.

Finally, Mari pulled back and gazed up into his eyes. She could see in his face that he shared her disappointment. And the compassion in his expression made her knees weak. She held his gaze, staring into those warm, green eyes. Intentionally or not, her eyes flicked briefly to his lips. Her hands tightened on his back, and he pulled her closer. She could feel his breath tickling her skin. He tilted his head down, their faces mere inches apart. Mari instinctively pushed up onto her tiptoes.

From somewhere down the front lane leading to the mansion, a car's engine roared to life.

Mari started. Trey took a half step back, and his arms dropped to his sides, though one hand lingered on her arm.

Mari glanced over her shoulder toward the front gates. A flash of color coming down the lane toward the mansion caught her eye. An orange car sailed past the last cluster of trees and into the open.

Mari's stomach clenched.

"Hey, look at that. It's a '69 Dodge Charger! That's a classic. You know—" Trey stopped. He must have noticed the change in Mari.

The orange Charger continued around the bend toward the fountain and the steps of the front entry. Mari glanced at the handful of thin trees surrounding the gardener's cottage. She suddenly felt incredibly exposed.

Turning back to Trey, she pushed against his chest. "Go. Go!" she whispered.

Despite the confused look on his face, Trey obligingly scrambled back around to the hidden side of the cottage, Mari following closely on his heels.

Once out of sight, she turned and peeked around the corner. Nose-Stud had parked in the valet roundabout and stepped out of the car. Mari couldn't see the front of the mansion, but Nose-Stud stood on the bottom step looking up at the entrance.

"Who's that?" Trey asked.

"That's one of the thugs Brax sent to kidnap me the day after he abducted my mom."

Trey grunted an acknowledgment.

"Oh, and I passed him at the security gate when I left work yesterday," she added casually.

"Did he recognize you?" Trey asked.

Mari shrugged. "Maybe. He chased me around half the west suburbs."

Trey pulled her out of view back behind the building and gaped at her.

Mari's brows went up. "What?" she asked innocently.

"You were in a high-speed—" He narrowed his eyes in her direction. "I assume it was at high speed?"

Mari nodded.

"—a high-speed car chase with one of the bad guy's hired goons, and you didn't think to mention it."

"I didn't want to worry you," she answered.

"You didn't want to wor—" He hung there, mid-sentence, before finally rolling his eyes. He pushed her forward to peer around the corner of the building again. She crouched slightly so they could look at the same time, his head just above hers.

Brax came down the steps to join Nose-Stud. Barely slowing his pace, Brax jerked his head away from the front entrance, and Nose-Stud followed him. As they neared the end of the mansion, Mari could start to make out their conversation.

". . . supposed to be here yesterday afternoon," Brax said.

"Sorry, boss. I was driving in when I saw her driving out. I tried to follow her. Then when I lost her, I came back, and you were already gone."

"What are you talking about? Who did you see?" Brax asked.

"That scientist lady's little girl." Nose-Stud paused, and a smirk spread across his face. "Though I'd say she's hardly a little girl, really." His tone was thick with suggestion.

Mari felt Trey's body tighten against her back.

"I'm glad you got away," he whispered.

"Me, too," Mari said, without looking up at him.

Brax had stopped moving forward. "She was here? Dr. Sandoval's daughter? Are you sure?" he asked.

Nose-Stud shrugged. "Pretty sure. She looked a little different. Maybe her hair was colored. But she nearly plowed into my car, and she had those same wide eyes. I remember those eyes from before." The creep sounded almost nostalgic. Mari wanted to puke.

Brax considered him, clearly trying to figure out whether or not to believe the guy. He thumbed over his shoulder toward the back of the mansion, in the direction of the parking lot. "What about her car? Do you remember what her car looked like?"

With a sinking feeling, Mari realized that her car was parked in the back lot, sporting the same forest-green paint job it did every day she'd brought it to work. And why wouldn't it? She hadn't wanted to call attention to herself by showing up with a different colored car every day.

"Sure, boss," the thug said with a nod. "It was a green compact. Maybe a Civic or something like that."

Brax moved quickly along the lane toward the rear lot.

Mari made to run from behind the cottage.

Trey grabbed her arm. "Where are you going?"

"I need to change the color of my car before they find it."

"Change the color? What are you talking about? If Brax finds you by your car, you're not getting out of here."

Mari pulled herself free of his grasp. "If he finds the car at all, I'm not getting out of here. I need to change the color so he doesn't recognize it."

Trey frowned, clearly still confused.

"It's a Banana Girl thing. Trust me." She dashed from behind the shed and stepped quickly through the trees lining the mansion's back lawn and parking lot. The sparse forest that encircled the outside edges of the mansion's property came within ten feet of the lot, but she'd be forced to take a circuitous route, and she'd have to cross a wide patch of lawn without cover.

No footsteps followed her through the brush. Obviously, Trey had decided against joining her on such an insane attempt. She didn't know what he could have done to help her, anyway. All she knew was that keeping her identity safe from Brax hinged on preventing his right-hand man from recognizing her car.

Brax and his goon scanned the nearest cars in the lot, looking for a green compact. Mari had the advantage of knowing exactly where she had parked—where she always parked—two-thirds into the lot, half-way down the row. She crouched behind a scrawny shrub a few feet off the edge of the lawn, directly across from the row she parked in.

After Brax and his lackey checked the first row, they weaved through the cars to inspect the second row. Mari waited until they turned away from her and moved up the aisle. She bolted from her hiding place. Hunching low, she crossed the open grass in half a dozen steps and ducked behind the first car she reached.

She peeked through the car's windows, looking for Brax. He was still looking the other way. Staying as low as possible, she moved down the middle of the row between the car's front bumpers. At one point, two cars had parked with their bumpers nearly touching, forcing her to shimmy on her stomach along the ground below the bumpers.

By the time Mari reached her car, Brax and Nose-Stud had just turned onto her row. She only had seconds to get the color changed. Crouching down, she inched along the warm cement surface until she could grab the door handle. The handle quickly scanned her prints and unlocked. She didn't dare climb up into the driver's seat for fear of being seen, though the temptation to jump in, start the car, and make a break for it was incredibly strong. Wriggling forward until she was sprawled over the front seat, she reached up and touched the color control screen on the main console.

Mari hadn't even had time to think about what color she wanted to change it to; she simply swiped until she found a color that looked different. It was a goldish-silverish color.

Just as she was about to activate the new paint job, she heard Nose-Stud call out, "I think I see it over there."

Mari's hand hovered over the console screen. If she activated it now, not only would the goon have seen the car while it was green, but its changing colors would definitely raise suspicions. She might compromise more than her own mission. She might compromise the Banana Girls' entire operation.

But if she got caught there, hanging halfway out of a green compact car, how would she talk her way out of that? And how could she keep from implicating the entire team, including Trey?

She squeezed her eyes shut and mashed her hand on the screen.

"Hey, Brax! There you are." It was Trey's voice. Coming from the direction of the research wing.

As Mari slid out of the car, the electronic paint shimmered and morphed from deep green to dark sand flecked with silver. She heaved a sigh of relief and pushed the door until it was partially latched. It was the best she could do—swinging it violently closed would make too much noise.

Approaching footsteps told her Trey's distraction wouldn't keep her undetected for much longer. She hit the concrete and rolled under a small pickup truck parked in the next space. A second later, she saw a pair of dirty deck loafers and faded blue jeans walk between Teen Banana and the pickup. They stopped a few inches from her face. A few seconds later, they were joined by a pair of oxfords and dress slacks.

"This isn't green, you idiot," Brax said.

"But, boss, I could have sworn it was green before. We turned around for half a second, and now it's not green."

"Tucker, just when I ask myself why I even keep you around, you make an observation like that." Brax's grating voice made Mari cringe, but at least it was directed at someone else at the moment.

"Boss, I'm telling you, it was—"

"Just shut up, Tucker, before you blather yourself into trouble," Brax said.

Another set of feet approached. "Brax, I'm glad I found you." Trey sounded out of breath. Mari hoped Brax would think it was because he had jogged out into the parking lot to find him, not because Trey had sprinted from the gardener's cottage, around the front of the mansion, through the fancy hallways, and out the back door to save Mari's skin.

"What do you need, Trey?" Brax asked through a polite facade.

"I have some of those potential customer lists that I thought you'd want to see," Trey replied.

There was a long pause. Mari wished she could see Brax's face.

"You chased me out into the parking lot to tell me about the customer lists?" Brax asked.

"Uh, yeah," Trey said without missing a beat. "They're really good lists."

Mari pinched her lips together to trap the giggle inside. If anyone could pull off the casual, nice-guy routine, it was Trey.

Brax let out a deep sigh. "Tucker, wait for me in the front room. I'll be there in a few minutes."

Trey and Brax walked away. Mr. Nose-Stud, Tucker, left last. Mari could almost hear the gears grinding in his brain, trying to make sense of what his eyes were telling him. Mari waited several minutes before she dared come out from underneath the truck. She couldn't risk staying too long for fear that the truck's owner would get in and drive away.

Rolling out from beneath the undercarriage, Mari lifted herself to a crouch and glanced around. She didn't see anyone in the parking lot. Should she just stand up and walk back into the building? She remembered that Tucker was going to be waiting for Brax in the mansion. Would he stay there? She couldn't risk accidentally running into him. Best to wait until he left.

Mari moved quickly, zigzagging between the cars, and scampered across the lot toward the gardener's cottage. She couldn't really think of anywhere else to hide where she'd be safe and could still know when Tucker was gone. Carefully situating herself on the forest-facing side of the cottage, Mari crouched down and sat on a medium-sized decorative rock. She waited there for what seemed like hours, periodically standing to stretch her legs and check around the corner for Tucker leaving.

About the time her stomach started complaining that it was way past lunch, she heard the Charger's door slam and its engine roar to life. She peeked around the edge of the cottage and watched the orange car wind its way back to the front security gate. She leaned against the wall and heaved a sigh of relief.

She waited a few minutes before walking back through the parking lot to the entrance at the far end of the research wing. Residual scents from lunch hung in the air near the cafe. Mari grabbed a muffin from the display case on her way past. She glanced at her normal table, hoping Trey hadn't been lonely without her. Well, she definitely hoped he had been alone, just not necessarily lonely.

Settling back at her desk, she called through the door to Carol, "I'm back. Anything pressing for me?"

"Just a handful of invoices to reconcile," Carol replied.

As Mari worked on those tasks, her mind churned over her predicament. She was down to the last day of Brax's extended deadline. Worse, his hired enforcer had just told him he'd seen her on Keating Mansion property. And worse than worse, they had checked the entire research facility and most of the mansion, meaning that her mother must be trapped back in Brax's wing again.

Footsteps sounded from the mansion's rear staircase, and Mari took a fortifying breath. She glanced up, expecting to see Chaz coming down the steps on his cellphone. Instead, Brax stepped toward her. He smiled at her like a wolf might smile at a cornered rabbit.

"Excuse me. Marina, is it?" His leer grew. "I don't believe we've formally met." The gleeful expression on his face clearly conveyed that he didn't mean the words he said. "This very important-looking document seems to have been misplaced." He set a sheet of paper down on her counter, and she recognized it instantly.

It was the form that Carol had left on her desk the week before. The one that needed Chaz's signature. The one that had allowed Mari to sneak up to Brax's wing.

She'd had it in her hand when she found her mother. But she hadn't taken it to Chaz. And she hadn't brought it back to Carol.

She must have left it in her mother's room.

"I hope you don't mind that I went ahead and got my cousin's signature. It's the least I could do considering the mix up. And the fact that it's a *week late*." His icy gaze pierced her as he emphasized the last two words.

Mari held perfectly still. She didn't twitch or even breathe.

He knew.

She was cornered by her mother's captor, and he knew.

How was she ever going to get away?

Mari refused to give him the satisfaction of watching her squirm.

Play to the end of the point, her mother had always told her. She wasn't willing to give up yet.

Mari stood and picked up the signed form. "Thank you very much, Mr. . . .?"

Brax smirked. "Keating. Braxton Keating."

Mari allowed her eyebrow to tick up slightly. She turned and walked toward Carol's office.

Halfway there, Brax spoke again. "Mari?"

Without thinking, Mari paused, but she resisted the impulse to turn around at hearing her real name.

Brax continued. "After you've given that to Carol, would you come upstairs with me? Chaz would like to have a chat with you."

Mari knew instinctively that if she went up those stairs with Brax, she wouldn't be coming back down.

She stood in the doorway and considered her boss.

Carol looked up at her. "What did Brax want?"

Mari set her jaw. She grabbed the office door and slammed it shut, quickly turning the lock. In the instant before it closed, she saw the look of surprise on Brax's face. It was priceless, really.

Pulling out her phone, she tapped out a quick message to Trey.

— Brax knows. Locked myself in Carol's office. Don't let Brax call the security gate.

"Marina, what's going on?"

Loud pounding came through the locked door. "Carol, I need you to keep Marina in there," Brax yelled. "She's not who you think she is. She's a corporate spy."

Well, he was right about the spy part.

Carol's brows pulled together.

Mari moved closer to Carol's desk and leaned toward her boss. "I need your help," Mari whispered.

Carol considered her for a moment then nodded. "What can I do?"

"Whatever she's saying, Carol, don't believe her," Brax called through the door.

Mari glanced around the small office. She could get out the window, but then it would be obvious that Carol had helped her—or at least hadn't stopped her. That would put Carol in danger with Brax.

"Don't you have any rope or cable or something I can tie you up with?" Mari whispered.

With a tilt of her head, Carol said, "Now, why would I have rope in my office?"

"If they think you let me get away . . ."

Carol's brows went up as the reality dawned on her.

"You need to scream when I hit you," Mari said quietly as she walked toward her boss.

"If you hit me, I *will* scream," Carol said with a wry smile.

Mari swung her hands together in a loud clap. Carol's squeal was more of surprise than pain. Mari scowled at her with a reproving look.

"Sorry. Try it again," Carol whispered.

Mari clapped her hands hard enough to hurt. This time, Carol's scream sounded like real pain. Mari nodded in approval. Keeping eye contact, Mari swung her fists down onto the desk with a loud thump. Carol timed her grunt perfectly.

"Fight her, Carol," Brax yelled. "Keep fighting her. We'll get help." Instead of sounding overly concerned, his voice carried a note of disappointment, like he was sorry to miss the fight.

Mari raised her fists again, but Carol grabbed her hands. "I can beat myself up," she said. "You need to get out of here."

A smile spread across Mari's face as Carol kicked her desk and let out a short yelp. Mari wrapped her boss in a tight squeeze. "Thank you, Carol. For everything," she said softly.

"Take care of yourself, dear." Carol pushed Mari toward the window.

As she slid open the window, Mari glanced back over her shoulder and grinned. Carol slammed a chair against the wall with a loud thud and a wonderful wail of agony.

A voice outside called through the door, but it wasn't Brax this time. "Carol, we're going to get the extra keys to your office door. We should have them in just a minute or two. Hang on." That was Trey's voice. It was a warning to make her escape.

Carol waved her away with a smile and the heavy smack of a binder against her desk. Mari jumped onto the grass and slid the window closed. She ran toward her normal parking spot, pausing for only a split second when she found a silver-gold car there. She jumped into the powerful compact and burned rubber toward the front gate. She took a deep breath as she rounded the last stand of trees and pulled up to the security gate with the somewhat harried look of someone who had to leave work early because of an emergency. Hopefully Brax hadn't thought to alert security yet, or all her acting would be wasted.

The afternoon guard glanced her way, nodded, and opened the gate before waving her through. With a very audible sigh of relief, Mari sped away from Keating Mansion. She took a slightly complicated route back to Club Banana, just in case Brax sent someone to follow her. Once she reached Midtown, she doubled back twice to make sure she didn't have a tail.

When the elevator door opened on the top floor, Mari was shocked to see Trey leaning against the wall, hands stuffed in his pocket, and that adorable crooked grin on his face.

"What are you doing here?" Mari asked.

"Hannah gave me clearance to come to your headquarters, remember?"

Mari rolled her eyes. "I know that. I mean, what are you doing here right now?" She stepped off the elevator and stopped half a foot in front of him, waiting. He did exactly the right thing and enveloped her in a crushing hug.

"When we finally got Carol's door opened and found her on the ground, Brax realized that you had escaped through the window. He was livid." Mari heard the smile in Trey's voice. "He pulled out his phone and muttered something about Tucker. So, I volunteered to follow you."

Pulling back, Mari looked up at him. "And he agreed?"

Trey grinned. "I drove the Trans Am to work today."

"But how did you get here before me?" Mari asked.

With an expression that said the answer should be obvious, he pointed at himself and said, "Trans Am."

Mari leaned into him again. "What are we going to do now? Brax knows who I am."

Trey tightened his grip around her. "We'll figure something out."

With a sigh, Mari released him and walked over to the penthouse door.

As they walked inside, Susan sat up quickly on the sofa. "What's the matter?"

"Brax knows who I am," Mari declared.

Anna twisted around to face them. "What? How?"

Mari walked around and sat next to Anna on the couch as she explained about yesterday's car chase and Brax's cornering her at her desk. All the while, Trey stood awkwardly behind her.

As she finished the story, Mari's chest began to constrict, realizing that she'd failed at her mission, and she still didn't know where her mother was. She swiped at the tears welling up in her eyes.

Anna cast a quick glance toward Hannah. There was something meaningful exchanged in the look. Anna scooted closer to Mari and put her arm around her. "Hang in there. We need to work this out."

The tears spilled out as she sat with her head on Anna's shoulder. Susan came and sat on her other side, wrapping her arms around Mari, too.

A failed mission and awkward blubbering probably weren't what these ladies had in mind when they agreed to let her take the assignment. It wasn't what Mari had in mind.

Katie stood and took a step in Trey's direction. Opening her arms wide, she said, "Do you need a hug, too?"

Trey rubbed the back of his neck. "Uh, I'm good," he answered.

Anna and Susan laughed.

"Katie . . ." Anna said in a warning but teasing tone.

Katie's expression was all innocence. "What? I'm only trying to be helpful."

Hannah stood from her corner seat and moved toward the circle of couches. "We need to talk about the mission." She spoke to her roommates before throwing a haughty look Mari's way. "Alone," she added coldly.

It felt like a punch in the gut. She had failed, and now she wasn't even allowed to be part of the discussion about her mother's destiny. As Anna and Susan retreated from their group hug, Mari nodded awkwardly.

She stood and looked around the room, "Okay, uh, I'll just go find something to—"

"Hey." Trey held a hand out to her. "I happen to have a black '82 Trans Am down in the parking garage that might be able to find its way to Rosati's Pizza."

Mari laughed and swiped at an errant tear. "That's perfect, because I was just thinking how a spunky, talking car would really come in handy right about now."

Trey smiled and motioned toward the door. That dimple in his cheek was enough to make her knees give out, especially when her knees weren't feeling all that strong to begin with.

"Have a great time," Katie called as they left the penthouse. She only sounded a little bit jealous.

Of course, the black Trans Am didn't drive itself, but in an effort to distract her, Trey did a passable impression of both KITT and David Hasselhoff that had Mari laughing all the way to the restaurant.

Trey held the door open as they entered the pizza parlor.

"This place has the best deep-dish I've ever had outside of Chicago," he said as they headed for a cozy booth near the back.

"You weren't kidding when you said you like pizza," Mari answered with a laugh.

Instead of sitting across the booth from her, Trey insisted that she slide over to make room for him on the bench next to her.

They had worked together alone in his office, they had crept along empty hallways at Keating Mansion, he'd even held her in his arms, consoling Mari in her time of need. But sitting next to him in a crowded pizza parlor, she suddenly felt very aware of his presence. Not that she hadn't already noticed the definition in his arms or the way his shirt fit across the chest, but those things suddenly became quite unavoidable.

They sat in silence for several moments until the waitress arrived. Trey ordered his favorite pizza, all the while assuring Mari that she would love it.

When the waitress was gone, he turned to Mari and simply smiled. But it was a sad smile. They both knew why.

She glanced down at her hands to avoid Trey's gaze, but a short sob escaped her lips. "Are they going to call off the mission?" she asked in a voice barely above a whisper. "And what happens to my mother?"

Trey put an arm around her. "Hey, it's going to be okay. We'll get her out."

With an accusatory glare, Mari said, "You can't know that for sure."

"No. I can't." Trey squeezed her shoulders. "But I can guarantee that I won't stop until we find her."

Mari looked up and gave him a watery smile. She wiped at her eyes with the napkin he offered. "Thanks," she said as she glanced up at him. The depths of his green eyes and the spicy scent of his cologne had combined to render her momentarily unable to process normal thoughts. She looked back at the table, her fingers fiddling with the back of her phone case.

They sat in mostly comfortable silence. Trey was kind enough not to force her to talk again until she was ready.

"Could she be back in the original room?" Mari finally asked.

He lifted a shoulder. "Possibly. That would be the last place we'd look. But how would they have known to move her out of the room on the exact day of the rescue?"

Mari inhaled sharply, remembering the forgotten form that had led Brax to her.

"What's the matter?" he asked.

"That was my fault," Mari said.

She explained the situation with the form that she must have left in her mother's room.

Trey made a pondering sound. "That was more than a week ago," he said. "Don't you think they would have done something if they suspected you?"

Mari shrugged. She didn't know what to think anymore.

As they fell silent, Mari's gaze searched his face. His eyes held kindness and understanding. And something else. When he glanced down at her mouth, she realized what the something else might be. Her heart hammered in her chest.

"Mari, I wanted to—"

"One large Monster." The waitress dropped the pizza onto the table, and Mari jerked back. She had been leaning much closer to his face than she should. "Sorry," the waitress muttered when she saw Mari's reaction.

Mari started to object that she really hadn't been about to do what the waitress thought she was about to do. But it was a hollow protest. Out of the corner of her eye, she saw Trey's smirk. She gave him a playful glare and scooted a few inches away under the guise of needing room to eat.

Despite Mari's inclination to disagree with Trey, the pizza really was delicious. And spending time with him made her heart feel lighter, despite the pit of hopelessness festering inside her. His strange way of cracking jokes or making witty comments made her laugh and sigh.

Throughout the meal, Mari would cast a quick glance over and catch him looking back at her. He'd quickly look away. Of course, he'd later catch her staring at him and she'd be forced to look away. She felt like a girl in junior high, as if this was the first time she'd ever sat next to a boy.

Each time she realized how light and relaxed she felt around him, reality came crashing back in on her. In the middle of one of those rollercoaster moments, when Mari went from laughing to fighting tears, Trey reached out and touched her hand.

"You don't have to fight it. My shoulder actually doubles as a tear-catcher. I won't tell any of those ninja-girls you hang out with." He finished with that crooked grin.

All Mari wanted to do was melt into his embrace. To completely abandon herself to the safety of his steady—and incredibly muscular—arms. She looked up into his eyes. There was no judgement, no indication that he thought she was weak. Just kindness. And desire.

Mari leaned toward him, tilting her head back ever so slightly. She watched his reaction, hoping she wasn't misreading his signals. His eyes widened a bit, as did his delicious smile. She could feel his breath on her cheeks—see the flecks of brown in his dark-green eyes.

"I think I'm going to kiss you," she said softly.

"I think I'm going to let you," he replied, moving even closer.

When their lips were a mere whisper apart, Mari's phone buzzed.

It was her mother's ringtone.

She pulled back, still staring at Trey, reality crushing her heart once again.

He, too, knew what that ringtone meant.

Her time was up.

Heart thudding with dread, she put in an earbud and reluctantly answered the call.

"Hello, Mari," Brax said with a taunting leer. "Or is it Marina? I'm so confused about what to call you now."

"Mari," she said.

Brax tilted his head playfully. "Ah, why so gruff? No warm greeting for a dear coworker?" Brax's stupid, singsongy voice grated on her nerves.

She glared at him.

"Oh, come on Mari, don't feel bad that you revealed your secret identity and completely ruined your plans to rescue your mother. I already had my suspicions. I couldn't figure how your mother had a purchase order form in her room. And of course, we've never had a rodent problem in the mansion before, so I took some precautions that afternoon."

Mari glanced momentarily at Trey. It was confirmation of their fears about the rescue. She quickly looked back at the phone, not wanting to reveal that she was with someone.

Mari's eyes prickled, welling up with tears. It was also confirmation that she had failed.

"Mari, Mari, Mari," he said, shaking his head. "Now I understand why you've been less than diligent about getting the swarm algorithms from your mother's lab. At first, I thought you must take some cruel joy in making your mother suffer."

Mari's breath caught in her throat. She fought the urge to look up at Trey; she could see him shaking his head out of the corner of her eye.

"But all this time, you've been trying to infiltrate my operation," he grinned. "Kudos for finding me. But I warned you about trying to be a hero. I'm afraid your mother will have to suffer for it."

The emotions rising inside Mari threatened to overwhelm her. She choked down a sob. "Please, no! Please don't hurt her."

"Mari, if I don't punish you, how will you ever learn?" He sounded like he was chiding a wayward child. "Besides, I'm getting tired of trying to convince you to be a good daughter." He lifted his hand, taunting her with a goodbye wave.

"Wait!" Mari croaked. "I'll get the codes for you."

Her sudden, rash decision must have surprised Brax and—a quick glance up told her—Trey as well.

Brax's eyes narrowed at her. "You're suddenly cooperative now?"

Mari swallowed hard. "I'm done trying to be a hero. I'll get the algorithms for you. Please, just give me my mother back."

Brax's mouth twisted as he considered her unforeseen change of heart. "Noon, tomorrow. I will send you the location. Do not disappoint me again."

He terminated the call.

Mari looked hesitantly over at Trey.

Would he agree to help her, or was she on her own now?

A tear ran down her cheek. "She's all I have, Trey. I can't lose her."

He took her hand and squeezed. "I know." His lopsided grin slowly grew. "All we have to do is convince those spy girls you hang out with."

A crescendo of begging, pleading, and shouting assaulted them as Trey and Mari walked back through the penthouse door.

Anna's voice carried over the others. "It's her mother, Hannah. How you would feel—"

"How dare you bring my mother into this!" Hannah yelled back.

"There has to be a way!" Susan paced behind the couch, waving her hands in the air.

The Banana Girls must have noticed Trey and Mari entering, but they didn't seem to care.

Hannah stood and pulled out her phone. "This discussion—not to mention this crazy mission—has gone on long enough. I'm calling Stacia to scrub it." She tapped the screen a few times and held the phone to her ear.

"We're supposed to make the decision together, Han," Anna said with a glare.

"We *are* supposed to make these decisions together, but we're also supposed to be rational. And none of you are right now," Hannah shot back.

Mari's eyes went wide. She had hoped to have a few minutes to talk to the team. To convince them to go through with what she'd just promised Brax. "Hannah, wait!"

Hannah ignored her, speaking into the phone instead. "Yes, this is Hannah McCarthy. I need to speak to Director Keller, please. Yes, it's important."

Mari looked around the room. Susan and Katie were scowling, while Anna simply shook her head.

After a few seconds, Hannah spoke again. "Fine, I'll hold."

Mari moved across the living room toward Hannah. "Please don't cancel the mission. I just promised Brax we'd get him the control algorithms by tomorrow."

"Are you crazy?! *Our* instructions—" she waved her free hand at her roommates "—from the beginning of this assignment were to prevent the nano-bots from being replicated. We should have scrubbed the rescue mission as soon as we found out Brax was already manufacturing them."

"Please, Hannah." Mari wasn't above begging. "Please."

"Hannah, we can't just give up on Mari's mother," Anna said.

Hannah shot a fierce glare at Anna, then turned to Mari. "I'm sorry, Mari. I don't want to be the bad guy here. But we're already behind the eight-ball. We have to come up with a plan for how to destroy the nano-bots they already have. That takes higher priority. It's out of my hands." Hannah still had the phone to her ear, waiting to speak with Director Keller.

Mari sunk onto a nearby sofa.

Could she get the algorithms on her own? Would Hanna and Anna try to stop her again?

"Maybe there's a way to do both," Katie chimed in.

Mari swung around to look at the petite girl. Katie's face was screwed up in concentration.

"Missions don't run on hope, Katie. We need an actual plan." Hannah's rejection brought all of Mari's hopes crashing down.

Panic rose in Mari's chest. She couldn't let Hannah cancel the mission. She couldn't let her mother be sacrificed, not if there was another way.

Mari stood slowly from her seat, eyeing Hannah. Could she get over the back of the couch and tackle Hannah before the others could stop her?

Mari leaned forward, preparing to pounce.

Trey must have seen the look in Mari's eye because he stepped between her and the thin blonde girl. "Hannah, if there's another option—one that could save Mari's mother *and* destroy the nano-bots—shouldn't we give it a chance?"

Hannah considered him for a long time.

The room was dead silent.

Suddenly, a small, tinny voice echoed from the phone's headset speaker. "Hello?"

Mari stared at Hannah, pleading with her eyes. Hannah stared back for a long moment.

"Hello? Hannah?"

Hannah glanced around the room. The girls were all entreating her in their own ways. Susan was waving praying-hands back and forth in front of her. Hannah looked back at Trey, who simply nodded his agreement with the others.

With a sigh, Hannah touched the screen to end the call. "You've got until she calls back to convince me. Start talking."

The adrenaline that would have taken her hurtling over the couch started to fade, and relief flooded into its place. Mari looked at Katie, trusting that she could quickly explain whatever idea she had to destroy the nano-bots while still—hopefully—rescuing her mother.

Katie smiled. "We could give Brax exactly what he's asking for. We could get the programming instructions for the nano-bots and send them to him."

Hannah's mouth nearly fell open. "That's your big plan? Give the bad guy exactly what he's asking for?"

"I wasn't finished," Katie continued. "I didn't mean we would give him the authentic programming. We get the code, and then we modify it a little bit."

Hannah's eyes narrowed. "Modify it how?"

Katie stood and began to pace the room, her eyes lit with excitement. "Well, it would have to be a two-part attack, because the executable needs to be separate. And it can't be obvious; we'd need to bury it in a subroutine somewhere." She was practically mumbling to herself at this point. "In fact, it would need to look completely innocent, because if they found out we—"

"Katie?" Anna prompted.

Katie stopped and spun around. "Yeah?"

"Convince Hannah." Anna swept an arm toward Hannah, who still held the phone in her hand.

"Oh, right." Katie moved back toward the group. "You see, if we modify the instruction code and send it to Brax, they're certainly going to check it first. We need the kill switch to be part of a separate set of code that we execute after the nano-bots are programmed."

They all stared at her in silence.

Her arms fell to her sides in frustration. "A self-destruct! We trick Brax into programming the bots to self-destruct."

Anna cocked her head to the side. "Will that work?"

"Sure," Katie said with a smile. "We'd need to make the modification small—a standard function call, or something like that. Things will work normally until we load the second half of the code. Then *poof*—nano-bricks."

"And how do we load the second half?" Hannah asked.

A slight grimace formed on Katie's face. "Uh, we have to place it on the Keating BioMed server—while the nano-bots are still interfaced."

The collective confidence of everyone in the room quickly dissipated, like air let out of a balloon.

"So, let me get this straight," Hannah began in her you-must-be-crazy voice. "First, we'll need to sneak into Dr. Sandoval's lab—again—and steal the algorithms. Then we'll need to modify it with a two-part time bomb and deliver it to Brax without raising his suspicions. Then—assuming he doesn't realize we're trying to trick him and actually installs the modified code—we'll need to get someone back inside Keating BioMedical where they'll need to locate the nano-bot lab and load the second half of the code onto the server and push it to the bots. Have I got everything?"

Katie nodded enthusiastically. "Yep. And arrange to make the trade for Mari's mom."

"Right, that one little detail." Sarcasm dripped from Hannah's voice. "I completely forgot about the one little thing we've been focused on for the last *two weeks*!" Hannah looked around at the rest of the team in disbelief. "This whole thing is crazy!"

The room was silent for a few seconds before Anna finally said, "Never underestimate a Banana Girl."

"I've learned that one," Trey added with a grin.

The other girls smiled. Hannah scowled at him and pointed a finger at Mari. "She's not a Banana Girl."

Mari felt the sting of those words. She also felt Anna and Susan move closer to her in an almost protective way. They stared Hannah down, unwilling to budge.

Hannah's phone chirped. She answered it, still holding their collective gaze. "Yes. Yes, everything is fine. I was going to consult with you on the mission . . ." Hannah paused for a moment. Mari squeezed her eyes shut, hoping against hope that Hannah wouldn't have the mission cancelled. ". . . but the girls and I worked out the details. We have a plan."

They held their barely contained excitement until Hannah finished her call. Katie and Susan rushed forward, squealing, and surrounded Hannah in a hug.

"I didn't say it was a *good* plan," Hannah said over the noise, a small smirk on her face as her friends squished her. She and Mari locked gazes and her smile vanished. She didn't say anything, but her look conveyed the idea well enough.

This plan better work.

Chapter Fourteen

"Tell me again why you needed me on this mission," Hannah asked as Mari swiped her access card.

"It's for old times' sake, Han," Anna said.

"The last time we were here, we had to drag a certain person from the building kicking and screaming." Hannah gave Mari a long, pointed look.

"I wasn't *screaming*," Mari said. She couldn't help a small smile at the memory of the kick she'd landed in Hannah's gut the morning they met.

The girls crossed the empty atrium to the bank of elevators. They had agreed—with the exception of Hannah, who said it was unnatural to be awake that early—that 5 AM was the ideal time because it was early enough to avoid even the earliest researchers, but late enough in the midnight shift to not interrupt any custodians. Mari had worked on a cleaning crew one summer in high school, and the easier work usually happened later in the shift.

Mari ushered them from the elevator toward the offices adjacent to her mother's research lab.

Anna stopped as they approached the outer door. "I think I'd better wait out here. Just in case."

Hannah and Mari continued into the office suite. "Don't turn on the office light; it'll attract attention. And see if you can turn down the brightness on the computer."

Mari nodded her understanding as she quietly entered her mother's office. Hannah positioned herself near the reception desk facing the entrance doors.

In the dark, empty office, Mari's keystrokes echoed loudly. She looked up and saw Hannah glare at her from across the hall. Mari shrugged an apology and tried to type softer. She guessed her mother's password on the third try. Her mother had never been secretive about security. As her only family, she had always made sure Mari knew her passwords in case of an emergency. Mari assumed this situation qualified as an emergency.

Four rapid knocks tapped on the glazed glass of the office suite. Hannah ducked behind the reception desk and motioned for Mari to hide. With a quick tap to turn off the monitor, Mari sunk down beneath the surface of her mother's desk. Several seconds later, footsteps thudded in the hallway. Mari held her breath as the footsteps came to a stop.

In the reflection of a framed picture on her mother's wall, Mari could make out a tall, rather disheveled student janitor standing with his hand on the glass door of the research offices. As he pushed the door open, a high-pitched yell sounded from somewhere in the maze of hallways outside. It sounded like Anna.

Fighting her initial instinct to race out into the halls to find Anna, Mari peeked around the side of her mother's desk. She could see Hannah still crouched low behind the reception counter. Hannah motioned downward with her hand, telling Mari to stay calm. A second later, the main door swung shut as the janitor went to investigate.

"Hurry." Hannah's sharp whisper cut across the open space between them.

Kneeling in front of the computer, Mari quickly turned the monitor back on and raced through folder after folder in her search for the necessary files. She didn't have time to copy the entire contents of her mother's hard drive, but she didn't have time to search every directory to find what they needed, either. In her original plan, she wasn't this rushed to get the information. Then again, she hadn't even gotten this far in her original plan, no thanks to Hannah and Anna.

Two levels down in the file system, she found a folder labeled "Working Code." Mari plugged in the flash drive and started the duplication process. One of the subdirectories was password-protected. Fortunately, her mother had used a familiar variant of her primary login. It only took two tries for that one.

There was another series of taps on the glass wall facing the reception area. A few seconds later, Hannah crept into the office and hid behind the desk with Mari.

"That was Anna's code to hurry," Hannah said. "How much longer?"

"It's duplicating the files right now."

With Hannah watching the progress, it seemed to go even slower than normal. Finally, the process finished and Mari ejected the flash drive.

"Put everything back the way you found it," Hannah instructed in a whisper.

"Why? No one else should be on this computer except my mother," Mari whispered back.

"It's standard procedure. You need to learn to follow the rules!"

"Fine." Mari readjusted the monitor's brightness and moved the mouse and keyboard half an inch to the left. Not because that's where they had been, but just because she wanted to prove to Hannah that she'd done something.

Hannah rolled her eyes, but seemed ready to leave regardless. They moved to the doors of the suite, and Hannah peeked out into the main hall. "Let's go."

They rushed toward the elevator. The closest elevator car was only two floors below them. Mari hoped it wouldn't take long. Half a second before Hannah pushed the elevator call button, the lift machinery engaged. Mari looked up at the floor indicator light. The elevator was moving toward them.

"Someone's coming up." Mari grabbed Hannah's arm and pulled her away from the elevators.

Mari and Hannah dove down the first side hall. They heard footsteps coming from a nearby corridor, so they ducked around the corner into a small alcove. A few seconds later, Anna flashed by, completely oblivious of them.

"Anna!" Hannah called out in a whisper.

The tall girl skidded to a halt and turned around. A smile spread on her face as she hustled to join them in their hiding place. "You got it?" she asked through labored breaths.

"I think so," Mari replied, suddenly aware of her own uncertainty and the risks these girls were taking for her.

Anna held a finger to her lips as the sound of clumsy footsteps approached. They grew louder then began to recede.

"I might be wearing him out." Anna's lips curved into a mischievous smile.

They waited until the footsteps had disappeared before leaving the safety of the alcove. At the main hall, Anna quietly nodded toward the elevators.

"Hey!" a voice called from behind them.

Without even looking back, all three girls ran down the hall. Loud footsteps echoed behind them. They couldn't take the elevator now; they'd be caught for sure. Mari pointed to a side door that led to the stairwell. They flew down two flights of stairs in a blur.

"Next floor," Mari instructed. The other girls followed her lead without hesitation. This must be how a well-oiled ninja-machine worked. Mari envied them for their trust and sense of purpose.

The three girls walked as calmly as possible out of the stairs into the main hall of the third floor. Mari fought to slow her breathing. "There's a smaller stairwell toward the back of the building. We'll have a better chance of getting away there," she said. Those would be better odds than trailing a sleep-deprived janitor noisily down the main stairwell.

Mari guided them in the direction of the back stairs. As long as the janitor on their tail didn't realize which floor they'd come out on, they might make it out without being caught.

Halfway along the hall, they passed a conference room with floor-to-ceiling windows. Too late, Mari realized that there was an informal work party going on inside the room. Half a dozen student custodians had gathered—their cleaning supplies resting in a pile near the door—to feast on several boxes of donuts.

The girls continued calmly on, facing straight forward. Out of the corner of her eye, Mari saw movement—fingers pointing at them—and heard exclamations of surprise.

"Just get past the conference room and start running," Mari said through motionless lips.

The instant they were out of sight, they all took off. Mari pointed to the back stairs as they approached the door. She could already hear the custodian party spilling out into the hall behind them.

Down two more flights of stairs they ran. If they could reach the lobby before being caught again, they stood a chance of making it out unscathed—relatively.

Mari stopped the girls at the exit on the ground floor. "Students pull all-nighters in this building all the time. Act like we've just finished a long project."

Anna grinned back at her, clearly enjoying herself. Hannah scowled, clearly not enjoying herself.

They walked down the main floor hall with faked exhaustion, but they hadn't taken more than four steps into the atrium before Mari realized they weren't going to make it out unnoticed. The disheveled janitor from her mother's offices stood blocking the main exit.

Mari wanted to turn and bolt, but Anna grabbed her arm with calming reassurance. "Steady," she whispered. They continued to walk confidently forward.

"Hey, you three need to—"

Anna suddenly turned to Hannah. "Would you say this counts as getting caught?" she asked.

Hannah pretended to consider her friend's question. "Yes, I guess it would."

Anna turned to Mari. "Sorry, little pledge. It looks like you got caught. You won't be joining the sisterhood."

The janitor gave her a funny look. "Do you mean—"

"But there was that clause about getting caught by a hot guy . . ." Hannah said as she and Anna both turned deliberately to look at the janitor boy. Mari was sure this guy would never qualify for what Hannah would consider "hot." Maybe cute—in a competent, nerdy sort of way.

He sputtered and blushed an adorable pink.

"Hmm." Anna put a finger to her lips. "I guess you're right on that part." She slowly looked him up and down.

Mari almost felt sorry for this guy, with the way they were working him over. He was way out of his league.

He chuckled nervously and ran a hand through his tousled hair. "Uh, so this is just a sorority hazing or something?"

"Sneak into a building during the night shift and don't get caught unless it's by a hot guy." Hannah lightly tapped his nose. The phrase rolled off her tongue so easily, Mari would have thought she'd practiced it a million times. "You've never heard of it?" she asked innocently.

Cute Janitor-Boy swallowed and shook his head.

The girls were already moving around him, pulling Mari along.

"Well, I suppose . . ." he stammered, "if it's just innocent fun . . . you can . . . go . . . I guess."

Mari had heard of girls who could sweet-talk boys into doing anything they wanted, but she'd never seen the ability wielded in the hands of such experts.

Mari walked out into the dim, predawn light with the code she needed to save her mother resting safely in her pocket.

Katie worked all morning, modifying the algorithms. Mari had received a message from her mother's phone an hour before the scheduled exchange. The pin for her mother's location sat squarely in the middle of an abandoned stone quarry south of the airport.

Was there some bad-guys support group that villains went to where they all agreed to make hostage swaps in creepy, dangerous places?

Anna and Hannah had been forced to go to their morning classes tired and grumpy. Well, Anna had gone tired; Hannah had gone grumpy.

Mari wasn't going in to work at Keating BioMed anymore, so she could have gone back to classes, but she wasn't willing to miss the exchange to get her mother. Plus, she was more than a week behind, so she'd just be lost, anyway. Katie had agreed to go to her linear algebra class again to take notes for her. Mari hadn't dared tease her about the reason. She figured she might need to check the quality of the notes, though.

As Susan was the only one who didn't have any classes on Thursday afternoon that semester, she volunteered to help Mari.

"I've never been to a hostage negotiation." Susan waved her hands a lot while she drove. Mari wished she'd keep them on the steering wheel. At least she watched where she was driving.

"It's not technically a negotiation, Susan. We send the algorithms, and Brax releases my mother. That's the plan, anyway," Mari said.

Susan nodded as she slowed the SUV on the narrow, rural road leading to the quarry. She squinted at an approaching sign. "I think this is it."

They turned off the small lane onto a wide gravel path. The rickety-looking gate of the rusted chain-link fence stood open. Susan looked over at Mari with wide eyes. She was certainly not helping Mari's nerves.

Mari leaned forward as they rounded a bend in the path, searching for the white van that Brax said would be here waiting for them. Her right leg bounced nervously. Susan glanced down at Mari's lap and smiled.

Susan steered Big Banana—currently painted dark blue—around the neglected piles of rock and sand. Every time she came around a corner, she'd take a small breath. At first, Mari thought that meant she'd seen something. But after half a dozen false alarms, Mari came to the conclusion that Susan just lived her life in a perpetual state of anticipation and excitement. It was fitting.

Mari and Susan both sucked in a short breath when they saw the white van parked at the end of the long, low conveyor. As they approached, its lights flashed. Mari glanced at Susan who shrugged back at her.

"I guess we should stop," Mari suggested.

She stepped out of the SUV and walked a few paces toward the van. A large figure wearing a baseball cap and sunglasses stepped out of the passenger side but stood close to the vehicle with the door still open, partially obscuring his face with his arm.

"I have what you want!" Mari yelled, holding up her phone.

"Send it, then!" the man yelled back.

"I need to see my mother first," Mari replied.

The man didn't move for several seconds. Mari began to wonder if he'd heard her.

Maybe it was all a ruse, and he didn't even have her mother.

The muscles in Mari's legs tensed, ready to make a run back to the SUV if the guy should move toward her. She squinted at the man. She couldn't make out much of his features, but it could have been one of Brax's goons.

Finally, he ducked his head in the van and said something to the driver. A few seconds later the side door opened and two figures stepped out. Well, one figure stepped out dragging another smaller figure behind him, who he dumped unceremoniously on the ground.

Mari's breath caught.

The smaller one was clearly a woman. Despite the weather still being warm in early October, the woman wore a large trench coat and broad rain hat.

The woman was about her mother's size. Mari wanted to believe that it was her mother. She wanted to rush forward to see if it really was her mother.

"There!" the man yelled. "Now send the files."

What choice did Mari have? She couldn't get any closer to the van without risking her own safety. But she had no way of knowing if it was her mother or not.

"Back away from her," Mari said.

The second goon, also wearing glasses and a hat, smirked as he backed away. He got back in the van and closed the door, leaving only the first guy.

"Send the files or the deal is off," he said.

Mari nodded. His tone told her that she'd better not push for anything else. She pulled out her phone and found the modified control algorithms. With a few more taps, she sent the file to her mother's phone.

The same moment that she saw the notification that it had been received on her mother's phone, the van's engine roared to life. The man jumped into the passenger seat, and the tires churned rocks and dirt into the air as the van spun a hard turn and fled the scene.

Mari rushed forward through the dust cloud and knelt next to the prone woman. She caught a glimpse of the skin of her hands, and her heart leaped for joy. It was the same olive tone as her mother's hands. She dragged the woman off the ground into a sitting position and pulled back the hat.

Unfamiliar eyes—wide with fear—stared back at her.

The woman was a good body double, but very obviously not her mother.

Anna had warned her this might happen. That didn't mean it was any less heartrending.

Susan rushed up to them. She knelt on the ground next to Mari. "Not your mother." She sounded dejected but resigned.

Mari looked down at the woman on the ground. "Who are you?" she asked.

The woman shook her head.

"Why were you here with those men?" Mari asked.

The woman continued shaking her head. "No hablo inglés."

Mari glanced up at Susan who shrugged back at her. Mari's Spanish was rusty, but at least Susan wouldn't make fun of her. "¿Quién es usted?" Mari asked.

"I didn't know you could speak Spanish," Susan said.

Mari smiled wryly. "Let's wait and see if she understands me before we get too excited."

"Me llamo Isabel," the woman replied. "¿Quiénes eran aquellos hombres?

"She says her name is Isabel," Mari translated. "And she's wondering who those guys were."

Susan frowned. "I guess that cuts the interrogation short. Maybe we can take her to a police station and see if she can give them some information."

The woman grabbed Mari by the arm. "No policía. Por favor, no policía."

"She says 'no police.'"

Susan grinned. "Yeah. I figured." Her eyes went wide with excitement. "Hey, I think I might be able to pick up this Spanish thing with a little more practice."

They helped Isabel to her feet. "¿Dónde podemos llevarle a usted?" Mari asked.

Susan tapped Mari on the arm. "And see if we can give her a ride somewhere."

"I just did," Mari said with a grin.

"Oh," Susan's smile fell. "I guess I might need a few more lessons before I'm fluent."

Later that evening, Mari sat on the long, white leather couch in the Club Banana living room, stewing over the events of the day. She had broken into her mother's lab, stolen top secret algorithms, delivered them to the bad guy, and still she had nothing to show for it.

Even knowing that the code had been modified with a self-destruct, it still felt wrong.

She grabbed a bright yellow pillow sitting nearby and punched it across the room. If only that could have been Brax's face.

From her spot on a sofa across from Mari, Susan shifted back and forth, swinging punches at an imaginary foe. "Feeling better?" she asked.

"Not really." Mari attempted a scowl in order to cover her grin. She wasn't quite ready to feel better yet.

Anna brought a tray of pastrami sliders from the kitchen and set it down on the coffee table. "You did everything you could, Mari. There was nothing we could have done differently that would have gotten your mother in the trade."

"I hate him," Mari said.

Anna patted her arm. "I know, sweetie. Let's put those feelings to good use."

The chime announced the arrival of a guest. Katie went to the door. "Mari, you have a visitor."

Mari twisted around to see Trey stroll casually in, a broad grin on his face when he saw her. She felt heat creeping up her neck. "He's not only here to see me. We have to plan for tomorrow night."

Each of the ladies made their own sound of disbelief or skepticism.

Trey came around the couch and sat next to Mari. "I heard what happened today. I'm sorry." He set a hand on Mari's knee. It was clearly meant to be a comforting gesture, but it sent jolts of electricity through her.

"Thanks," Mari said, trying her very best to keep her composure.

Anna glanced down at his hand. She gave him a polite but patronizing smile. "Trey, would you be a dear and get us something to drink? There's some raspberry lemonade in the fridge."

Trey jumped up. "Sure. No problem." He was either very eager to please or eager to have something to keep himself busy. Perhaps both.

Once he was out of earshot, Anna quietly said, "You've been forced to spend lots of time with Trey so far, and that'll need to continue at least until tomorrow night if this plan's going to work. You're good with that?"

Mari glanced over at Trey searching the kitchen for glasses. A small smile touched her lips. "Yeah."

"I wasn't asking whether you were enjoying it." Anna's tone told Mari she might have misunderstood the question.

Mari turned back to Anna, trying to pay more attention. "What do you mean?"

"I'm sure you've noticed that we're pretty casual about Rule Number One, but there's a reason it's number one. I just wanted to make sure you aren't getting in too deep, too fast. Feelings can get unnaturally amplified when you're paired with a guy on a mission." Anna paused as they both looked back at Trey heading their way with the lemonade. "Especially an attractive one," she finished in a whisper.

Trey leaned down and set the glasses on the table in front of the girls.

"Oh, waiter," Katie called to Trey from across the room, "I'll take one of whatever they're having."

He gave Mari an absolutely adorable, conspiratorial grin. "Coming right up." He went back into the kitchen for more lemonade.

"I'm definitely experiencing the amplified feelings part." Mari gave Anna a small shrug. "But I think it'll be okay."

Anna nodded her understanding, and Mari knew she was just playing her role as caring mother. "Well, I would say the feeling is probably mutual from Trey," Anna said.

Mari felt a blush creep to her cheeks. "Really? Why do you say that?" she asked in what she hoped was a casual tone.

Anna turned to face Mari fully. "He probably never told you the details about his mission. He was meant to infiltrate Keating BioMed and sabotage the nano-bot production efforts at all costs," she explained. "He was never authorized to help rescue your mother. In fact, he has basically put his job on the line by helping us deliver the algorithms to Brax. If we don't successfully destroy the nano-bots, his career as an agent will pretty much be over."

As if Mari's emotions hadn't already been a swirling mess, she felt a sudden surge of new feelings for Trey that were difficult to describe—the attraction was still there, for sure—but there was an intense gratitude mixed in, too. Plus a gritty determination to make sure they didn't fail at the mission. All Mari wanted to do in that moment was walk over, wrap her arms around him, and stay that way for a very long time.

Anna and Mari both watched as Trey delivered a glass of lemonade to Katie, who was busy working on the code for the second half of the nano-bot time bomb. She thanked him and asked him something, presumably to hold his attention.

Mari didn't dare elaborate on her new, more complex feelings for Trey; that would only worry Anna more. She decided to move the conversation in a different direction. Still watching Trey and Katie's interaction, Mari quietly spoke to Anna, "I can't even imagine how Katie does on missions; it's like she's a completely different person around guys."

Anna laughed lightly. "Hannah and I may have invented Rule Number One, but Katie has definitely tested its boundaries."

"Has she ever . . ." Mari didn't want to wrongly accuse Katie, but she needed to know if there was history there, ". . . stolen a guy from you?"

A knowing smile spread on Anna's face. "It does sometimes seem like she's trying, doesn't it." Anna turned to look at Mari, her expression still casual, albeit slightly more serious. "I hope you know she would never actually do it. The few times it's worked, she's immediately turned the guy away. In her own unique way, it's how she shows her loyalty. She's trying to protect us from guys who would stray."

Trey had already started inching back from Katie, clearly wanting to end the conversation. Katie tried one more flirtatious laugh, but Trey turned and rejoined Mari and Anna. Behind his back, Katie's expression changed from a playful smile to a self-satisfied smirk and an almost imperceptible nod to no one in particular.

Anna gave Mari a similar nod of satisfaction. "Apparently he passed."

Mari looked at Trey with newfound appreciation. How had she been so lucky to find such an amazing guy?

A few seconds under Mari's gaze, and Trey turned self-conscious. "What?"

Mari shook her head, clearing her mind of thoughts of a future with Trey in an attempt to focus back on the mission.

"We were just talking about the timeline for tomorrow night," Anna replied without missing a beat.

Trey clapped his hands together. "Great. What's the plan?"

"You've received your invitation to the party at Keating Mansion?" Anna asked.

"Yep."

"And it included a plus one, I assume?"

Trey nodded and shot a quick glance at Mari.

"Then we just need to decide who will be going with you." At this point, Anna turned deliberately to Mari.

Mari felt her cheeks heat, but she didn't demur. Trey winked at Mari. She knew he was doing this to help rescue her mother, but the look on his face told her that he would have invited her to accompany him to the party, regardless. Assuming they had ever met in the first place without all this craziness.

Mari didn't even want to consider that possibility.

"Mari shouldn't be the one going," Hannah called from her corner.

Mari blinked. It felt like she'd been slapped. She stood and glared at Hannah. "Why not?!"

"It's too dangerous. Brax knows who you are and what you know. He could very easily lock you up with your mom. Don't you think he'd do it?"

"We've already given him the nano-bot algorithms. What else could he want from me?"

Hannah gave a noncommittal shrug and looked back down at her tablet.

Mari's blood boiled, and her hands balled into fists at her sides. "You just don't think I can do it!"

Hannah dropped the tablet into her lap. Though there was still an edge in her voice, her blue eyes held an expression of genuine concern. "This isn't a game, Mari. We're talking life-or-death risks," she said softly.

Hot tears welled up in Mari's eyes. "Is it because I'm not a Banana Girl?"

Hannah motioned with her hand toward the other girls. "We're not just playing spies here. We've trained for years to do what we do." She paused as if unsure how to put the next part into words. "I don't want you or your mother to get hurt." Hannah's cheeks pinked a little, and she returned her attention to her tablet. "I just think it's too dangerous for you, okay?"

As much as Mari wouldn't have believed it, Hannah actually seemed worried about her. Mari sank back down into the couch, her indignation ebbing away.

Anna shared a look with the others. "What do you two think?"

"It's too late to send anyone else but Mari," Katie said. "She's tough. I think she can do it."

Susan gave two enthusiastic thumbs up accompanied by a big smile.

"What about you, Trey?" Anna asked.

His expression was thoughtful. "I want it to be Mari," he said finally.

Anna looked toward the chaise lounge in the corner. Without even looking up from her tablet, Hannah lifted her shoulders ever so slightly. Mari realized there must be some major history between those two because they could communicate almost telepathically.

Focusing her attention back on Mari, Anna pinched her lips into a stern line. "We think you can do this. The question is, do you want to?"

Mari took a deep, fortifying breath. "Yes. I want to be the one to do it."

Anna nodded firmly, as if that settled the matter.

She turned to Trey. "So, you and Mari will drive to the party in one of your fancy cars—"

Trey jumped in, looking at Mari with excitement in his eyes. "I'm thinking my blue '67 Mustang, or maybe the yellow Corvette Stingray—"

Anna spoke over him. "—whichever car you choose, you'll be sneaking Susan and me onto the grounds of Keating Mansion with you."

When all eyes turned toward her, Susan smiled and waved as if she was a beauty queen on a parade float.

"We will infiltrate the lab, upload the second half of the nano-bot code, and find Dr. Sandoval." Anna turned to Trey. "You'll need to disable the latch on one of the doors in the research wing. And I think Katie has a few recon bots for you to strategically place somewhere in the mansion."

Trey nodded. "Will do."

Mari waited for Anna to give more assignments. When she didn't, Mari asked. "What about Hannah and Katie?"

"Katie will be remotely monitoring and managing the code upload, recon bots, and drone video. Hannah will be the point on communications and dispatch. She'll also control the drones and pyrotechnics, if necessary," Anna added.

Mari looked around at her new friends, each wearing an expression of optimistic determination. She wasn't sure how the final act of the mission would play out, but she was grateful to be in such good company.

Anna pointed at Trey. "Make sure you're back here on time tomorrow night. You don't want Cinderella to be late for the ball."

CHAPTER FIFTEEN

"WHY WON'T YOU JUST believe me that you look terrific in all of these dresses?" Trey asked with a sigh.

Mari shot Trey a smile and did a quick twirl before turning back to the mirror. Truthfully, she could barely believe her eyes. The full-length red gown hugged her in all the right places, including some places she hadn't even known she had. Even wearing black high heels, the hem brushed the ground. Not that anyone could have actually seen the tranquilizer serum hidden in the heel of her right stiletto, but having the shoes covered by the dress added to Mari's peace of mind.

"Remember, your primary goal tonight is to keep Chaz's attention," Hannah said.

"If he's a warm-blooded male, it shouldn't be too hard," Trey muttered.

Hannah turned to Trey. "And if Brax is there, you'll need to keep him occupied and away from the research wing."

"Check," Trey said with a nod.

Katie approached, holding a tiny earpiece in her palm. "Connected and ready to go. Let's test it."

Mari placed the device in her ear.

"Can you hear me?" Katie whispered.

"Yes," Mari whispered back. "But it's probably because you're standing right next to me."

Katie giggled. "Hold on." She walked into her tech room. "How about now?"

Mari heard her whisper as if she were still standing beside her. "Works great." Mari replied. "Can you hear me?"

Katie gave her a thumbs up around the corner.

"You're sure you disabled the lock on the auxiliary entrance?" Hannah asked Trey.

"Double checked it," Trey answered.

"And you put the recon bots in the ductwork?" she asked.

Before Trey could answer, Katie stuck her head around the corner. "Affirmative on that. I'm already in the security system."

Hannah turned to Mari. "What about the tranquilizer in your heel? Did you fill it?"

Mari sucked in a few shallow breaths, fighting another attack of butterflies in her stomach. Anna came and put an arm around her, turning toward Hannah. "She's nervous enough, Hannah. We've already gone over everything. She'll be fine. Besides," Anna pulled back, still holding one of Mari's hands, and looked at her in the mirror, "she's on her way to a ball, and she looks stunning."

"Amen to that," Trey called out. "And she'll be going with a prince."

The girls laughed, helping ease Mari's jitters.

Anna looked around the room. "I think we're ready." She turned to Hannah. "You'll be our lead on radio comms."

Hannah nodded.

Anna turned to Susan. "Ready to cuddle in the trunk?"

Susan smiled and tilted her head down onto Anna's shoulder.

Trey in his tuxedo and Mari in her red formal crammed into the elevator with Anna and Susan in their ninja-blacks.

Anna and Susan got in the back seat of Trey's car. Trey walked around and opened Mari's door. "Your carriage awaits, Your Highness."

The butterflies were back, but for an entirely different reason.

The western sky burned bright pink and orange as they wound their way out of Midtown and farther and farther into the affluence of the suburbs. A few miles from the mansion, Trey pulled off on a short side road. Everyone got out, and Trey opened the trunk.

Susan climbed in first and got comfortable. "Wait! Trey, there's no trunk release in here," she said.

He hunched over and peered inside the trunk. "Is there supposed to be?"

"If you need Anna and me to go all ninja on the bad guys." Susan swung a karate chop toward his head. "We can't do it from inside the trunk," she said.

Trey and Susan both looked at Anna.

"We do need a way to get out of the trunk. Cars these days have release cords on the inside," Anna explained.

"I know that," he said defensively. "But this is a '67 Mustang. It's a classic."

Mari's panic inched up several notches. Would this put the mission in jeopardy? She wasn't willing to miss another chance to save her mother. "What if we let you out when we get there?" she asked.

"A black-tie gala at a multi-millionaire's mansion will definitely have valet parking," Trey pointed out.

"I guess we can hold the trunk down from the inside," Anna offered.

"On these roads?" Susan sounded skeptical. "What if we hit a bump, and it latches?"

Anna shook her head. "Maybe this isn't going to work."

Mari's lungs constricted; it was getting more and more difficult to breathe. There had to be a solution. "My purse!" she said, holding out her small black clutch.

The other three stared at her.

"I'll leave my purse in the car. Then after the valet parks it, I can go back with the excuse that I forgot it. Then I can let Anna and Susan out of the trunk."

Susan and Anna looked at each other. "That's a long time cramped in a trunk," Anna said.

"We could play *I Spy*," Susan said with a laugh.

Anna giggled as she climbed in with her friend. "Sure, but you always spy the hardest things. And you never give me any hints."

"I'll go easy on you this time," Susan shot back as Trey closed the trunk.

Mari was extra-sensitive to the bumps on the last few miles of road to the mansion. They rounded the turn and slowed at the guard station. Mari fidgeted with the clasp on her purse while they waited for the guard to check Trey's invitation. Trey placed his hand over hers and squeezed gently. After a quick glance in the back seat, the guard waved them through.

Mari let out a long breath as they passed through the gate and drove to the front door. She stowed her clutch under the seat while Trey came around the front of the car, racing the valet to open her door. He helped her stand and casually handed the valet the keys.

Her heart was in her throat as she slipped her hand through his arm and they mounted the front stairs. She winced as she considered Anna and Susan still trapped inside the small trunk.

"Not that I mind you checking out my massive bicep, but you're cutting off the circulation to my arm," Trey said through a smile.

Mari looked down at his arm and released her stranglehold on his crumpled sleeve. "Sorry."

He shot her his crooked smile and placed his other hand on hers. "You'll be great."

The butler showed them through the marble front entryway and escorted them down the hall of the old mansion's south wing into the grand ballroom. Mari had been told that Keating BioMedical sometimes used the space as a conference room for company meetings. Tonight, it was decked out in all of its dazzling glory. Extravagant gold drapes adorned the tall windows, and three gorgeous chandeliers hung in a row from the ceiling. Round tables covered in white linen dotted the room, and a small wooden dance floor spread out in front of a dozen-piece orchestra at the far end.

"It looks like we're at the party," Trey said to her. Actually, he said it for Hannah's benefit, as Mari could clearly see where they were.

Hannah's voice whispered in their ears. "Excellent. Anna, how are you two doing?"

"We're just fine; thanks for asking. Susan has me stumped on *I Spy* again, though. So there's that."

Susan's voice sounded equally strained. "Well, Anna made the rule that it has to be something we can see, so I gave her the clue 'very, very dark gray.'" A long pause was followed by grunts and the sound of shifting bodies. "If it's not too much trouble, now would be an amazing time to come get us."

Mari glanced up at Trey, and he nodded.

She brought a gloved hand up to her mouth. "Oh!" she said dramatically. "I forgot my purse!"

Trey raised an eyebrow at her.

"That was laying it on pretty thick," Hannah muttered over the radio.

Mari blushed as she turned back to the door.

"You'll need this." Trey covertly placed the spare key in her hand as she brushed past.

She ducked her head in acknowledgment—and a little embarrassment—and walked out of the ballroom.

She rushed past the butler with an airy explanation about her purse in the car and stumbled out onto the front stairs. With great effort, she kept herself from running down the steps.

Near the bottom of the staircase, one of the valets approached her. "Can I help you, ma'am?

"Oh, it's nothing; I just forgot something in the car," she replied as she flew past him.

The valet followed quickly on her heels. "I can get it for you, ma'am," he said.

"No, it's no trouble," Mari called over her shoulder. She increased her pace in an effort to lose him.

"Really, I insist." The valet caught up and matched her strides. "What do you need me to get for you?"

Hannah's harsh whisper came over the comm. "Get rid of him."

What could Mari do?

She stopped, flustered. "Oh . . . um. Well, you really shouldn't ask a girl about her personal items. It's not very gentlemanly." She was definitely grasping at straws with that one.

The young valet blushed. "I apologize, ma'am. But I'll need to escort you to the car. I can't allow you in the parking area alone."

Mari nodded, but she felt her desperation rising as they continued toward the parked cars.

Then she remembered.

Falling slightly behind the valet, Mari kicked off her stiletto and swiftly slid the tranquilizer prick-pin out the heel.

"Ooh, you have a mosquito on you." She swung and landed the tip of the heel on the back of the valet's neck.

"Ow!" He put his hand on the spot and turned to Mari. He looked down at the high heel in her hand. "Why would you kill a mosquito . . . with . . . your . . . high . . . hee—"

He slumped forward into Mari's arms, nearly bowling her over. She dragged him toward the cover of the shrubs that grew around the walls of the mansion.

"What's happening? Did you get him?" Susan's voice was excited. "Oh, I hate being stuck in a trunk."

"I had to use one of my tranquilizer heels on him," Mari explained through her exertion.

"Smart thinking," Hannah grudgingly acknowledged.

"I'm almost there," Mari whispered. She hoped Susan and Anna didn't hate her too much for how long they'd been crammed in the trunk.

Mari found Trey's Mustang and made one last glance around the area before inserting the key and popping the trunk. Aside from a few whispered gasps for fresh air, the ladies weren't any worse for the wear. Together, they hefted the boxes of Anna's custom fireworks and disappeared into the darkness of the mansion's back lawn.

On her way back into the party, Mari stopped to peek at the sleeping valet. With any luck, he would only remember the mosquito sting.

As she walked up the front steps, she could hear the chatter on the comm between the infiltration team—Anna and Susan—and the support team—Hannah and Katie.

"We're just inside the rear auxiliary entrance," Anna announced.

"Mari, you need to get back into the ballroom to distract Chaz," Hannah said.

Instinctively, Mari nodded then immediately felt silly. How did spies live this kind of life all the time? "On my way," she said quietly.

Katie chimed in. "I've got a great view of everyone on the recon bots. Nice job, Trey."

An indistinct combination of a throat clearing and a grunt came over the radio. So that was how spies did it. Mari wondered if she could ever learn everything they knew.

Back in the ballroom, Trey was deep in conversation with a group of men dressed in stylish suits. Chaz was among them. That made her job much easier. She walked up and put her hand through Trey's arm.

"Got it," she said, shaking the small purse.

He stared down at her with a longing gaze, as if he hadn't seen her in days or weeks, instead of merely minutes. "Dance with me?" he whispered.

His request took her by surprise. Was he working off of a different game plan? How was dancing with him going to distract Chaz? Mari decided to roll with it. Glancing quickly around the group—lingering particularly on Chaz—she replied, "I don't want to interrupt."

Chaz said nothing—he didn't even seem to have noticed that she'd spoken—but the intensity of his gaze devoured her.

Polite murmurs of approval from the other gathered businessmen indicated that they didn't mind if she accepted Trey's offer.

Again the decision.

Chaz or Trey.

She should be dancing with Chaz, keeping him busy.

But she would much rather be in Trey's arms.

Mari turned to Trey, completely prepared to turn him down, and she was again confronted with his deep green eyes. And that longing.

He held out a hand. "Trust me," he whispered.

"Okay," she said quietly.

Trey took her hand and led her out onto the floor. To the crooning sound of the lively music, he spun and twirled her as they circled the ballroom. As the end of the song died away, the band transitioned to a slower mood.

Trey's arm tightened around Mari as he pulled her even closer. She knew she should be focusing her mind on something, but at the moment, all she could feel was his hand on her back, his breath on her cheek, and the beat of her heart.

"I don't hear Chaz." Hannah's voice jolted Mari from her stupor. "Mari, aren't you supposed to be distracting Chaz?"

"She is," Trey said softly.

"How? Is he close by?" Hannah asked.

"She's pretty much mesmerizing every man in this room," Trey replied with a grin.

Mari felt her cheeks pink.

There were groans from the ladies on the comm, and something whispered that sounded like, "He's got it bad."

Mari looked up through her eyelashes. "Every man?" she asked shyly.

Trey nodded solemnly. "Every. Last. One."

She felt her head spin with intoxicating power. She looked at Trey's lips, at that adorable grin that was as crooked as ever.

A movement over his shoulder caught her eye. Chaz and Brax were huddled near one of the ballroom's side serving doors, talking and gesturing toward the research wing.

Mari's fantasy came crashing down around her.

What was she doing?

She was here to rescue her mother, not charm Trey Brooks.

And certainly not to fall for him.

"Trey, something's going on." Mari heard the worry in her own voice.

"That's true. But I kind of expected it as soon as I saw you in this dress."

Too flustered to acknowledge his flattery, Mari pressed on. "No. Brax is here. He was just talking to Chaz. I wonder if they suspect something. Are Anna and Susan okay?"

The few seconds of silence felt like an eternity. "Yeah, I guess we're fine," Susan whispered. "We found the nano-bot lab, and Anna's loading the kill code. But I can't cover all of the approaches to the lab, and we're really exposed here. We could use another pair of eyes."

Trey held Mari's gaze for a long moment. They both knew who should do what. Trey pulled her closer. "Be safe," he whispered in her free ear. Trey held her for another half a breath before letting go. He strode the length of the ballroom as he spoke softly into his hidden mic. "Tell me where you are, Susan."

Even after he disappeared from her view, Mari felt the reassurance of being able to hear his continued conversation with the team.

Chaz and Brax finished their animated conversation, and Brax slipped out through the ballroom's side door. After a quick glance around the room, Chaz moved to follow Trey out the main doors. Mari maneuvered herself into Chaz's path and looked up innocently as he approached. "Hello, Chaz."

Chaz flashed her his perfect smile, though it seemed rather forced. "Hi, Marina. I'm glad you're here tonight. I hope you're enjoying yourself."

"Yes, I am." She wondered if he would take the bait or if he'd need more persuading.

"Listen, Marina, I'm sort of busy right now. Maybe I could—"

Channeling her inner glamour girl, Mari grabbed his arm and let her fingers trail down his sleeve until they reached his hand. "... but I would be enjoying myself even more if . . ." She glanced slowly over her shoulder. It was difficult to pretend this level of flirtation and allure, so she tried to imagine how Anna or Hannah would do it. Or Katie.

Chaz's face broke into a broad, wolfish grin. "I suppose I could spare one dance."

Even though this had been the plan all along, Mari felt cold ice in her chest as she pulled Chaz by the hand, leading him out onto the dance floor.

When they reached an opening on the hardwood floor, she turned toward him. Chaz's other hand snaked around her back and held her tight. She fought the urge to push him away. For the sake of the mission, Mari needed him to stay with her.

Chaz confidently whirled and spun her around the floor in time with the music. Truth be told, Chaz was a much better dancer than Trey. Where Trey was rough and energetic, Chaz was smooth and sophisticated. Together, she and Chaz glided circles around the other couples.

"You've never allowed me to properly apologize for not having dinner at the Corinthian last week," Chaz said.

"It's okay, you already apo—"

"How about a weekend at my beach house on Hilton Head Island?"

Was there an easy way to reject a millionaire? She opened her mouth, but he didn't let her reply.

"Or if that's too boring, we can do a week at my villa in the Caymans. Just say the word."

Mari stared at him. In that moment, she realized she could get anything she wanted from this man. For a while, anyway.

That kind of power was intoxicating.

But it wasn't enough to satisfy.

"That's very kind, Chaz. But I don't think we should," she said.

"Is it because of Trey?" Chaz asked.

Mari didn't know how to answer that. A change of subject seemed the best bet. "I do love this part of the house," Mari said as she looked up at the ornate ceiling. "I remember it from the tour. I'm glad we finally get to dance in it."

Chaz focused his gaze on her. He seemed to be trying to figure her out. Mari forced herself to remain calm under his scrutiny. This was just a role she needed to play.

"I'm glad you like it. You certainly are the belle of the ball, it would seem," Chaz said.

For most of the dance, she had tried to ignore the whispered conversations over the radio comms. She was vaguely aware that Anna was uploading the second half of the nano-bot self-destruct code.

Katie's voice came over the comm from her computer room at Club Banana. "Uh oh. It looks like you've tripped one of the security systems," she called out. "They're sending a guard your way. You need to get out of that lab!"

Mari forced a smile and tried to concentrate on what Chaz had just been saying.

"Anna, let's go," Susan whispered.

"Hang on. I've almost got it," Anna replied.

The atmosphere in the party felt surreal compared to what Mari knew was happening just a few hundred feet away. She forced her mind back to Chaz, trying to think of something to keep his attention.

"I bet when we first met, you had no idea we'd eventually . . ."

Voices echoed in Mari's earpiece.

Slamming doors. Yelling.

A gunshot.

A scream.

Mari instinctively jerked her head toward the research wing.

Chaz did the same.

For a split second, it felt completely normal. Why wouldn't they both look toward the sound of a gunshot? But her brain slowly caught up. The only gunshot noise in the ballroom would have been the one in Mari's ear.

Unless Chaz also had an earpiece.

At that exact moment, Chaz must have reached the same conclusion about Mari. His eyes narrowed as he stared down at her, all the false warmth evaporating from his gaze. He stopped dancing and reached for her arm, gripping it tightly. "I think we need to have a little chat," he said through a fake smile.

With a slight jerk, he pulled her from the dance floor toward the doors. Mari searched the room for Trey, but remembered that he was probably in the research wing helping Anna and Susan.

She was on her own.

Mari tried to pull away from Chaz, but his grip only tightened on her arm. They passed several other guests on the way out of the ballroom. Would they help if she screamed? Or would that only put her mother in more danger?

As Chaz pushed her down the hall, he lifted a hand to his earpiece, speaking into his sleeve. "Security Level Three, ASAP."

Hannah's voice in Mari's earpiece sounded as frantic as she'd ever heard it. "Susan! Anna! Please respond. What's your status?"

"Susan's been shot." Anna's voice was desperate. "We need to—"

Chaz yanked the miniature comm receiver out of Mari's ear.

Mari's breath caught.

Susan was hurt.

"My cousin, Brax, told me the most interesting story a few minutes ago," Chaz said quietly as they maneuvered through the halls and up the grand staircase. "He said that our most esteemed guest is actually your mother."

Mari's blood ran cold.

He knew about her mother.

That meant he knew about Mari, too.

He gave a particularly painful jerk on her arm as they turned toward the second-floor staircase. Mari clinched her jaw shut to not cry out. She didn't want to give him the satisfaction.

Chaz continued, "I didn't want to believe him. I told him it couldn't be true." He paused to look down at her. There was nothing left of the picture-perfect Chaz. An unfamiliar, ruthless face had replaced the attractive one. "But apparently, I was wrong."

There was no way out of this.

Mari stumbled in her high heels as Chaz dragged her onto the third-floor landing and toward the east wing.

Brax's wing.

Two burly men in suits met Chaz at the head of the staircase. "Follow me," he said.

"Chaz, please don't do this," Mari cried. "I'm begging you. Please, let my mother go."

"I might let her go, after I'm certain we have what we need."

Mari's heart sank. If he meant to double-check the code Mari had sent to Brax, he'd discover her duplicity. She struck a defiant tone. "You can't have the nano-bots! Protecting innocent lives is more important."

"That's exactly what we're trying to do, Marina," Chaz said as they rounded the corner to her mother's room. "If we can provide the nano-bot technology to vulnerable countries like Ukraine and Israel, we can save thousands of innocent lives."

Mari gaped at him. "You abducted my mother so you could use her research as a weapon?"

"It's for the greater good. Can't you see that?"

"No. I can't. All I see is a greedy, selfish man who doesn't care about anyone else but himself and his bottom line."

Chaz jerked back as if she'd struck him. Then his expression hardened. "How stupid of me to think you'd understand." He pushed open the door to her mother's room and shoved Mari inside. She tripped and fell onto the hardwood floor.

"Wait here," he called over his shoulder to the guards as he flicked on the lights and closed the door behind him.

Mari scrambled to her feet. She choked back a sob when she saw the small figure huddled in the back corner of the bed.

The form on the bed stirred and turned toward her. "Mari?" her mother croaked, squinting against the sudden light.

"Mamá!" Mari threw herself into her mother's arms. She turned back to Chaz. "Let her go!" Mari sobbed.

Chaz moved toward the bed, looking down at her in silent contemplation.

"You would do anything for her, wouldn't you?"

An icy chill ran down Mari's spine. She slowly nodded.

Chaz smirked down at her. "Wouldn't I love to find out if that's true." He grabbed Mari by the arm and lifted her from the bed.

Her mother let out a squeal and hid herself in the corner.

"Who else is here tonight? What have you done to the nano-bots?"

"Nothing!" Mari squeaked.

"I don't believe you!" he bellowed.

Mari flinched and glanced toward her mother.

The smile on Chaz's face grew. "Well, let's see if your mother would be willing to do anything for you."

He grabbed Mari by the throat and pinned her against the wall. Then he spoke to her mother. "Give me full access to program the nano-bots or your daughter will never leave this room alive."

"No. No. No!" Mari's mother cowered with her hands over her ears.

"She won't," Mari rasped, digging with her fingers into the skin of Chaz's hands.

"Shut up!" Chaz released Mari's neck and backhanded her onto the bed. Her mother screamed again, amplifying the pain in Mari's skull.

Chaz grunted in frustration and lifted Mari by her arms. "I'm tired of waiting." He shook her. "I will kill both of you!" he screamed.

Mari lifted her tranquilized heel, quickly flicked the needle out, and stamped down with all her strength on Chaz's foot. The syringe sunk through the leather of his shoe. He yelled in pain and released her.

With a snarl, he reached a hand into his tuxedo jacket. But before he could even pull out whatever weapon he had in there, Mari hiked up her dress and planted a ninja kick square in his chest. Chaz flew backward into the wall and slumped to the floor. A small dot of blood bloomed on his white shirt where the tranquilizer needle had pricked him a second time.

He didn't move.

Mari stepped forward and slapped him hard across the face, partly to make sure he was completely knocked out, partly to vent her anger.

She rushed to her mother and helped her out of the bed. Her mother was shell-shocked. She stood, but barely. Walking steadily on her own was out of the question.

Together, they hobbled to the door. Mari stopped and fished her earpiece out of Chaz's pocket.

". . . Mari? Can you hear me? Please respond." Hannah's voice sounded tired. "Mari?"

"I'm here," Mari said.

"Mari! We heard a scuffle on your radio. Are you okay?"

"I'm fine. I have my mom. We're back in her original room, but there are two security guards outside the door. Can we get a little help?"

"I'm busy . . . at the moment," Anna said between grunts.

"What's going on? How's Susan?" Mari asked.

"Can't walk too well, but I'll live," Susan answered weakly.

"We can't get to you," Anna explained. "More guards are heading our way. Meet us at the car."

Mari took a deep breath. She and her mother were on their own. That was nothing new. Then she remembered—not quite alone. "Hannah, can you give us a distraction with some of Anna's fancy fireworks?" she asked.

"Definitely. Just give me some directions from the outside." Hannah replied.

"East wing. Third floor. There's a short hall toward the front of the mansion that ends in double windows. Can you hit that small of a target?"

"Do you want a small, medium, or large distraction?" There was a note of amusement in Hannah's voice.

"A few small ones to get us started. But then definitely a large one. And give me a countdown to the big one; I need to time it right," Mari said.

"Now's as good a time as any to start the fireworks show, don't you think, Anna?" Katie asked over the comm.

"Yes, please," Anna replied. "The more distractions the better."

Mari pulled her mother to the door and quietly checked the handle.

Locked, just as she'd expected.

She could hear the fireworks exploding on the back lawn. Hopefully, that would divert the security guards' attention.

"Vectoring the big one toward you now, Mari. You've got about ten seconds."

Mari lifted her hand to the door. A prisoner would bang to get out. The warden would knock assertively to signal the guards.

She rapped four times in a short staccato.

Hannah's voice counted down in her ear. "Five . . . four . . . three . . . I hope you don't waste this chance . . ."

The door opened, and Mari landed a nose-shattering punch in the guard's surprised face. At that exact moment, Hannah's guided firework-missile hit the window at the end of the hall with amazing precision. The glass shattered with the impact, and shards of wood and glowing embers of red and gold streaked and skidded across the floor.

Mari leaped forward with a modified roundhouse kick and caught the other guard in the back with the tranquilizer pin. He stumbled forward, only to be slammed backward by Hannah's final bloom of exploding distraction.

As Mari walked back to the first guard and stepped on his thigh with her tranquilizer high heel, she heard Hannah's voice again. "Did it work? I still have a few medium ones if you need."

"Nope. That was perfect. Thanks, Hannah," Mari replied, grabbing her mother.

They made their way cautiously down the hall toward the auxiliary stairwell at the end of the wing. When they stepped out onto the back lawn, the warm night air was filled with reds, purples, and golds exploding all around her. Mari shepherded her mother to Trey's car and placed her gently in the back seat.

She closed the door and turned back toward the mansion, straining to find Anna and Susan through the chaos of fireworks and spectators. She wondered how long she should wait before going to help them.

Movement behind a nearby luxury sedan caught her eye. "Susan? Anna?" she whispered into the semidarkness. She crept around Trey's Mustang and stared across the gap in the row of cars. She didn't see either of the Banana Girls. Or Trey, for that matter. Every muscle in Mari's body tensed, wanting to do something to help, but not knowing what. She turned at the sound of a footstep behind her.

Brax's sneering face loomed over her. His large hands closed around Mari's neck. "Didn't your mother teach you it's not nice to take something that doesn't belong to you?"

Mari fought for breath. She swung at his face, but his arms were longer than hers. She aimed a destructive punch at the back of his elbow. He shifted his arm to dodge the blow, but it was enough to loosen his grip on her neck. Mari kicked straight forward and landed the tranquilizer heel in his gut. She wished she could have popped him one in the chest, but he was too close, and her dress got in the way.

He released his chokehold and stumbled back. He steadied himself and reached inside his jacket. "You've been nothing but trouble, you little—"

Mari spun and kicked the gun out of his hand. It bounced twice and skidded under a sporty convertible.

Brax snarled and lunged at her. His punch caught her in the shoulder and knocked her off balance. She careened into a nearby car and rolled away. Scrambling to her feet, she backed off, putting a safe distance between them.

She looked down at the tiny spot of blood on the stomach of his tuxedo shirt. The tranquilizer should have started working by now.

"How many doses is my heel good for?" she muttered into the comm.

"About four, maybe five," Katie replied.

Now Mari regretted tranq-ing Chaz twice.

Or the valet boy at all.

She carefully slipped off her high-heels and flung them toward Trey's car. Then she hiked up her dress and rolled it inward against her thighs.

She would have to deal with Brax the old-fashioned way.

Brax leered at her, licking his wolfish lips as he circled.

Mari lowered herself into her familiar fighting stance. She breathed tentatively through her bruised windpipe and glared across the small open space at her foe. "I plan to hurt you for what you did to my mother," she declared.

He lunged at her with a powerful swing. Mari ducked and deftly swiped a kick against the side of his knee as he passed. Brax stumbled into the hood of a red Jaguar.

He spun around and charged her again. One of his wildly swinging arms caught her on the side of the face. She landed a punch to his ribs but quickly backed away.

"How long before the guards find us, Mari?" Brax coughed through his sneer. "A minute. Maybe two. You're mine now. You won't be leaving these grounds ever again," he taunted.

"If I don't, at least I'll have the pleasure of smashing your pathetic face into as many luxury vehicles as possible."

He roared and hurtled toward her, aiming a blow for Mari's head. She sidestepped and shoved him headlong into the window of a silver Mercedes. She grabbed the staggering man and slammed him facedown on the cement, wrenching his arm behind his back. He twisted and writhed, his thrashing limbs slapping harmlessly against her sides. She dug one knee into the base of his neck and pulled his other arm behind him, and the flailing subsided.

Mari looked around, wishing she had something to tie his hands with.

"Hey gorgeous, would this be helpful?" Trey stood next to her, dangling his undone bowtie in front of her.

With a quick smile, she snatched it from his hands. "It's about time you showed up," she said as she cinched the fabric around Brax's wrists.

"I was busy helping," Trey replied with his crooked grin.

"Helping?"

"He found us," Anna answered as she came around a nearby car, shouldering a limping Susan beside her.

"Susan, are you okay?" Mari asked from her perch atop Brax.

"The guard was like, 'halt!' and I was like 'what?!' and then he was like *PEW*,"—she lifted an imaginary gun and pretended to shoot—"and I was like,"—she tried to demonstrate how she had lunged sideways, but Anna held her tightly. Susan winced. "Anyway, yeah, I'll be okay."

Anna rolled her eyes and helped Susan climb in the back of the car with Mari's mother then quickly slid in next to her.

Trey helped Mari to her feet and pulled her close. He lifted her chin with a gentle finger. "He did this to you?" Trey asked as he eyed the marks on her cheek and throat.

Mari nodded.

"Well, being an only child, it was always my job to take out the trash." Trey grabbed Brax by the ankles and dragged him to the back of his Mustang.

The sounds of partygoers gathered on the back lawn drifted toward them as Mari helped him lift the unconscious man into the trunk. She glanced around the empty parking lot, expecting to see guards converging on them any second.

Trey guided her to the passenger door of the Mustang. "We need to get out of here."

With a forlorn gaze up at the third floor of the mansion, she said, "I wish we could stuff Chaz in the trunk, too. Are we going to let him get away with all of this?"

Trey's expression turned apologetic.

Anna stuck her head out of the back window. "There's no time. We'll deal with Chaz another day."

Mari jumped into the front seat and held on tight as Trey burned rubber for the front gate.

At least the Banana Girls would get one bad guy today.

Chapter Sixteen

"Mamá, can I get you something to drink?" Mari walked out onto the patio of her childhood home and found her mother sitting on a lawn chair, staring out at the trees.

Almost a week had passed since they had escaped Keating Mansion together. Her mother's bruises were nearly gone, but, of course, there were other scars that would take longer to heal.

They had spent an afternoon at the police station filing reports and giving witness testimony. And they'd spent several days just lounging around the house, doing nothing. Her mother had gone to some sessions with a counselor, but neither of them had gone back to campus yet.

Mari knew that time was coming soon.

To respect her mother's wishes, she'd probably need to move back to her apartment near campus. Mari had been dreading that. She knew her mother wanted her to be independent, but to Mari, independent felt like code for being lonely.

"Mamá?" Mari prodded.

Her mother glanced up, shaken from her reverie. "Oh, Mari. No, I'm fine, thank you." She reverted to gazing at the trees swaying in the wind.

Mari turned to go back inside, but her mother caught her hand.

"Sit with me, Mari."

Mari pulled another chair up next to her mother's. "What is it, Mamá?"

"I missed seeing the trees," her mother said absently.

Mari looked out at the trees of their backyard, the ones she'd climbed in as a child, and nodded her understanding.

Her mother turned to look at her, really examining her face. "And I missed my sweet Mari. I thought of you every day. Every moment. Having you sneak into my room began to feel like a mirage or a hallucination in the days after. I tried to will you to come back again."

Mari reached out and took her mother's hand, enjoying the warmth and the closeness of the most important person in the world to her. Mari would miss that when the time came to go back to regular life.

"You probably couldn't imagine me as a ninja-girl."

Her mother laughed and shook her head. "You've always had a bit of ninja-girl in you."

Mari smiled at memories of adventures she'd had in the backyard that must have tried her mother's patience.

"Mari? I know I've always pushed you to be strong on your own. I've pushed myself that way, too."

Not knowing what to say, Mari simply continued to squeeze her mother's hand.

After a few seconds of silence, her mother turned her gaze back to the trees. "I guess what I'm trying to say is that I don't want you to feel like I'm pushing you out. I still feel like it's important for you to be independent," she looked Mari in the eye again, "but only when you're ready."

Mari felt her insides swell to the point she would burst. She didn't think she could smile any bigger. She knelt next to her mother and engulfed her in a tight hug. "I'm so glad you're safe, Mamá."

"Thank you for rescuing me, my sweet Maricita," her mother whispered.

Mari's tears mingled with her mother's as their cheeks pressed together.

Her mother pulled back and lifted a hand to Mari's face, gently brushing the strands of hair away. "You're so strong and so brave. I've always seen that in you. But I don't think you saw it in yourself. That's why I've always challenged you and pushed you, not because I thought you couldn't do it, but because *you* thought you couldn't."

Before starting college, Mari had wanted so badly to stay close to her mother. She hadn't been ready to grow up; she'd been scared of being an adult. Now she finally realized that her mother hadn't pushed her away; she'd pushed her ahead.

Mari nodded, pressing her forehead against her mother's.

In that moment, she knew she needed to move forward, not hold back.

"I think I'm ready to be out on my own," Mari said. "But maybe I could come back to visit once in a while."

Her mother beamed at her. "You'd better visit more often than that."

Mari stood on the penthouse balcony, enjoying the panoramic scene of midtown Atlanta. The murmurs of the ravenous weekend lunch crowd drifted up from the street below. Cars revved and idled as they crisscrossed each other. In the distance, steel and gray melted into a carpet of mottled green as skyscrapers gave way to suburbs.

With one last glance and a deep sigh, Mari turned away. She would miss living the high-life here with her new friends. But her mother was safe, and it was time to return to normal life. She'd waited until the girls were in the middle of their morning workout to sneak in, pack her things, and take one last look.

Chatter and laughing from the hall told Mari that her last look might have taken too long. She hurried across the living room, but before she could grab her suitcase and make her escape, the front door opened, and the four Banana Girls spilled in.

"Hi, Mari. Welcome back," Katie said on her way into the kitchen for some hydration.

Anna touched Mari on the arm. "How's your mom doing?" she asked.

Mari nodded. "Oh, she's good. Almost ready to get back to normal."

"We missed you at training this morning," Susan said as she limped to one of the couches.

Mari attempted a casual response as she blocked her suitcase with her legs. "Yeah? What was the training?"

"Well, after the regular hand-to-hand warm-ups, we were going to do ballroom dance—particularly appropriate considering last week's mission." With an over-exaggerated sigh and feigned swoon, Susan flopped gingerly onto a nearby couch. "But it wasn't working, so we ended early."

"Really? What wasn't working?" Mari hoped if she kept them talking, they wouldn't notice what she was up to. She wanted to avoid awkward goodbyes; that's why she'd planned to leave while they were gone.

"It was working fine," Anna called from the kitchen. "But Katie kept giggling every time I tried to dance with her." Anna rolled her eyes. "The silly girl."

Katie walked over to stand next to Mari, holding out a finger while chugging her drink. When she finally lowered her glass, she jumped into the conversation. "I told you I could get plenty of boys to come over and help us."

"You can't invite just any boy to Club Banana," Hannah said from her seat. "Especially not to our training room. You know that."

Katie's mouth turned down in an adorable pout.

Mari gave her a sympathetic shrug as she attempted to subtly inch her suitcase toward the door.

Katie leaned to look behind Mari's legs. "Wait, why do you have a suitcase?"

"Oh. Uh . . ." Mari looked down.

"Are you leaving?!" Katie yelled.

Anna stuck her head in from the kitchen. "No. She can't leave now. I was about to put some bananas on the grill."

The other girls groaned in unison. "Please, not grilled bananas again," Susan said.

"I'm going to get it right this time," Anna answered indignantly.

Katie pointed at her luggage. "No, I mean she's *leaving* leaving." The way Katie said it made Mari feel like she had just been caught on a mission without a disguise.

"What?!" Anna called from the kitchen.

Mari mustered a small smile. "Well, I just thought it was time to leave. You were all so nice to take me in while I was alone. Not to mention helping me rescue my mom. But I need to go home now."

"Are you moving back in with your mother?" Hannah asked.

"She invited me to, but no, I'm going back to my old apartment," Mari said.

"Do you have a roommate that will miss you if you don't move back?" Hannah pressed.

It was just like Hannah to twist the knife in her back. Did she know how alone Mari had felt before all of this? How alone she would feel again? Mari stared at Hannah. "No," Mari answered.

"If you're still going to be out on your own, it seems like you could choose to live anywhere, right?" Hannah said.

"Yeah . . ." Mari wasn't sure where Hannah was going with this.

"Don't you like it here?" Hannah asked defensively.

"No. I mean, yes. I love it. But isn't Club Banana just for . . . you know . . . Banana Girls?"

Susan and Katie shared a dumbfounded look, as if they couldn't believe what they were hearing.

"Anna!" Katie called, not taking her eyes off Mari.

Anna walked into the room, balancing several drinks in her hands. "Yeah?"

"Didn't you tell her?" Katie asked.

Anna smiled sheepishly. "I was waiting until we were all together."

This goodbye had already veered from awkward to painful; Mari wasn't sure she could take much more. "Tell me what?"

Anna set down the drinks and stood up straight. "Your undercover name is no good. You're going to have to change it."

"My . . . undercover name?"

"Yeah, Marina. It doesn't match the rest of ours. It doesn't end in -ana."

Mari's brows furrowed, and she pointed at the other girls one at a time. "Hannah . . . Anna . . . Susan."

"Susana, actually," the redhead corrected.

Mari frowned. She moved on to the final Banana Girl. "Katie . . .?"

Katie smiled proudly. "My official mission name is Katiana, but that's only because the girls wouldn't let me be Katana, which I'm sure you know is a Japanese Samurai sword. Don't you think that would have been a much cooler sounding—"

"Katie . . ." Anna prompted.

Katie's open mouth turned to a grin. "Sorry."

Mari's brain could barely process what they were saying.

Anna smiled patiently. "You see, you can't be Marina anymore; it just wouldn't match. And you know how we feel about things matching."

Susan and Katie both nodded vigorously.

"If you're going to be one of us," Anna continued, "your mission name needs to end in -ana."

"You mean . . ." Mari looked around at the four girls, a lump rising in her throat. ". . . you want me to be a Banana Girl?"

Anna nodded.

"Definitely," Katie added with a huge grin.

Mari choked out a laugh to avoid crying. She felt the glow of the smiles around her.

"How about Mariana?" Susan suggested.

Mari pretended disappointment. "Aww, I was just getting used to Marina," she said.

"Hey, you don't have to join the team. No one's forcing you," Hannah huffed.

"Hannah . . ." Anna's voice had that warning tone that only she could use on the sophisticated blonde girl.

Hannah scowled at Anna, though as she turned back to Mari, her face softened. "We really would like you to join us."

Coming from Hannah, that felt like a tearful, begging plea for her to stay.

"It feels like you're one of us already," Susan said. "This is just making it official."

"Actually, to make it official, Stacia will need to convince her bosses," Hannah explained. "Plus, Mari will need a more in-depth background check, and a secure bank account for her salary, not to mention the week-long boot camp and small arms training requirements—which we could obviously do in the shooting range below the garage . . ."

Mari put her hand to her mouth. She and her mother had been on their own for so long. She hadn't ever expected to find the same acceptance and support anywhere else, especially not at college. She blinked against the prickling in her eyes, but it was a losing battle.

The four ladies stared at her in anticipation.

She nodded through her tears. "Yes," she whispered. Then she shouted, "Yes!"

They instantly crushed her in a giant group hug.

Even Hannah joined in.

Getting through all the assignments to catch up in her classes had been difficult, but holding herself hostage in the library every night that week had helped. Friday night, Mari didn't get back to the penthouse until well past dinner. The others had gone to see a movie together.

Mari dumped her books and laptop on the table and headed to her room. Pajamas seemed about right after the day she'd had.

She almost missed the note taped to her bedroom door.

Rooftop

Two minutes

Come alone

Having officially been a Banana Girl for less than a week, Mari wasn't exactly sure how new mission assignments were given, but this didn't seem like their style. Besides, the handwriting was distinctly masculine.

How many guys had access to Club Banana? Or had the girls been in on it?

Unable to pass up investigating a mini mystery, Mari climbed the stairs leading to the private rooftop terrace.

A warm breeze whispered through the ivy walls and slatted roof. The terrace was empty except for a single, white-draped table and two chairs. The elegant place settings, flickering candles, and crystal glasses provided an interesting contrast to the hoagie sandwiches on the plates.

Mari turned at the sound of footsteps.

Trey approached, holding a red rose. "You said anything was good, as long as it wasn't Mexican food."

Mari laughed and took several steps toward him. "That's true. So, you thought deli sandwiches would be the perfect candlelit meal?"

"Hey, we already did pizza. After this, I'll be fresh out of ideas." That self-deprecating grin made her knees go weak.

He handed her the rose. Mari lifted the beautiful flower and inhaled deeply of its fragrance. She hadn't taken the training course on using her allure as a weapon yet, but maybe she could project enough charm on pure confidence alone. She stepped closer and looked up at him, batting her eyelashes playfully.

Trey took the flower back from her. "On second thought, you're going to need both hands for this." He set the rose on the table and pressed a button on the remote.

Mari raised a brow at him.

"We only got one dance at the ball," he said, his hands extended.

Music began to play from the terrace speakers. "One and a half, actually," Mari replied.

"Well, I want more," he said as he took her into his arms.

Mari wrapped her arms up over his broad, muscular shoulders and intertwined her hands behind his neck. The sweet musk of his skin enveloped her.

Her body tingled as he pulled her closer to him.

She looked up into his warm, green eyes.

"I think I'm going to kiss you," she said in a husky whisper.

"It's about ti—"

Mari smothered whatever else he planned to say with her eager lips.

But without her venomous high-heels, tiptoes were a must.

ORIGIN STORY AND NEXT BOOK

That's the end. I hope you enjoyed the first Banana Girls' book.

As you might have guessed, there's more back-story about how Anna and Hannah met and started the Banana Girls than I included in this book.

If you would like to read Spies Never Share, the exclusive Banana Girls' origin story novella—including Anna and Hannah's first mission and the first guy they fought over—you can get it here: www.myleschristensen.com/banana1

After that, the Banana Girls action continues with Spies Never Swoon, where Anna must come to the rescue of a handsome European prince.

And if I could ask one big favor—it would really help my book succeed if you would leave a review on Amazon and Goodreads. Thank you so very much!

Acknowledgments

I'm not sure that I can thank a dream, but as this is just an acknowledgments section, I suppose I can acknowledge that the initial idea for this book series came from a dream that I had about my daughter and her friends (one of whom has a name that rhymes with my daughter's). And that's where it all began.

I appreciate the early feedback that I got from my beta readers: angela_lee, bingeingonbooks, and maddy216. Y'all definitely helped the book pivot in a better direction (and love triangles stink, right?).

Thanks to Courtney at Courtney Larkin Editing. I can never seem to get those comma rules; I'm glad you know them.

Thanks to the folks at Indie Book Covers on Facebook. Without your feedback, I would have gone completely off-track with the direction my cover was headed (though I really still like that art I found).

Thanks to my parents, wife, and daughter for giving opinions on covers when I was completely at a loss for what to do with the new feedback I was getting.

I definitely need to thank my youngest sons who were patient enough to let me read the final proof copy out loud to them so that I could find those last few typos. And I couldn't help but notice that you two seemed to end up liking it, even though it was mostly about ninja girls (and a little kissing).

As always, my biggest thanks goes to my sweet wife who puts up with my endless rambling about plot ideas and writing roadblocks. Hopefully I didn't spoil the story for you too much, sweetheart.

MYLES CHRISTENSEN LOVES TO write exciting adventures because he loves to read exciting adventures. The hopeless romantic in him will usually sprinkle a teensy bit of romance into his stories. While writing, he listens to music that matches—and sometimes inspires—the storyline.

His mild-mannered alter ego is a product development engineer, university professor, and game inventor.

He lives in Utah with his wife and children. He writes cozy thriller/suspense under the name M. Taylor Christensen.